Praise for *Sins*

"Fast-paced, tense, and fi... novel attests to Mason and Marlowe's skills and ability to collaborate on a taut, intriguing, and satisfying story."

—*Publishers Weekly*

"Another winner! Mason has outdone herself with this page-turning, emotional romance, rich in historical details and plot twists."

—*RT Book Reviews*

More Praise for Connie Mason

"You'll hardly have time to take a breath as you race through this action-packed, delightful tale…everything her fans expect—a rip-roaring adventure with sensual love scenes and three-dimensional characters you care about."

—*RT Book Reviews* on *Love Me With Fury*

"Mason delivers exactly what her fans expect by creating a world filled with adventure, sensuality, history, and characters whose biting verbal repartee keeps her fast-paced plot flying."

—*RT Book Reviews* on *Highland Warrior*

"Connie Mason never disappoints her readers…You'll love the exciting and sizzling adventure."

—*Fresh Fiction* on *Highland Warrior*

"Connie Mason gives us a fast-paced story that delivers exactly what romance readers are looking for—action, villains, and, of course, passion."

—*Joyfully Reviewed* on *Highland Warrior*

"A sizzling Highland romance…Sexy, smart, engaging."

—*The Romance Reader* on *A Touch So Wicked*

"Filled with all the components of a great romance: likeable characters, an engaging plot, and sizzling passion."

—*Examiner.com* on *The Dragon Lord*

Praise for Mia Marlowe's *Touch of a Thief*

"Absolutely terrific!"

—Victoria Alexander, #1 *New York Times* romance bestseller

"Mia Marlowe proves she has the touch for strong heroines, wickedly sexy heroes, and love scenes so hot they singe the pages."

—Jennifer Ashley, *USA Today* bestselling author of *Lady Isabella's Scandalous Marriage*

"Sensuality, sexuality, passion, and mystery blend into a wonderfully entertaining tale."

—*RT Book Reviews*

"Witty, sharp dialogue...both historical and paranormal readers will love this crossover tale."

—*Publishers Weekly* starred review

Sins of the Highlander

Enjoy

Mia Marlowe

SINS OF THE HIGHLANDER

CONNIE MASON

with MIA MARLOWE

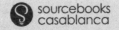

sourcebooks
casablanca

Published by Sourcebooks Casablanca, an imprint of Sourcebooks, Inc.
P.O. Box 4410, Naperville, Illinois 60567-4410
(630) 961-3900
Fax: (630) 961-2168
www.sourcebooks.com

Printed and bound in Canada.
WC 10 9 8 7 6 5 4 3 2 1

Connie and Mia dedicate this story to you,
their readers. Without you, no magic can happen.
Thanks for bringing your imagination along for the ride!

Chapter 1

THE PEAT FIRE HAD BURNED OUT AND THE ASH GONE gray, but Rob MacLaren didn't feel the least bit cold. Not while his hot-blooded woman writhed under him. Their breaths mingled in the frosty air of the bedchamber. Fiona tilted her hips, welcoming him deeper, and he bit the inside of his cheek to keep from emptying himself into her.

It was too soon.

He never wanted it to end, this joining, this loss of himself in the woman he adored.

Rob raised himself up on his arms and gazed down at her. The candles had burned down to nubs but still flickered enough to cast her in soft light. He could see his wife clearly. Her strawberry nipples peaked, with cold or arousal he couldn't be sure, but he loved looking at them just the same.

"What are ye doing, daftie man? 'Tis too cold!" Fiona raised herself up and clung to him for warmth.

"That's what ye get when ye marry a man on Christmas Day—a cold bridal night." He gently pushed her back down, and she sank into the feather tick.

"It doesna have to be cold." Her skin rippled with gooseflesh. "Come back under the covers, love."

"I canna. I need to see the lass I wed," he said. "I want to watch ye melt for me, to see your face when ye make that wee kitten noise just afore ye come."

"Wee kitten noise, is it?" She shook with laughter. "Have a care, husband, lest I bare my claws."

She raked her nails across his chest, and the sensation made his balls clench.

He lowered himself and kissed her, devouring her lips and chasing her tongue. He withdrew for a heartbeat for the sheer joy of sliding slowly back into her slick wetness. Then he raised himself again and reached between them to stroke her over the edge.

"Oh, Rob." Her inner walls clenched around him, and he felt the soft tremor that signaled the start of her release. "When ye do that, I don't care a fig if it's so cold I catch my death…my death…my death…"

Her voice echoed round the chamber and faded into the distant thatch overhead.

Rob jerked awake.

He wasn't in his bridal bedchamber. He was lying on stone-hard ground with a stone-hard cock still primed to make love to the woman in his dream. Stars wheeled above him in a frigid sky. His band of men snored nearby.

And the fact that Fiona was dead slammed into him afresh.

He'd married her two years ago at Christmas, and she'd been gone by Epiphany. Twelve days, he'd been a husband. Only twelve.

And now a night didn't pass without his wife visiting him as some phantom, sometimes tender, sometimes terrifying. She lived in his dreams, but always he was powerless to hold her to earth.

She was so vibrant, so real by night, he suffered all the more in the waking world with the knowledge that he'd not find her there.

One of the men in the clearing let out a loud snore and mumbled in his sleep. It was hours till dawn, and even more till Rob could accomplish what he intended in the coming day. But he would not seek sleep.

He couldn't bear to lose Fiona again so soon.

∽◈∾

Rob narrowed his gaze at the stone kirk across the glen. The bagpipes' celebratory tune ended with an off-key wheeze. He and his men, concealed on the edge of the forest, had watched the bridal procession and the arrival of the groom's party. Now he heard nothing from the kirk. The only sound was the harsh cry of a jay from the branches above him.

The ceremony must have been beginning in earnest. Rob snorted, his breath like a curl of dragon smoke in the chilly air.

"'Tis time, Hamish."

"I wish ye'd reconsider." His friend shook his head, his scruff of red beard making him look like an alarmed hedgehog. Hamish never let his beard grow beyond the stubble stage. A metal worker couldn't chance much facial hair. Even his eyebrows were habitually singed off. "If ye go through with this, folk will say ye're...that ye're—"

"Mad? They say that already." Rob mounted his black stallion. The beast sensed his agitation and pawed the dirt, restive and spoiling for action. "I see no other path before me. Now will ye help me or no?"

"Aye, Rob, ye've no need to ask, but—"

"Then get the men ready to ride. I hope to be in a wee bit of a hurry when next ye see me." He shot his friend a mirthless grin and spurred his mount into a gallop across the glen.

It was possible the next time Hamish saw him, Rob might be in no hurry at all.

He could very well be dead.

⁂

The smell of incense was so cloying, Elspeth Stewart feared she might faint dead away. But a bride must stand before the altar.

She drew a shallow breath and swallowed hard. That was better. As the priest droned on, she sneaked a glance from under her lashes at the man who would be her husband.

Lachlan Drummond.

Tall and commanding in his dress plaid, he wasn't altogether unpleasing. His face was tanned, and the lines at the corners of his eyes suggested he'd squinted into countless northern suns. Those lines didn't trouble her. They proved the laird was a man of action, not like the dainty fops who visited from the English court from time to time.

No, it was the deep grooves between his brows and the hard set of his mouth that gave her pause.

"Dinna fret yerself," her mother had assured her when she complained that she didn't know her betrothed well enough to even speak to him if she met him in Queen Mary's court. "An arranged match is a safe match. Yer father has chosen the Drummond for ye, and ye'll do well to bide by his wishes."

The queen had approved too. She'd angered so many of the nobles with her other policies, she didn't dare gainsay two of them on something as inconsequential as the marriage of one of her ladies-in-waiting.

Inconsequential to everyone but me, Elspeth fumed.

An exchange of breeding cattle, a grant of grazing rights, a promise of fealty between their clans; that was really all that was being solemnized now. It was certainly no marriage as she'd ever imagined it.

Or Seen it. Elspeth was gifted with a bit of the Sight, and never in all her prescient dreams had she seen this match on her horizon.

This loveless ceremony was as far removed from the tales of courtly devotion in her precious little book of sonnets as the distant moon.

Yet when the priest asked Lachlan Drummond to pledge his faith to her, his voice was strong, the tone pleasing. He even sent her a quick private smile.

Elspeth jerked her gaze back to her folded hands. Her cheeks burned as if she had a fever.

She wondered if her mother was right.

"Passion," Morag Stewart had said, "is a dish that flares hot, but then goes cold as a tomb often as not. An arranged match is like a cauldron set to simmer over a low fire. A nourishing broth heated evenly warms a body from the inside out."

Elspeth wasn't sure how she could do the things her mother said her husband would expect of her. Bizarrely intimate things. Of course, she'd seen horses mate, and dogs too, but she never suspected people did something as…primitive as the mere beasts.

And now she'd have to do it with a man she barely knew.

Silence jerked her back from her musings. The priest had asked her a question and was waiting for a reply. She blinked stupidly at him. What had he said?

Suddenly the double doors of the nave shattered. A man on a large black horse was silhouetted in the opening for a heartbeat. Then he urged the stallion into the kirk and charged up the center aisle.

"Mad Rob!" she heard someone call out.

Half the horseman's face was painted with woad, and his cobalt eyes burned as brightly blue. With his dark hair flying and the fierce expression of a berserker on his features, he certainly looked mad.

"The MacLaren," shouted another.

Her bridegroom was silent, but a muscle worked furiously in his cheek.

Her father reached for the horse's bridle, but the MacLaren shouted a command, and the stallion reared, pawing the air. Then it lashed out with its hind hooves, and everyone scrambled out of reach of the slashing kicks.

Elspeth watched in disbelief as the man drew a long claymore from the shoulder baldric strapped to his back and laid the flat of the blade across Lachlan Drummond's chest. Riding a horse into the kirk was bad enough. Mad Rob had broken the sanctity of holy ground by drawing his weapon. All the other men had laid their swords and dirks outside the doors, which now hung drunkenly from the hinges.

Elspeth half expected the Almighty to strike the blasphemer down with thunderbolts from the altar.

"Twitch so much as an eyelash, wee Lachlan, and I'll take yer head," Mad Rob said as pleasantly if he'd offered Drummond a plate of warm scones.

Then he leaned down and scooped Elspeth up with his other arm and dropped her belly-first across his kilted lap.

She was too astonished to be afraid. All the air fled from her lungs with a whoosh. Her head and arms dangled on one side of the restive stallion, and her legs kicked on the other. She couldn't rail at the man, since she was busy fighting for breath, but she struggled to free herself from such an undignified position.

"Hold still, lass, lest my hand slips and I lop off a bit of your groom."

Now fear sliced into her. She froze and looked at Lachlan. The madman's blade had slid up to his chin. Her bridegroom hadn't taken his black-eyed gaze from Mad Rob's face.

"I'll be going now, Drummond," Rob said in the same reasonable tone a man might use to discuss cattle or the weather. "If ye've the stones for a fight, ye may collect yer bride at *Caisteal Dubh*. But dinna show your face till month's end. Come for her sooner or try to follow us now, and I might have to kill her."

Elspeth couldn't look up at her captor's face, but she heard a wicked smile in his voice.

Kill her reverberated in her mind.

And all she'd thought she'd lose when she woke this day was her maidenhead.

The madman wheeled the stallion around, and

Elspeth hooked an elbow around his knee lest she fall as the kirk and the people in it ran together in a blur of colors. Her mother keened like a lost soul over the din of shouts. The stallion clattered back down the aisle and shot out into the crisp November air, making a beeline for the distant forest.

With every jarring stride, Elspeth's ribs took a pounding. Then she felt both the MacLaren's hands at her waist. He lifted her without slowing the stallion one jot, controlling the beast with his knees and will alone.

"Can ye ride astride?" he shouted.

"Aye." She threw one leg over the horse's neck and settled herself before him, matching his rocking movement to keep her seat. She dug her fingers into the horse's mane. Trying to leap off at this speed would mean a broken neck. There'd be another chance to escape later.

For she must escape. A month, even a night, with this madman would mean ruin.

Lachlan Drummond would surely come for her. He'd be obliged to, according to the contract between him and the House of Stewart. And her father and his men with him.

She twisted and glanced under MacLaren's arm. Men were milling before the church, not giving pursuit, clearly taking Mad Rob's threat to kill her seriously.

Once they reached the trees, a shout went up behind them. Rob pulled the stallion to a stop. Elspeth gasped a shuddering breath as his arm around her waist tightened. They turned to see her bridegroom and her father mounting up to follow.

"Apparently, they hold your life less precious than your honor, lass," the MacLaren muttered. "Hamish! Tell the lads to lay the trails. Now ride."

A half-dozen other horsemen appeared from their places of concealment in the trees. They circled the small clearing, obliterating any betraying tracks, and then they all hied off in different directions to confuse Drummond's men and cover Mad Rob's escape.

Elspeth and her captor rode wildly over hill and down dale, eeling through copses of spindly trees. The MacLaren's horse was hill bred. Not as showy as the palfrey Elspeth had ridden to her wedding, but hardy and deep chested and apparently willing to run till it dropped if the man on its back demanded.

Shouts of discovery rose behind them. The men in pursuit must have split up, and someone followed their trail. Elspeth's heart nearly burst from her chest with hope.

"Hi-up!" Mad Rob bellowed at the stallion, and it leaped into a burst of speed as if being chased by a thousand demons but feared the man on its back even more.

The MacLaren leaned forward. Elspeth bent over the horse's neck, Mad Rob's hot breath searing her nape, and held on for her life. They dodged trees, leaped over fallen trunks, and splashed through a burn in full spate. The world ripped by her in a green blur.

Her pearl-studded snood peeled off as the wind whipped past them. Her long brown hair uncoiled and fluttered behind her. She hoped it was flying in the MacLaren's face, but a quick glance back showed it waving over his shoulder like a banner.

When they reached a rise, Mad Rob paused long enough to look back. A dozen horsemen were in pursuit.

"Drummond is a better tracker than I credited him," he muttered.

Elspeth drew several gasping breaths, trying to still her pounding heart after their mad dash. She squinted at their followers but didn't see her father's dun mare in the pack.

"Your horse carries two," she said. "Surrender, and I'll convince them to spare you."

"Drummond wouldna know mercy if it bit him on the arse."

"Ye'll never outrun them."

"Then we'll go to ground."

An angry swarm of crossbow bolts buzzed around them. Mad Rob whipped the stallion's head around, and they plunged down the far side of the hill.

When they reached the bottom, he reined the horse to a slow trot along the base of the hillside.

Elspeth tried to wiggle free as soon as they slowed their pace.

"Hold still," he snarled. "Dinna try me, wench. I've nothing to lose."

She settled then, taking hope from shouts of the men following them. Their voices echoed from one rise to the next. The horses' hoofbeats on the far side of the hill sounded like approaching thunder.

Mad Rob seemed not to hear them. He just kept scanning the craggy slope. Then he turned the stallion's head back up the incline, making for an outcropping of dark granite.

"They're almost upon us!" Elspeth shouted. "Surrender and live."

He didn't slow his determined flight toward the rocks. Then when they almost dashed into them, Rob brought the stallion up so short it nearly sat on its haunches.

"Get ye behind the rock." He nearly threw her off the horse and leaped down behind her. He pushed her between a pair of cottage-sized boulders, leading the stallion behind him. "To the right."

There was a yawning hole in the hillside, a cave whose entrance was hidden by the rocks. Elspeth staggered into the darkness as the MacLaren and his mount followed. The ground was uneven beneath her feet.

The cave was cool and dark and ripe with must. She extended her hands before her lest she walk into a wall.

"How did ye know—?"

Mad Rob clamped a hand over her mouth and pulled her back against his chest. "Not a word if ye wish to keep breathing." His whisper tickled her ear.

She stood perfectly still, inhaling the scent of leather from his gloved hand. She heard his soft breathing and the stallion's trappings creaking as the horse shifted its weight. Then in the distance, she made out the tattoo of hoofbeats and muffled shouts as the men who were pursuing them overran their hiding place.

Then those sounds faded, and all she could hear was the pounding of her blood coursing through her veins. The heartbeat of the man standing behind her thudded against her spine. He relaxed his hold and removed his hand from her mouth.

She turned to face him and shouted out: "I'm here! Hel—"

His mouth descended upon hers and swallowed up her cry.

She'd been kissed sweetly before, stylized expressions of courtship during some of the dances favored by Queen Mary's court.

This kiss bore no resemblance to those. This was a ravishment, a demanding plunder of her mouth.

He stole her breath, but she was so surprised by the sudden invasion, she didn't think to pull away. She froze like a coney confronted by a fox.

He filled her with breath from his own body, warming her to her toes.

I should be revolted. I should be screaming to get away.

But then his mouth went suddenly soft and beguiling on hers. Elspeth had never imagined the like.

How strange, this shared breath, this mingling of souls.

Without conscious thought, her fingers curled around his collar. She received a flash of Sight. Not exactly a vision. More like a deep Knowing.

Rob MacLaren had a hole in his heart, a void nothing could fill.

He no longer seemed mad to her. Just empty. Her chest constricted in empathy.

An image forced itself into Elspeth's consciousness, creeping in softly but with determination. The willowy form of a woman with long coppery hair took shape in her mind, distant and hazy. Elspeth couldn't see her face. The woman turned and fled into the mist.

She sensed deep sadness in MacLaren, an ache

that wouldn't be stilled. A loss for which there was no comfort.

He'd abducted her from the altar, but she couldn't feel anything for him but pity.

As the Sight faded, pain seared through her brain. It always did when she was touched by her gift, but it paled in comparison to the nameless hurt he bore. Elspeth reached up a tentative hand to comfort him, palming the cheek that wasn't covered with woad.

He wrapped an arm around her waist and tugged her closer. Her lips parted. His tongue swept in. Her belly clenched, and a warm glow settled between her legs.

He left her lips and began kissing her chin, her cheeks, her neck. "Ach! Ye're sweet, lass."

Pity dissipated like morning mist. Instead, little wisps of pleasure followed his mouth's path. The stubble of his beard grazed the tops of her breasts, and her nipples tightened almost painfully. She sucked her breath over her teeth to keep from crying out in pleasure and surprise when his palm covered her breast, the pressure sweet even through the stiff boning of her pink silk bodice.

She'd been sickened by the thought of submitting to Lachlan Drummond's intimate caress. Now her whole body thrummed with life. She tingled with awareness as Rob touched her.

She'd never understood how a maiden could allow herself to be ruined before. Unruly, unwelcome urges seared through her. The sensations were so unlike her, she wondered if they were somehow part of what she'd Seen of the copper-haired woman.

To her amazement, she ached to lie down beside this man. To feel his body cover hers. To give to him what Lachlan would have taken.

This was madness, but she couldn't bring herself to end it. With each kiss, his sadness lessened and her pleasure increased. She'd never dreamed she'd experience such astonishing delight.

Only a little longer, she told herself as bliss sparked across her skin. His kiss was like a draught of heady wine. The discomfort that usually accompanied the Sight was leaving, but her head still felt fuzzy. Was it clouding her judgment?

One kiss more. Then I'll stop.

She splayed her fingers across his chest. His muscles were like a brazen shield beneath his shirt and plaid. He growled with satisfaction. She smoothed her palms up to his shoulders and down his arms.

And encountered sticky wetness on the left side.

"You're bleeding," she whispered. One of the crossbow bolts must have found its mark.

He dipped his head and mumbled into the well between her breasts. "'Tis nothing."

It was enough to recall her to sanity. To serve Queen Mary, she must be either a pure maid or the wife of a nobleman. If she couldn't remain the first, she'd never be the last. She pulled away from him.

"Truly, 'tis naught but a scratch. Come, lass."

He folded her into his arms again and delivered a string of kisses along the curve of her jaw.

"No!" she said

When he tried to kiss her again, she delivered a ringing slap to his cheek. Reason flooded her mind again. Perhaps he was called "Mad Rob" because he could entice others to insanity. She jerked herself out of his arms.

"Now keep away from me," she ordered.

He chuckled mirthlessly. "Lass, I've killed dozens of men. Do ye really think ye can stop me from whatever I may decide to do with you?"

He took a step toward her, his eyes glittering fiercely in the dark.

Chapter 2

ROB ADVANCED STEADILY, STEELING HIMSELF TO IGNORE the way her brows drew together in fear.

"A man doesna name a horse he might have to eat come winter," he said, his voice silky with menace. "And he doesna befriend one he's taken hostage."

"Then why did ye kiss me?" she asked, scuttling backward over the cave floor.

He stopped. It was a fair question, and he had no answer. He didn't know what was wrong with him. He'd thought that part of him dead. Oh, he still woke with a cock-stand, and occasionally the thing rose of its own accord when he caught sight of a well-turned ankle or the swell of a breast, but he always tamped down the urge. He'd not truly desired any woman since Fiona.

Then he found this Elspeth Stewart in his arms, and all he wanted to do was rut her blind.

He curled his lip in a snarl. He didn't want to feel those things for anyone but his wife. Certainly not for Lachlan Drummond's woman.

When he first conceived this plan, in the blackest

part of his mind he'd thought to wound Drummond by ravishing his bride. But when it came down to the actual doing of the deed, he didn't know if it was in him. Even if he was able to raise his cock long enough to take her maidenhead.

He'd done his share of lying and thieving and killing.

He'd never taken a woman unwilling.

But Elspeth Stewart hadn't seemed particularly unwilling. At least, not at first. And he'd already proved his body was up to the task if he should decide upon ravishing her.

Rob smiled because it seemed to unnerve her when he did. "I kissed ye because it seemed the best way to shut ye up at the time. Though I didna expect ye'd like it so well."

Her eyes narrowed at that. "I didna like it."

"Liars go to hell, ye know."

"So do men who steal brides from the altar," she snapped back, still retreating, bunching the train of her velvet skirt in one hand to keep from tripping on it. Then she reached the rear of the cave and could flee no farther.

"Oh, rest easy on that score, lass. I was bound for hell long before this morning's work." Rob closed the gap between them and laid his hand at the base of her throat.

She didn't fight him, which showed intelligence. He might hurt her unintentionally if she struggled. Her pulse raced like a hummingbird's wings.

Plenty of men *would* kill her now, he knew. He'd certainly travel easier without her. Hidden in this remote cave, her body would likely never be found.

He could claim she ran away from him and must have perished in the cold with no shelter from the elements. If their places were reversed, Drummond would certainly kill his hostage and get away clean.

Rob tightened his grip experimentally. It would be easy enough, with a little neck like hers. One good twist would do the trick. She'd feel little pain. The symmetry of the idea appealed to him.

Even the good Lord said "an eye for an eye."

But that would mean punishing the innocent for the sins of the guilty. And Rob wasn't quite mad enough to see justice in that.

She swallowed hard beneath his hand. He loosened his grip but didn't release her.

He'd seen men sniveling in the dirt over less threat to their persons, yet she didn't plead. He slanted a gaze of grudging respect toward her.

"Will ye no' beg for your life, Elspeth Stewart? Aye, lass," he said with a nod when her eyes went wider, "I ken who ye are."

"No, I'll never beg." She stood straighter and met his gaze squarely. "Why should I give ye what ye want?"

The lass has spirit. Rob liked that.

Fiona'd had spirit too.

But Fiona wouldn't be pleased with what he was doing now, he was certain. A half-heard sibilance curled round the cave. He released Elspeth and cocked his head, straining to listen, willing the small voice to come again. Was that Fiona trying to speak to him?

So often, while lying on his lonely bed, he thought he heard his wife singing to him just on the edge of sound. If only he could listen hard enough, if only he could follow the song to wherever she was, heaven or hell or that slice of a moment between sleep and wakefulness, it mattered not—

"Let me tend your wound," the flesh-and-blood woman before him whispered. "You're bleeding badly."

Elspeth Stewart's voice brought him back.

Now that she mentioned it, his arm did sting a bit. He'd thought the steady drip on the cave floor was water pattering from the stone vault overhead. It turned out to be blood trickling from the fingers of his left hand.

"Let's get you into the sunlight where I can see what's needed," she said, taking his good arm.

"Clever, lass, but no," he said. "We'll no' need to leave the cave just yet. Yer bridegroom might turn back this way. Come with me."

❧

Elspeth drew a deep breath and followed her captor back along the cave's main corridor. At least he no longer seemed disposed to harm her.

Madmen were changeable as weathercocks. One moment he was making love to her mouth and the next he threatened to squeeze the life out of her. She'd have to tread warily to avoid setting him off again.

He turned sharply down a narrow passage she'd missed when she was backing away from him.

"The outside entrance is hidden by rock, and inside, the cave hides its secret room the same way," he explained. After a tight turn, the cave expanded into a high-ceilinged second chamber.

A shaft of golden sunlight poured from an opening

high overhead, illuminating a small pool of water bubbling in the center of the vaulted space. Moss clung to the rock walls, creating a natural underground hothouse. The air was several notches warmer here than in the other chamber of the cave.

Elspeth halted midstep. She'd never dreamed once about her wedding with Lachlan Drummond, but she'd been in this very room shrouded in the mists of the Sight more times than she could count. She'd never Seen *why* she was in this cavern, but the fact that she recognized her surroundings gave her confidence it was Meant. The realization steadied her.

"I know this—" She stopped herself.

How would a madman respond to claims of foreknowledge? He might demand she look into the future for him, and that was not how her gift worked. She could not summon it at will. The Sight came when it would, in hazy impressions or blinding flashes, and showed her what it pleased, not what she asked. Elspeth rarely shared that part of herself with anyone since doing so marked her as different, maybe even fearsome. She decided not to chance telling him of it.

"How did you know this was here?"

"I've reived a herd or two in these parts," he admitted, speaking in a normal tone of voice now. The moss climbing the walls seemed to absorb the sound and freshened the air with the green breath of growing things. "It's good to know where the hidey-holes are. I spent most of a week here once when Drummond's men would have stretched my neck if they'd caught me. The water is good."

He knelt at the edge of the spring and splashed water on his face. The blue clay he'd painted himself with ran off his skin in indigo runnels. Then he dunked his whole head and came up, shaking like a spaniel. Dark hair flying, he sprayed the space with droplets of sparkling water.

The woad swirled in blue ribbons around the spring and then disappeared under the rock shelf into an underground stream.

Now that he wasn't painted for battle, Rob MacLaren looked younger, not so many years older than she. His jaw was firm and sported a shadow of a dark beard. His mouth slanted across his face in a sensual, cocky half smile. He was tall, well favored, and muscular. She'd have thought him handsome beyond the lot of mortals if he hadn't abducted her from her wedding.

However, his eyes stopped her cold. They were the brilliant blue of a loch in high summer, but the soul behind them was deadened by grief. He was a man who might do anything.

No wonder folk named him "mad."

Elspeth knelt to drink, dipping with both hands. The water tickled down her throat, bracing and sweet. The cool water steadied her. "Take off your shirt, and I'll tend your wound."

"After I see to my horse. He's served me well this day. I'd be worse than a knave if I repaid him sore."

He left her alone, diving back into the dark corridor to fetch the stallion. Elspeth walked the perimeter of the chamber. There seemed to be no other way out except the small opening far over her head. She was as good as in prison with nothing to do but watch the sunlight track across the cave's floor.

Rob returned, leading the horse. He unsaddled his mount, but left him haltered and tied him to a narrow column of rock rising from the floor of the cave.

"Guess no one's been here since me," Rob said as he stooped to pick up a discarded leather bucket. "I was wondering where I'd left this."

He filled it and gave his horse a drink. The stallion whickered his thanks and then fell to munching oats in the nose bag Rob settled over his head.

Tending the horse seemed to settle the MacLaren. Elspeth was grateful. She wasn't sure how long she'd stay alive with a madman. Rob sounded like any other Highlander when he crooned soft endearments to his horse.

He patted the stallion's arched neck. "Aye, Falin, eat yer fill. There's a good lad."

"Falin? So he has a name?" Elspeth said. "I thought a man didna name a horse he might eat come winter."

Rob chuckled. "I'd be eating my shoes before I butcher this fine fellow. Falin's too valuable. He'll strengthen the MacLaren herd for generations to come."

"So ye gave him the name of a demon?"

"Ye didna see him before he was broke. He earned the name, believe me. Even now, he'll suffer only me to ride him."

"He let *me* ride him," Elspeth pointed out.

"Aye, well, I didna give either of ye any say in the matter."

Rob shrugged off the blue and green MacLaren plaid draped over his shoulder and peeled out of his shirt. His brawny chest and arms were thickly muscled, and whorls of dark hair swirled round his brown nipples. Blood oozed from one thick bicep.

He settled next to Elspeth near the spring.

"Do your worst," he said sourly.

"I'll have you know I've doctored my father before, so I'll have none of your sauce." She examined the wound, which appeared to be a straight-edged gash. She couldn't tell for certain till she cleaned it up. "Do ye have anything we might use for a bandage?"

"No."

"What about a needle? This wants stitches. And spirits, if ye have aught."

"That I do." He stood and went over to rummage in his saddlebag again. "Mayhap a bit of your skirt will serve as a bandage."

Her bridal dress had seen hard use already. But with nothing else readily available, she had little choice.

Elspeth's mother had been particularly partial to the wine-colored velvet skirt and decided adding pink silk piping at the hem would be the perfect way to mate it with the pink bodice to make it special for the wedding. Elspeth wouldn't be able to rip the thick velvet, but the silk was much frailer. With silent apologies to her mother, Elspeth picked at the hem until she parted a few of Morag Stewart's fine, even stitches and ripped a length from the bottom.

When she looked up, Rob was staring down at her exposed ankles, need straining his features. She tucked her feet under the velvet, realizing there were other ways the MacLaren could harm her that would probably grieve her family more than finding her dead.

"Looks like something else will want stitching as well," he said, his voice strangely tight.

"I'll see to turning my hem after I tend ye. The gown's no' bleeding, ye ken. But should my ankles be exposed again, I need ye to avert your eyes, as a gentleman should."

"As ye will." He settled beside her with sewing supplies and a flask of whisky from his saddlebag. "But ye're mistaken, mistress, if ye think me a gentleman."

A sizzling retort danced on her tongue, but she reminded herself that baiting a madman was a fair definition of lunacy. Instead, she dipped the pink silk into the cool spring and then dabbed at his wound.

"Ye were fortunate," she said. "The bolt grazed ye and went through clean."

"Drummond's a tetchy bastard. Shooting off crossbows when his bride is in the line of fire," Rob said with a black frown. "It might have just as easily been ye who caught the business end of a bolt."

She narrowed her gaze at him as she gave his arm a thorough scrubbing. The same thought had occurred to her. She'd already decided Lachlan must not have been thinking clearly when he gave the order to shoot, but she didn't appreciate this man pointing out her betrothed's error. She enjoyed Mad Rob's yelp when she poured whisky on the wound.

He grabbed the flask from her and took a swig, muttering about wasteful females.

"If ye're so concerned for my safety, perhaps ye might have thought of that before ye dragged me from the altar," she said. He was the villain, not Lachlan. "I'll thank ye not to disparage the man who will be my husband."

"Why is that, by the bye?" He cocked a brow at her. "Did wee Lachlan court ye sweet?"

"That's none of your affair," she said brusquely. There'd been no courtship at all, sweet or otherwise. "And why do ye name him small? He's as tall as ye."

He snorted. "Men are measured in all kinds of ways."

"Aye, in kindness and courage," she said with conviction.

"And in other ways," he said with a smirk. "Granted, I've no sure knowledge, but men like your intended, who are small of spirit, are often deficient in other things as well. But perhaps as a maid, ye're ignorant of such details."

Innocence and ignorance didn't always hold hands. Elspeth had heard some of the other ladies-in-waiting tittering behind their fans over who among the queen's courtiers was naturally well endowed and who padded their codpieces with rolled-up stockings. Only Highlanders didn't follow fashion and wore nothing beneath their kilts but what God gave them. Her gaze flicked to Rob's lap.

A hot blush crept up her neck. Where had that come from? She wasn't the sort to ogle a man's groin.

At least, she hadn't been.

"Kindly remember, sir, I am holding a needle with intent to use it."

"Duly noted," he said with a smile in his voice. He reached over with his right hand to stroke her arm.

Even though her chemise and a detachable silk

sleeve separated them, she felt the heat of his palm on her skin. All the small hairs on her arm pricked to attention, and her flesh shivered with expectancy.

"Are ye cold, Elspeth?"

"Aye, but I dinna expect ye to care." She jabbed the needle through his skin with more force than necessary.

He didn't so much as twitch, though his hand squeezed her arm slightly and his lips tightened in a grimace.

"This will hurt ye more than it does me," she said as she pulled the thread through his skin.

"Nay, lass, you're but tickling me," he said, his eyes never leaving hers. His thumb rubbed back and forth over her forearm.

"What are ye doing?" she demanded.

"Hmm?" He blinked, all innocence.

She looked pointedly down at his hand. His thumb stopped.

"I was just distracting myself a bit from the pain," he said. "Ye're fair soft."

"Ye're accustomed to scratchy wool. That's just the silk ye feel."

"No, I can imagine ye beneath your clothes," he said. "I'm thinking your skin puts silk to shame."

"Aye?" She jabbed him again.

He groaned. "Aye. Your father may let ye tend him, lass, but ye must admit, ye've no' got a healer's touch."

"And what's a healer's touch like?" she asked, working quickly to push the needle through and tie off another knot, closing his wound with each stitch.

"Light as a feather. Like this."

He moved his hand from her arm to her breast. His

fingertips brushed the bared skin above her bodice in teasing strokes. She held herself still, beguiled by the sensation. She'd never have guessed her body would react so to a man. She should be afraid, she knew, but her only fear was that he'd stop.

His touch moved down, between the stiff boning of her bodice and the soft, thin chemise, circling her nipple slowly through the cloth of her undergarment.

Oh, how he made her ache. He tormented that needy skin with his nearness. She fought the urge to squirm into his touch. When he finally flicked a nail over it, a jolt of wickedness shot from her breast to her womb.

Warning bells jangled in her head.

"Stop." She covered her breast with her own hand. "That's no' a healer's touch."

His smile was sin incarnate. "Ye've the right of it there, lass. That's a lover's touch. And ye've had only the smallest bit of the pleasure, only a taste of what I would give ye an' ye allow it."

"No." She scrambled to her feet to put some distance between them. "An' ye try to take me, I'll scratch yer eyes out, Rob MacLaren."

"I'd not take ye. Not a step further than ye wish. I ken ye're a virgin and wanting to stay that way," he said earnestly. "But there's great delight for a man in the giving of pleasure, ye see. And ways around a maidenhead that'll leave ye still pure when we're done."

She'd forgotten to breathe as he spoke. Now she sucked in a quick breath.

"Shall I pleasure ye, Elspeth?"

Chapter 3

SHE BLINKED AT HIM, LIKE A SMALL BROWN SQUIRREL caught in the gaze of an adder. Then she gave herself a shake.

"No, of course not!" she said, backing away from him again. "Ye've stolen me away from my own wedding! How could I suffer ye to touch me so?"

"It didna seem to me that ye were suffering." Rob never claimed to know much about women, but he recognized waking passion when he saw it.

"I hardly know ye."

"Ach." He nodded. "Then I take it ye must know Lachlan Drummond well."

With a few quick steps, she managed to put the spring between them. "We met at the altar, if ye must know. He was my parents' choice."

"Well, that's a point in your favor, lass. Otherwise, I'd mistrust your judgment." Rob liked the way her cheeks flamed with color. "But still ye intended to bed him this night, did ye no'?"

Her brows drew together in distress. "He'd be my husband. I'd have to."

"So enthusiastic," he said, his tone laced with sarcasm. "And here I thought ye were a besotted bride."

"I never said I was besotted."

"If your heart's no' engaged in your marriage, then ye shouldna be averse to a wee bit of lust outside of it," he said, advancing around to her. She made him feel pleasurably male again. He decided to listen to his groin and not stifle the urge.

Lust wasn't the same as love. Surely it wouldn't be a betrayal of Fiona if he used his body to wreak vengeance on his enemy. Especially not if he convinced Lachlan's bride to succumb willingly.

"Ye interrupted the ceremony before the vows were complete. I'm no' even officially a wife, I dinna suppose," she said, still circling the spring to keep her distance from him.

Her nipples stood out beneath her bodice, whether from cold or the memory of his touch, he didn't much care. They were a fine sight in any case. He ached to suckle them.

"I'm a maiden, which means I need to refrain from lust of any kind."

"Ye dinna strike me as doing especially well with restraint," he said, switching directions and gaining on her by doing so. "I've kissed ye, lass, and ye seem prone to passion. I felt the way your body responded to my touch. Ye wanted me, if ye dinna mind my saying so."

"Would it matter to ye if I do mind?"

"No' in the slightest. Truth must be spoken or 'twill burst out of us, lass."

She caught a toe in her broad skirts and went down

on the rocky cave floor. Rob ran around and knelt over her. "Are ye hurt?"

She looked up at him, her eyes enormous. He noticed they were hazel, the sort that picked up whatever hue was near. Now they were the same shade of green as the moss ringing the cavern. She shook her head at him. "The only thing that can hurt me here is you."

She balled her fingers into fists but kept them clenched on her lap. He sensed she wanted to strike him but wisely contained herself.

"Why are ye doing this to me?" she demanded with a hint of a suppressed sob.

"That should be obvious. Your intended husband owes me a debt he canna repay."

"So I'm to suffer for it?"

"No, I intend that *he* should suffer the loss of you."

"Then…" Her voice tremored, and she swallowed hard. "Ye do intend to kill me still."

He sat down beside her. Tears trembled on her lower lashes.

Deliver me, O Lord, from a woman's weeping.

"No, 'tis no' in me to do ye harm," he said softly. "Though wee Lachlan couldn't have known that. I threatened to kill ye if he followed, and yet he came after us. If I were ye, I'd think twice over giving your loyalty to a man who puts so little thought to your safety."

She chuckled mirthlessly, pulling her knees to her chest and hugging them to her. "As if ye care for my safety."

He gazed into her eyes. There were little flecks of gold ringing her pupils.

Now that she wasn't running from him or terrified by him, he realized Elspeth Stewart was really quite a beauty. Her lips were full and lush. By some trick of musculature under her smooth skin, the corners of them turned up naturally in a beguiling half smile, as if she were hugging a delicious secret to herself. There were soft hollows beneath her rosy cheeks, a sign of the bone-deep loveliness that only ripens with age.

"Lachlan Drummond is a lucky bastard," Rob said with conviction.

"I dinna imagine he'd agree with you." She picked absently at her frayed hem. "He did lose his bride at the altar remember."

"Aye, so he did." Rob leaned closer. She smelled faintly of heather and evergreen boughs. Scent was an extravagance. He wondered where she dabbed the fragrant oil. The thin skin of her wrists? The pulse point at her white throat? Or maybe in the sweet hollow between her breasts?

Thinking about all those soft, forbidden places made him feel rampantly, throbbingly male. He wanted to search out those tender spots, bury his nose in them, and lave them with his tongue.

She scooted away from him, but he closed the distance between them so he was still sitting beside her.

"Then what do ye intend to do with me?" she asked in a small voice.

"Most men in my position would take your maidenhead and be done with it." If he listened to his swollen cock, he'd be on her in a heartbeat. She might fight him at first, but she'd melted under his kisses before. She would again.

"If you intend to ravish me, you'll have to gag me."
Her chin lifted in defiance. "Because I'll scream my
bloody head off."

"Will ye now?" He lifted a hand and ran his fingertip
across the lace at her bodice. He'd been no monk prior
to his marriage, but losing Fiona had made him realize
it was possible for a man to forswear women. Since he
lost her, he'd not been tempted by a single lass.

Except this Stewart maiden.

But this was a special case. It didn't count as a
betrayal if his heart wasn't engaged, did it?

"As I recall," he said as his fingertip skimmed the
tops of her breasts, "I enjoy the sounds a woman
makes when I pleasure her."

"Ye'd not enjoy these sounds." She slapped his hand
away. "And if ye take me, there'd be no pleasure."

"As a maid, ye canna know that," he said, lifting
one of the long locks of her chestnut hair to his
lips and inhaling her scent. "And I dinna think ye'll
scream, not in the way ye mean, in any case."

"Ye'd have to tie me up and force yourself on
me, because I'd fight ye, tooth and claw," she said
with assurance.

"Now there's a thought," he said. "I've heard some
lassies enjoy being tied up."

He could picture her in his mind, bound tight, her
breasts bared, her legs splayed with her soft core wet
and ready. She'd be helpless before him. He'd make
her beg for release. He stood and walked to his horse
to retrieve a length of rope.

"Shall we give it a try?"

"No!" she said, scrabbling away. "Please, no."

"Dinna fret, Elspeth. I'll no' force ye," he crooned softly, as if she were a frightened mare. He settled beside her. "That's no' my way."

The image of her bound form faded only slightly in his mind, but not in his groin. If only he were a little more mad, it definitely *could* be his way. He shook off the lurid fancy and focused on the matter at hand.

"But I do intend to tie ye to me," he said. "We'll travel by night, so we need to get some sleep now. And I'll no' find rest if I'm worried ye may be trying to hie yourself off to your betrothed."

He looped the rope around her waist before she could protest.

"Where are you taking me?" she asked.

"To my home, to *Caisteal Dubh*, o' course. Though we canna take a direct route. Ye'll be safe enough there."

"The Dark Castle?" she said with a shudder. "The name doesna bring me comfort. Is it haunted?"

"No," he said curtly. Not unless he counted the way Fiona haunted his dreams. "'Tis named for the black stone it's made of."

"Not for its black-hearted laird?"

He frowned at her. "If ye dinna make a fuss, I'll spread my cloak for ye. Twill be more comfortable than the cave floor. Will ye be good now?"

She nodded with obvious reluctance. "And ye'll not...?"

"No, lass. I've never taken a woman unwilling, and I'll no' start with ye. I give ye my word." He grinned wickedly at her. "O' course, there's them who says the word of a madman isna worth shite."

She seemed to ponder that for a moment. "Are ye truly mad, then?"

"D'ye think a madman would know?" he said, trying to make light of her question. He rose and fetched his cloak and warm plaid to make a pallet for them. In his mind, he still struggled to close the door on the image of her trussed up and bound, awaiting his pleasure. He'd never imagined the like before, and it made him wonder about himself. "Sometimes, aye, I think I am mad."

That deepened her frown.

He slammed that door in his mind so hard the hinges rattled. Could there be any pleasure between them if she continued to stare at him so warily, as if he had two heads?

"A man is judged by his action, so by those lights, aye, I expect I am mad. In some ways," he admitted. "But no' completely, ye ken. If I promise ye something, I'll deliver. Lie down, Elspeth."

She stretched out on the cloak, stiff limbed and watching him as a mouse eyes a cat.

"Turn on your side."

She bit her lip, but she did as he bid. Rob knotted the other end of the rope around his own waist and lay down behind her.

"Lift your head."

When she did, he slid his arm under her neck.

"There ye are, lass, as fine as ye could wish. A pillow for your head and all."

"Aye, never let it be said the MacLaren didna care for the comfort of his captives," she said tetchily.

"Ye've the right of it now. We'll deal together well,

ye and I." He pulled her close and spooned his body around hers. Then he covered them both with the end of his thick plaid. She wouldn't be able to twitch a muscle without his knowledge, so he could catch the sleep he'd need for the coming night without fear of her escaping.

She lay stiffly, every muscle clenched. But Rob kept his breathing even, and she relaxed by finger-widths until he heard a very soft, very ladylike snore.

Poor lass. She probably didna sleep much last night with thoughts of the wedding dancing in her head.

Rob settled a hand on her hip, and she didn't stir.

However, he did. His body roused to hers again. His cock swelled, and his ballocks tensed, but he held himself perfectly still. He'd made a promise, after all.

As he sought sleep, it occurred to him that the best revenge on Lachlan Drummond wouldn't be to kill his betrothed. Or to rape her. Or even tie her up and torment her into surrender, pleasurable as that might be.

If Rob could seduce Elspeth Stewart into giving herself to him willingly, his enemy would be thoroughly shamed. The name of Lachlan Drummond would become a byword, held up for ridicule by all as the cuckolded bridegroom. Bards would compose songs about it, and folk would laugh at him over many a winter fire.

Drummond would be so furious, he'd respond to Rob's challenge of single combat at last.

And then Rob would send him straight to hell. Even if he had to go through the flaming gate with him.

༄

One good thing about Mad Rob MacLaren, Elspeth thought when she woke. *He throws off more heat than a roaring fire.*

She pulled the plaid up till it covered her nose. A few moments earlier, her disorientation in the darkness was so complete, she might as well have been blind.

She became aware of the hard male body curved around her back. And the thick ridge of him pressed against her buttocks. His breathing was deep and even and fluttered the small hairs on her nape in its warm breeze.

She supposed she should be grateful. Many men would have taken her maidenhead without a moment's qualm.

And without his heat, she'd have passed a miserably uncomfortable night.

But she didn't want to feel any gratitude toward this man. Even if she were rescued now, the damage was done. Her reputation was in tatters.

No one would blame Lachlan Drummond if he wished to cry off.

Would they send her to a nunnery?

Elspeth was as good a Christian as the next Scottish lass, but life in a cloister didn't bear thinking of. To be penned away, never to run free on the heath or wear a pretty gown...

Or lie beside a man.

Rob shifted in his sleep and pulled her closer to him. Her body glowed with something that had nothing to do with shared warmth.

No, she was not suited for life in a religious order. Her brief time with Rob MacLaren had proved that. Her body and its bewildering needs were far too strong to be overruled by even the strictest monastic discipline.

She was meant to be someone's wife.

And now that she thought about it, she realized Lachlan Drummond wouldn't abandon her. She represented too many heads of cattle and rich grazing lands. Her father was laird of a powerful clan, the queen's own cousin, albeit a distant one. Alistair Stewart offered too strong a political alliance for her bridegroom to give up her without a fight.

The realization didn't please her as much as it ought.

Would she never be wanted just for herself?

"Are ye awake, lass?" Rob's whisper tickled her neck.

She sat up, keeping the plaid wrapped about her against the cold.

"Good," he said, moving with confidence in the darkness. "It's time we were away."

Away. Perhaps if she managed to steal away from Rob and return to Lachlan on her own, she'd prove herself to be courageous and strong.

And pure. A woman who'd been defiled surely wouldn't have the will to free herself.

Her betrothed would realize she was worth far more than beeves and grain and bonds between clans. Elspeth Stewart was valuable, in and of herself.

"Aye," she said softly. "Let's away."

Chapter 4

WHEN MAD ROB DECIDED TO LEAVE A PLACE, HE didn't let anything slow him down. In the black cave, Elspeth couldn't see her own hand when she held it before her face, but the MacLaren seemed to know exactly where he was going. The rope at her waist jerked her along to keep up with him as he led the stallion out.

Once they cleared the cave's mouth and stepped into the crisp, star-splashed night, Elspeth worked the knot at her waist, but it held firm. "Will ye no' untie me?"

"No. Hush now."

Rob climbed up on the rocks and surveyed the countryside, lying flat so as not to present a silhouette that might catch someone's watchful eye.

If there was anyone watching.

Elspeth cocked an ear. Wind rustled through the heather down the valley. Small animals scurried to their burrows for the night. She startled when an owl screeched nearby, but she didn't hear any sounds that might be attributed to a group of men.

The search party must have given up for the night and camped in the rough, so they could look for her trail at first light. With any luck at all, she and her captor would stumble upon them in the dark.

"Please untie me. I willna run," she said, crossing her fingers behind her back. A promise to a man like Rob MacLaren surely didn't count. She'd run like a hind if she got half a chance.

"I thank ye kindly for your parole, but no." He slid down from the boulder and began inspecting the stallion's hooves. "I'll keep ye on a tether, lass."

"But…" Would the wicked man make her say it? "I need some privacy before we travel."

"It's a long rope." Rob didn't even look up from adjusting the stallion's girth. "There are bushes aplenty on the other side of the rocks."

She shot him a glare that should have burned off his eyebrows, but since he didn't deign to look at her, he suffered no ill effects. Elspeth snorted at him, pulled the cloak he'd let her keep tighter around her, and stomped around the boulders. As soon as she was out of his sight, she bent down and picked at her hem, ripping off a small piece. She'd leave it draped on a bush for Lachlan to find.

The rope at her waist drew taut, and she felt a tug.

"Dinna try to work free, or I'll have to come round there," he called out. "And it may not be at a time of your liking if I do."

"I'd name ye a pig, Rob MacLaren, but t'would be an insult to swine everywhere," she muttered as she relieved herself.

She needn't have worried. As she started back

around the rock, he said, "Best ye give me a moment as well, unless ye've no wish to guard the innocence of your eyes."

He was gushing on the other side of the boulder, his stream loud enough to pass as the stallion's. Then after a few moments, the rope at her waist jerked.

"I assume that gentlemanly summons means it's safe for me to return," she said.

"Safe? No' exactly, but aye, come ahead, lass. Will ye be pleased to break your fast? I've a few bannocks and a rind of cheese."

She accepted the crusty bun and nibbled a bit on it. Then she decided to share the last bite with the stallion. If she intended to escape, taking Falin was her best chance.

She held out the crust to the horse, keeping her palm flat. He nosed her cautiously then accepted her offering, his velvet lips and warm, sweet breath brushing her hand.

But when she grasped his mane and tried to swing up onto his back, he shied away with a little kick. She stumbled backward, trying to avoid his hooves, and landed on her bottom while the horse snorted and rolled his eyes at her.

"Ye didna listen to what I said, did ye?" Rob asked, watching unconcernedly from his seat on the rocks. He took a swig from the flask of whisky, offered it to her, and then popped it back into his sporran when she declined. "I told ye Falin will suffer no one to ride him but me. That was a warning. If ye persist, he'll do ye damage."

"Ungrateful wretch," she hissed to the stallion as

she scrambled to her feet, rubbing her backside. He whickered back at her, laying his ears flat.

Perhaps the beast did deserve the name of a demon.

Rob mounted him smoothly, and the horse didn't so much as swish his long tail. The MacLaren leaned toward her and offered his a hand to help her up.

She folded her arms across her chest.

"Perhaps I misjudged the seriousness of that fall on your arse." He shot her a devilish grin. "Will ye no' be able to ride astride?"

"Of course, I can ride," she said, narrowing her eyes at him. "I just dinna want to ride with the likes of ye."

"Verra well, Mistress Stewart," he said, nudging Falin into a brisk walk through the narrow boulders and down the slope. "If ye wish to stretch your legs, who am I to gainsay a lady?"

The rope pulled her after them, and she trotted to keep pace. She stumbled once when her foot found a hole, but managed to keep her feet. They moved briskly along the valley floor, heading north. Every hundred yards or so, Elspeth tore off another bit from her skirt and dropped it behind her.

"Is this what passes for chivalry to a MacLaren?" she finally asked when her wind was nearly blown and she was reduced to heaving breaths.

"Oh, aye, my father always told me to give in to a lady's wishes. A man lives longer that way."

"I didna say I wished to run along behind you."

"Or maybe my father said it only seems longer," Rob said, twisting in his saddle to look back at her. He slowed Falin to a sedate walk.

"My wedding shoes were no' made for such hard use," she muttered. Like her dress, whose hem was now hopelessly tattered, her cunning kidskin slippers were probably scuffed beyond redemption. They were so lightly soled, she felt each pebble on the balls of her feet.

"May I remind ye, my lady, that walking is your choice?"

"None of this is my choice, MacLaren." Now that their pace had slowed, she felt the cold more keenly. Wind whistled down the valley, slicing through the wool cloak Rob had let her use as if it were made of thin silk.

"My father dragged my mother all the way from Ireland," Mad Rob said, "and I'll wager she didna complain as much as ye."

"Well, I dinna suppose your father stole your mother from her wedding."

"Ach, no. He took her from a nunnery, and she didna care to go at first either," he admitted. "But dinna fret. She came round to his way of thinking in the end, and it was all for the best."

"Charming tale," she said with sarcasm.

"Aye, I always thought so. If my mother had kept her veil, I wouldna have been born."

"What a loss to the world that would've been!"

She'd picked off all the silk piping from her hem. It could be easily explained as an accident of the rough road and his own fault for making her walk.

When he faced away from her and kept plodding, she untied one of the sleeves from her bodice beneath the cloak and let it drop to the ground. In another fifty paces, she considered undoing the other one as well, but decided against it. She'd likely be able to explain the accidental loss of one sleeve, but not two.

He reined the stallion to a stop so she could catch up to them. "Ye ride with me now."

She looked away, continuing to defy him. If she walked, they'd travel more slowly, and it would be easier for the men tracking them to catch up. She'd picked as much of her hem as she dared, both for modesty sake and because she feared Rob might discover what she'd done. Angering a madman was never wise.

"Come, lass." He held out his hand.

She was tempted to take it, because she could no longer feel her toes, but he needed to know she wasn't his spaniel to come and go at his bidding.

"Have it your way, then." He leaned down, caught her around the waist, and swung her up into his lap, her bum to the sky. He gave her bottom a swat, and embarrassed warmth coursed through her. She gave a yelp, more from surprise than pain. "Nothing like a good tanning to warm a body."

He didn't strike her again, but he kept his hand on her buttocks.

"Let me up," she demanded.

"Will ye stop ignoring me when I tell ye what ye must do?"

"Aye," she spat out.

He grabbed her waist and lifted her to ride astride before him. Then he kneed the stallion into a trot.

Her teeth chattered in the cold.

Rob spread the MacLaren weave over her and snugged her tight against his chest. "Better?"

"Better than freezing to death, I suppose." Elspeth didn't know how much warmer the extra wool made her, but she decided the heat from his body was worth a bit of her dignity. His thighs around hers set her blood flowing at a brisk pace.

Rob kicked the stallion into a canter, and they flew across the heath.

Elspeth remembered that her mother had insisted on tucking a handkerchief into the sleeve of her chemise.

"A bride always needs a handkerchief," Morag Stewart had said, her eyes tearing up. Elspeth hadn't been in danger of weeping at her wedding, but she felt the pressure behind her eyes now when she thought of her mother and how worried she must be.

"What woods are those up ahead?" She turned her head to ask and, as she'd hoped, it drew his attention. While he was telling her, she managed to pull out the kerchief and let it fly away from them without his notice.

When they reached the line of trees, he slowed to a trot.

"Not that I care if ye're lost," Elspeth said, "but I thought MacLaren lands were south of here."

"Aye, they are. Clever lass. Most wenches canna tell up from down."

"Then why are we going the opposite direction?"

"We canna go by a route your bridegroom will expect, can we? When they search for ye at daybreak, they'll all head south. So, o' course, we'll go north."

"Then we'll never reach *Caisteal Dubh*."

Surely not everyone in that stronghold would agree with their laird's decision to take her prisoner. She'd find someone to help her there if Lachlan and her father didn't catch up to them first.

Rob made a tsking noise. "Oh, ye of little faith. I've arranged for a way to swing south in safety."

Elspeth's chest constricted. He'd planned this abduction down to the last detail. Who knew a madman could be so devilishly clever?

They slowed to a walk and entered the forest, following game trails.

"Why are ye doing this?" she asked. "What did Lachlan Drummond ever do to ye?"

His arm around her waist tightened, and she felt his whole body clench, but he didn't answer. He was silent so long, she wondered if he hadn't heard her.

"There must be a reason," she said. "Because no one would abduct a man's bride without one." *Not even a madman*, she added silently.

"Sure of that, are ye?" The bitterness in his tone cut like a blade.

"Aye. I think I have a right to know why ye've taken me."

"Where have ye been the last two years?" he demanded. "In a hole in the ground?"

"Hmph. If ye must know, I've been in Edinburgh with the queen," she said, straightening her spine. "I'm one of her ladies-in-waiting. That's something ye might have considered before ye kidnapped me. Ye've not only angered my betrothed, ye'll have every Stewart hand against ye, as well. My father has a long reach, and the queen will take what ye've done very ill."

"If news of Drummond's deeds didna reach the

court, this willna either," he said flatly. "And if your
father didna know the measure of the man he was
giving his daughter to, then he canna be a verra
canny sort."

She bristled at that. Her father was the Stewart, laird
of a powerful clan. "My father is a great man."

"Your father made a deal with the devil, and unfortunately, ye get to pay the bill."

They came to a fork in the trail, and he turned the
stallion's head to the left onto the track heading down.

"Trust me, lass. By and by, ye'll thank me for keeping
you from becoming Lachlan Drummond's wife."

Elspeth curled her toes inside her left slipper and
managed to wiggle it off without his knowledge. It
fell under the stallion's hooves and was pressed into the
path, marking their way as clearly as if she'd stopped
and drawn an arrow.

Chapter 5

"WINE!" LORD DRUMMOND BELLOWED AS HE ENTERED the solar.

Old Normina shuffled forward with a horn and a wineskin of the best vintage to be found in the laird's cellars. She'd anticipated he'd demand more than mead this night after chasing all over creation for his lost bride. Without a word of thanks, the laird knocked back the horn in one long swallow and held it out for Normina to refill.

Not that she expected thanks. A laird couldn't be bothered to notice the likes of her. It was enough to have a roof over her head, a full belly, and a warm place to sleep. At her age, she was grateful for small comforts.

Lord Stewart followed him into the comfortable, tapestry-bedecked room. He pulled off his gloves, shrugged off his heavy cloak, and glowered at his would-be son-in-law. Without being told to do so, Normina scurried over to offer him a drink.

The Drummond didn't suffer servants who couldn't correctly divine his needs or the needs of his guests.

Then Normina took her place in the corner and

propped herself on a little straight-backed chair. That way, she'd be ready if called upon, and out of the way and of no more consequence than the boar hound lolling before the fire, if she was not.

"Well?" Lord Stewart said, his fists bunched at his sides. "Are you going to try to tell me this isn't about that sorry business from two years ago?"

"Who knows with a madman?" the laird said.

Lady Stewart appeared in the doorway, her eyes red rimmed from a long day of praying and weeping. She ran to her husband. "Tell me you found her, Alistair."

"Not yet, love," Lord Stewart whispered and took her into his arms to comfort her.

Normina didn't move to offer Lady Stewart wine. She'd not taken a bit of nourishment all day, though Normina had tried to tempt her with a number of dainty morsels. After her laird's disappointing news, the lady wasn't likely to change her mind now.

"But you will," she pleaded, her face pressed against his chest. "Promise me you will."

"Aye, we'll start again at first light. Lachlan thinks he knows where he lost them, and we'll begin there to pick up the trail. We'll find her, Morag." Lord Stewart patted her hair, bound in a snood, and then pulled her away from him. He pressed his lips to her forehead. "Now, to bed with you, and let us men worry about our plans."

"She's my bairn, Alistair," Lady Stewart said as she backed out of the room, her hands covering her face, her shoulders slumped. "My last, rosy-cheeked bairn."

Lord Stewart watched his wife leave, his mouth in a grim line.

"Dinna have children late in life, if ye can help it, Lachlan. Mothers get overly attached to that last little hatchling." Alistair Stewart swiped his eyes and coughed to cover an unmanly sniffle. "'Struth! Fathers do too. If it's a lass especially."

Normina had birthed five bairns, two lads and three lasses, and nary a one lived long enough to see ten summers. Her husband was gone now too, but that was the lot of all flesh. The cradle swings above a grave, and beds are empty at the last.

But how lovely it would have been to have had a daughter to comfort her last years. Someone to bring her a cup of willow-bark tea when her old bones ached or to give her grandchildren to dandle on her knees.

"Drummond, you know I want to believe your version of the tale, but MacLaren has naught against me or my house." Lord Stewart slumped into one of the leather chairs by the fire. "Why else would he do this if not for revenge against you?"

"I swear on all that's holy, I never intended hurt to MacLaren's wife."

Whenever Lord Drummond raised his hand to pledge to God, Normina cringed a little. A body never knew when the Almighty might smite a blasphemer, and she didn't want to be near when it happened.

"It was Christmastide, and spirits are always high then. I'll admit too much mead had somewhat to do with it," Drummond went on. "But it was meant as a harmless prank. Have ye never been part of a bride snatching?"

"Other than this one, ye mean?" Stewart said, his tone low and graveled with anger.

"'Twas nothing like this. I never unsheathed a blade. Never desecrated a kirk. 'Twas all in good fun," Drummond said, striding with nervous energy from one end of the solar to the other. "We caught the lady outside the walls of *Caisteal Dubh* and thought only to make some sport of her husband. That's all. I swear it."

Normina remembered Lady MacLaren. A kind young woman. Terrified, of course. Who wouldn't be if they were being held against their will? But well spoken, all the same. And clean. She was no trouble to look after at all.

Pity she was here for such a short time.

"God's feet! I was a friend to Rob MacLaren's father all his life. And he knows it," Lord Drummond said. "I'd broken bread in that castle hundreds of times before the old laird passed."

"And yet he bears ye ill will."

"We'd have returned her unharmed. She was in the tower for her own safety." Lord Drummond's black eyes snapped. "If I'd had any notion that fool of a woman would leap from the window, I'd never have locked her away in there. Believe me, Stewart, it was a tragic misunderstanding, the kind of thing they sing about in ballads."

Normina jerked her gaze away from her master lest he meet her eyes and know her secret thoughts. She had no misunderstanding about what happened to Lady MacLaren. Anybody with ears could've heard her piteous cries while Lord Drummond was with her in that locked chamber.

There was only one reason a woman might leap

from a tower window. Her spirit had already taken flight, and her body needed to catch up with it.

"I'd not be surprised if some bard hasn't already composed an outlandish version of the tale," Drummond said.

Normina kept her eyes carefully downcast. It wasn't her place to question her laird or to judge her betters, no matter how awful his sins.

It was God's place to do that. It seemed the Almighty took His time when it came to the nobility, but He always got round to such things eventually.

Normina hopped up to refill her laird's drinking horn and hoped she'd be there to see it when God finally demanded a reckoning from Lachlan Drummond.

From a safe distance, of course.

❦

Falin whickered and tossed his head as they plodded through the forest. Elspeth didn't blame him for skittishness. She loved to ride in the woods by day near her home. But by night, in this wood, every stump grew a boggle's face, and the trees' naked branches stabbed the sky like bony witches' fingers.

Movement caught the corner of her eye, and she turned her head to see several dark shapes keeping pace with them. Her breath hissed over her teeth.

"Aye, we've attracted the notice of a wolf pack," Rob said softly. "Pay them no mind."

Several pairs of feral eyes flashed at her from the deeper darkness.

She jerked her gaze away and fastened it on Falin's bobbing head. The stallion's ears pricked forward. His nostrils quivered. Then he whinnied and picked up his pace without Rob's direction.

"No, my brave heart, we'll not show them your heels," Rob crooned to the stallion as he reined him back. "There's a good lad. There'll be no running."

If the horse panicked and bolted, Elspeth and Rob would likely be sheared off his back by a low-hanging branch. And a man or woman afoot before a wolf pack had very little hope.

The wolves began calling to each other in short yips and howls.

Rob unwrapped the plaid that snugged Elspeth against him. "Can ye reach my boot knife? 'Tis on the right side."

Elspeth leaned down to fetch it and saw a big gray fellow dart closer, matching their speed.

He slipped through the trees like a wraith on silent paws, his long tongue lolling. His teeth flashed in the stippled moonlight. Even in this dimness, Elspeth could see the wolf's ribs protruding from his shaggy coat.

"They're starving," she said.

"Aye, most all the cattle and sheep in the Highlands have been sold off to the Lowlands for the winter," he said woodenly. "Like as not, this pack's not seen a meal for some time."

She felt for the knife in Rob's boot and drew it out, careful not to let the haft slip from her fingers.

"I've got it," she whispered.

"Cut the rope that binds ye to me," Rob said calmly, then his tone turned harsh with disgust. "Ach, I should have remembered there were wolves in these woods during these months."

"If ye hadn't stolen a man's bride, ye'd have no need to remember such a thing."

"Ye'll be sure to let me know if always being right ever begins to pall, won't ye?" he said as they continued to trudge along. "Tell me, lass, when ye were a little girl, were ye the sort to play outside, or did ye sit by the fire and spin all day?"

Elspeth's eyes widened as she sawed through the rope at her waist. Didn't the man realize what was happening?

"What on earth does that have to do with our current predicament?"

"I was just wondering if ye've ever climbed a tree, because I think the skill might come in handy verra soon."

"Oh, aye." Perhaps Rob wasn't so mad after all. "I can climb a tree like a squirrel."

Elspeth heard the metallic rasp of metal as Rob unsheathed his claymore.

"There's an oak overhanging the path in ten paces," he said. "If I give ye a boost, do ye think ye can swing up to that thick branch?"

The wolves began a howling chorus around them. They'd located the only fresh meat in the forest, and it was time to sing about it.

"Give me a boost, and I'll fly up to it," Elspeth said, drawing her legs up under her so she was hunkered on Falin's back instead of sitting astride. He danced sideways as he felt the unusual movement of his riders.

"Ho there, lad, easy now." Rob kneed Falin forward.

One of the wolves found some bravery and lunged at Falin's haunches. The stallion kicked at it. Rob kept

Elspeth from toppling off by balancing her hip with one hand.

The predator rolled and slinked away, snarling but unhurt.

"Do ye want the knife?" Elspeth asked.

"No, keep it," he said. "Just in case."

In case. Elspeth didn't want to contemplate what that meant. As they drew near the oak tree, she slid the small blade down the busk of her bodice, between the boning.

"Get ready." Rob's voice was steady and reassuring, but her heart still pounded like a smith's hammer.

She pushed the cloak off her shoulders, letting it drape over the stallion's withers, so her arms would be free. Cold was the least of her worries.

She'd have only one chance to leap to safety.

They drew even with the oak.

"Now!" Rob shouted.

He hefted her backside, and she sprang up and grabbed at the branch with both hands. The rough bark dug into her palms, but she didn't let go.

The sudden movement made the pack dart in, snapping at Falin's heels. He bucked and reared and danced backward on the path.

Elspeth was suspended over nothing but air, with writhing, furry bodies below. She swung her feet up to hook a knee over the branch, but not before the biggest gray wolf leaped up and grabbed a mouthful of her broad skirt. A lesser fabric might have ripped, but the thick velvet held fast.

Elspeth clung to the underside of the branch, which bowed under the additional weight. The wolf shook its whole body, like a terrier with a rat, trying to bring her down.

The bough creaked and popped, and she feared the limb might give way.

"Hang on!" Rob shouted and slashed, not at the wolf, but at the layers of her velvet skirt and chemise from which it was suspended. The beast fell to the ground with a yowl.

Elspeth scrambled and lifted herself to the upper side of the thick branch.

Another wolf leaped up, coming within finger-widths of her bare foot. She tucked it up and scuttled along the branch till she reached the trunk and stood upright, looping an arm around its comforting solidness.

One wolf continued to lunge and tried to scuffle up the trunk. Elspeth caught a whiff of his stinking breath as he snapped at her, but unless he sprouted wings, she was out of reach.

"Whatever happens, dinna come down till I say," Rob ordered as the pack turned its attention from her to the man on the prime piece of horseflesh.

The wolves formed a ring of snarling muzzles around Rob and Falin. Their breath rose in a haze, like a smoke ring from a giant's pipe. Elspeth counted fifteen big beasts with several smaller ones hanging back in the deeper shadows, yipping encouragement.

Rob pivoted the snorting stallion in a tight circle, so he could keep an eye on the restive crowd. The wolves called to one another, coordinating their coming attack. The sound raked Elspeth's spine like a claw. The unholy chorus rose and then stopped suddenly, as if the song was a thread snipped off with shears.

"Come, ye sons of bitches!" Rob growled into the sudden silence. "If ye want us, ye must take us. I give ye worm-eaten bastards leave to try!"

Elspeth had seen fearsome things in the hall of dreams. The Sight had sometimes taken her repeatedly to the aftermath of a great battle of some sort, and she woke from such bloody visions sickened to her soul. But she'd never seen anything as terrifying as the sudden attacking leap of the wolves on this man and his horse.

They came in waves, snarling and snapping. One managed to land on the stallion's back behind Rob, going for his unprotected neck. Falin screamed and reared, lashing out with his hooves, and the wolf slid off, raking the stallion's flanks with his claws. Rob's blade sang a song of blood and whipped around to shear off the beast's head.

Falin's kicks sent a few wolves flying as Rob laid about with his claymore. Man and horse, they fought in concert. They fought for their lives.

As the battle wore on, Falin stumbled on fallen wolf carcasses but managed to keep his feet. The ground was black with blood. Rob roared as he slashed his blade, sounding as wild and vicious as any four-legged predator.

The numbers of the pack dwindled. As the eastern sky lightened to pearl gray, hope rose in Elspeth's heart.

Then the largest wolf charged and leaped. His flying lunge knocked Rob from Falin's back. They rolled together, tooth and claw, man and blade, off the path and into the thick underbrush, disappearing in a growling, swearing mass.

Chapter 6

LACHLAN DRUMMOND AND ALISTAIR STEWART REINED their horses to a halt at the top of the rise. The sun eased over the southeastern hills, but it promised no additional warmth. The day was breaking cold and bitter as a spinster's bed.

"This is the last place we spotted them," Drummond said, scouring the valley from south to north. A light frost painted each leaf and blade of grass with a crust of white. "They weren't that far ahead of us at that point. Then once we reached here, they were nowhere to be seen. We headed south, thinking he'd try to confuse us by the river."

Stewart frowned at him and glared in the direction Lachlan pointed.

"We followed the watercourse for several miles, looking for a place he might have crossed over, but there was no sign of them. It was as if they'd vanished." Drummond shook his head and made the sign against evil. "I'm not a man given to fancies, but if ye told me they were swallowed up into the hollow hills, I'd believe ye."

"Ye'd best hope not," Stewart said, leaning on the pommel of his showy saddle. "If we canna find my daughter, our accord is off. All of it."

There was too much riding on his alliance with the Stewart clan for Lachlan to let it fall apart. "Now, see here—"

"No. You see. I'll no' make an ally of a man who canna even defend his bride at the altar."

"Your men were there, as well as mine. Why didna one of ye stop the MacLaren?" Lachlan said. "For the same reason I didna. There were women and children about, and none of us were armed. There was nothing to be done but let the madman get away, and well ye know it."

The older man shook with suppressed rage. "I'm no' talking about what happened at the kirk. Why didna ye post guards outside? Or ride patrols through your woods?" He turned an accusing eye on Lachlan. "Most importantly, why did ye no' settle this matter with Mad Rob before he dragged my Elspeth into your quarrel?"

"What would ye have had me do?" Lachlan urged his horse forward, hoping a change of scene would change the topic. He heard Stewart's horse follow him down the slope.

"What he wanted. All the man asked was satisfaction," Stewart said. "Ye should have met him in single combat afore it came to this."

"Aye, that would have been grand. First, the lady dies in my keeping, and then I kill her husband." Lachlan slanted an assessing gaze at the other man. Obviously, the Stewart had been listening to his wife whine all night and needed to purge her words from his head. A man would have followed the logic of the situation through to its unhappy conclusion. "Ye're no' thinking clearly, Stewart."

"I'm thinking ye're afraid to face the MacLaren."

"A man with a clear conscience fears nothing." Lachlan glared at his bride's father. "If ye were any other man, I'd kill ye for the insult."

"Ach, well, dinna stand on ceremony. Whenever ye feel man enough to try it—"

"Whist, man. Do ye hear yourself? What would your daughter say if she saw us at each other's throats like a pair of rabid hounds?" Lachlan turned his horse's head south once he reached the base of the hill. "It will no' help Elspeth if we…"

A spot of color caught his eye, near an outcropping of dark granite. It was far too late in the season for any blooms.

"The bride wore a rosy-colored bodice, did she no'?" Lachlan asked. He'd noticed, because the swell of Elspeth's breasts had pinked to almost the same hue when she caught him looking at them during the interrupted ceremony.

"Aye," her father said morosely. "With a deep wine skirt. Velvet, Morag said. It was one of Elspeth's court dresses. The best she had. I mind when she first…"

Even though Alistair Stewart droned on, Lachlan had stopped listening. He urged his horse up the incline, switching its flanks with a short crop to speed it along. When he reached the rocks, he dismounted and picked the patch of silk off the gorse bush. He rubbed it between his fingers. A tight, fine weave in a luxurious cloth.

Definitely part of his bride's dress.

But it hadn't been there when he and his men had thundered past. He'd stake his holding on it. The MacLaren must have holed up someplace and doubled back on them.

He looked north, narrowing his eyes. Another little swatch of cloth waved on the heather.

Clever girl. Perhaps she did deserve to be the mother of his children, after all.

Of course, if she quickened too soon in their marriage, the brat might be MacLaren's spawn. There was no doubt in Lachlan's mind that Mad Rob had lain with her already.

Why else would he have taken her?

Much as it galled him to take another man's leavings, Lachlan needed the hefty dowry and other benefits the match brought him. But he'd not abide a cuckoo's egg in his nest.

Even if Elspeth didn't become pregnant, women died of one ailment or another all the time. He might do well to speed her along with one.

He'd avoid another accident if he could help it, though. Might remind folk of MacLaren's wife.

There was an old hag in the next glen who had slow-acting poisons that she assured him were unde-tectable, if ever he had need for one.

But for now, he had to find the little Stewart bitch and marry her.

"Alistair," he called down to his bride's father, "I found a sign. Your daughter's heading north." He waved the little piece of silk in the air. "And she's alive!"

After all this trouble, she'd better be.

✎

Elspeth screamed.

The last thing she saw before Rob and the wolf disappeared into the brush was his long claymore flying into the air, end over end. It came to rest in the middle of the path, point stabbing the ground, blade quivering right in front of Falin's nose.

"Oh, God!" Elspeth covered her mouth with her hand. Without his sword, what chance did Rob have against the beast?

Without the man on his back, Falin lost heart for the fight. The stallion reared and wheeled and took flight back down the game trail in the direction from which they'd come, with what was left of pack hot after him, howling like demons from the pit.

Elspeth couldn't see Rob and the big gray. The woods were too dense, and daylight came slowly to the forest. But she could hear them.

And that was probably worse.

It was awful. Sometimes it was hard to tell whether the wild, fierce sounds came from the wolf or from the man.

Or to know which of them screamed.

Then suddenly there was silence. Not a twig broke; not a bird sang. She held her breath. Her heart pounded in her ears.

"Rob?" she said softly.

No response.

"Rob!"

No one answered her.

She hunkered down on the branch, trying to decide what to do. She still had Rob's boot knife. And his claymore stood in the middle of the path. She doubted she could even lift it, let alone wield it.

Tears gathered at the corners of her eyes. Mad Rob may have ruined her wedding and her reputation, but in a scrape, he'd made sure she was safe. He'd done all he could to protect her.

Her chest felt as if someone had dropped a lodestone on it.

She suspected Rob was dead. Horribly dead. No matter what he'd done to her, she was heartsick about that.

What about the wolf?

There was no sound of padded feet moving stealthily toward her.

But she couldn't remain in the tree forever. Eventually, the pack would tire of chasing Falin and return. She needed to be long gone by then. The cloak had been dragged from the stallion's back during the melee and was draped over a thornbush.

She'd freeze without that. Especially since now there was a wide swath missing from her skirt and chemise that bared her right leg to mid thigh.

How Mother will scold me when she sees how I've ruined my beautiful wedding dress, she thought disjointedly.

As if it signified anything.

She swung herself down, dangling from the bough again. She still had a ten-foot drop, which wouldn't have troubled her if she'd had both shoes.

Elspeth released her hold and tried to land mostly on her right foot. Her ankle turned, and she went down hard.

And found herself nose to nose with a dead wolf.

She scrambled to her feet. There were several carcasses littering the path. She ought to have felt revulsion, but she was numb.

Then she limped over to retrieve the cloak and throw it around her shoulders. Her ears pricked to a new sound.

Someone was humming. She recognized the tune as one of the bawdy drinking songs her father and his men sang late at night after they were all deep in their cups. Sounds of crackling underbrush accompanied the song.

"Father?" she asked shakily.

"If ye're asking whether I'm your sire or a priest, the answer is no to both."

The voice was gravelly but it belonged to Rob.

He finally appeared, working his way through the timber, and burst back onto the game trail.

"Oh, Rob, ye're alive!" Elspeth put both arms around his neck and hugged him close. "I was afeard ye were gone, but ye're alive!"

"Aye, lass," he said with a sinful grin. "Completely alive."

She was suddenly aware of the hardness of his groin against her belly and pulled back away from him. She noticed then that he was covered with blood, and her alarm must have shown on her face.

"Dinna fret. It's not my blood. At least, not mostly."

"Ye wicked, wicked man. Why didna ye answer when I called to ye?"

"Did ye call?"

"Aye."

He put a hand to the back of his head, and it came away with fresh, bright red blood.

"Seems I took a wee nap after the wolf knocked me into a fallen log. Fortunately, I woke with only a pounding head. He didna wake at all."

"How did ye manage that?"

"My belt knife in his ribs might have had somewhat to do with it." He stooped to clean the blade on the brown grass before he returned it to the small sheath at his waist. Then he did the same for the claymore and shoved it into his shoulder baldric. "I'll have my boot knife back, if ye please."

She stepped back a pace.

"I ken where ye stashed it, lass." His gaze flicked pointedly at her bodice. "Dinna make me go in after it. Unless, o' course, ye wish me to."

She retrieved the small blade and cast it down. It quivered upright between his feet.

"Ye've some skill with a blade."

"I've three older brothers."

"I suppose Falin's fled," he said, looking down the path.

Elspeth nodded.

"Aye, well, he's always had a coward's heart," Rob said. "The silly beastie."

"The rest of the wolves went after him," Elspeth said, feeling the need to stand up for the stallion. "He was no' a coward. He bore us in safety a long way. He fought well and hard with ye. But he stood by ye till *ye* left *him*! And now the wolves will…" She swallowed back the lump in her throat. "And ye dinna care."

She thumped his chest with her fist once.

"Ye dinna care at all, ye brute." Her face crumpled, and tears coursed down her cheeks. The tension of the last few days broke over her like a wave, and she wept without shame for a horse that wouldn't even let her mount him.

"Hush, lass. Ye dinna need to cry. The tears will freeze on your cheeks." Rob grabbed a corner of the cloak and swiped at her face. "Falin will be fine, ye ken. He can run like the wind."

"Ye didna see them after him." She cried harder.

"He's probably outrun that mangy pack and is well on his way back to his own stable by now," Rob said. "Which is more than I can say for us. We need to be gone before the wolves decide we can't run nearly so fast and turn back."

"What about you? Your head is wounded." She put a hand around his neck and felt a gash beneath blood-matted hair.

"There's no time to clean me up and make me pretty. Come, lass. Let's away."

He took her hand and started down the trail. They hadn't gone ten paces when she cried out.

"What is it?" he asked.

"I stepped on something sharp," she said, balancing on one leg and plucking a thorn from the ball of her bare foot.

"Where's your shoe?"

"I dinna know."

A guilty flush washed over her. She knew exactly where she'd abandoned that shoe.

But why should she feel shamefaced before her abductor? True, he had risked his neck to save hers. That counted for something, but she couldn't tell him the truth about her missing shoe. If she did, she'd have to admit to leaving a trail of silk all across the valley floor, and there was no telling how a madman might take to that news.

She glanced around. "It must be about here someplace."

"Well, we haven't time to look for it." He grabbed up the piece of velvet he'd cut from her skirt and wrapped it around her foot several times. Then he rummaged in his sporran and came up with a length of leather lacing. He bound the velvet to her foot and calf.

"No' exactly fashionable enough for court, but better than going unshod in this weather."

Wolf song reached their ears, distant, but close enough to be worrisome.

"Come, lass. And step lively."

This time he didn't have to tell her twice.

Chapter 7

ANGUS FLETCHER SQUINTED AGAINST THE GLARE OF the winter sun on Loch Eireann. His longboat was provisioned for the journey. He'd already talked to his neighbor in the next glen, Rory Comyn, about looking to the needs of his barnyard beasts while he was gone. Rory agreed, but even so, Angus would have to count the hens twice when he returned. Everyone knew the Comyns had sticky fingers.

Now if only his passengers would arrive when Rob MacLaren said they would.

Sailing the loch was a fickle enterprise in the best of times. It was a long, narrow stretch of trouble, bounded by the central Highlands all round and so deep in spots, no one knew for certain whether there was a bottom. Then there was the changeable current that might turn a boat about if a man weren't careful or turn it all the way over if he didn't show Loch Eireann the proper respect.

Winter didn't help matters either. The loch water was fresh, but Angus had never seen it freeze solid.

Sometimes warm, sometimes frigid, the pesky current turned the waters over too often for that.

Then, too, some folk believed an *each uisge* lived beneath the loch's dark water. Angus had never actually seen a water horse, but he didn't discount the existence of one. It didn't do to disregard the spirits of a place. The faerie folk had claimed Loch Eireann centuries before he eked out a living on its shores. The water horse would remain hidden in its depths long after Angus was worm food.

When Rob first approached him about this trip, Angus was happy to finally have a chance to repay his friend. But he had tried to convince him to go east instead. Sailing in that direction, the loch emptied into the lovely River Earn, which flowed all the way to the Firth of Tay and the shining sea beyond. It was said to be a grand trip.

A man ought to see something of the world, and the Firth was as far away as he could imagine.

But the MacLaren was adamant. He'd go west to Lochearnhead or not at all.

Angus glanced at the shadows thrown by the morning sun, gauged how much time they had until the current switched, and then it wouldn't matter what Rob wanted. There'd be no gainsaying the wind and standing waves.

"Well, if the MacLaren will no' come to us, we must see what's keeping him," Angus told Fingal, his deerhound.

The burly highlander threw a cloak over his shoulders, picked up his walking staff, and strode into the forest. The shaggy, long-legged hound loped beside him.

❧

"There's another sign!" Elspeth's father called out and urged his mount forward. He leaned from the back of his dun-colored mare and scooped a ragged pink sleeve from a tangle of blackberry bush. Stewart brandished the cloth for Lachlan to see as if it were a victory banner, a tentative smile on his face.

Lachlan Drummond was less hopeful about their search. True, Mad Rob hadn't made good on his threat to kill the girl if they followed. And she seemed to be watched lightly enough to be able to leave markers on her way. But once they caught up to the MacLaren, Drummond wouldn't give a pair of coppers for Elspeth Stewart's chances.

A cornered boar has little to lose and may as well take a tusk to the nearest thing to him.

Revenge would be best served if Mad Rob gave them reason to hope and let them catch up to him before he slit the girl's throat before their eyes. Then he wouldn't care if they tore him to pieces. He'd have had his moment.

That's what Lachlan would have done if their positions were reversed.

Drummond kicked his horse into a canter to close the distance between him and Stewart.

"We're gaining on them." Alistair folded the rosy sleeve with care and squirreled it away in his sporran along with all the other bits of silk they'd collected. "I can feel it."

"Aye, but I'm wondering if it isna too easy. The girl is leaving so many clues, we may be playing right into the fiend's hands," Drummond said, giving his black beard a thoughtful tug. "I'm thinking we ought to call in the support of our allies. The MacLaren's sins aren't just against us, ye ken."

"I dinna follow, unless ye mean Elspeth. He's besmirched my daughter's honor more than ours." Stewart continued toward the forest, looking for another scrap of silk. "Who better than her father and betrothed to defend her?"

"The MacLaren has acted against the queen's wishes by interrupting the wedding," Drummond said. "Mad Rob invited us to collect Elspeth at *Caisteal Dubh* at month's end. Wouldn't ye like to see his face when we arrive there flanked by the queen's own guard? After all, there's some that would say what he's done rises to the level of treason."

The possibility of his enemy dying a traitor's death gave Lachlan a warm glow of satisfaction.

"No, I canna think of that," Stewart said. "We have to find Elspeth now. Her mother willna be satisfied to wait. Not even on the queen's pleasure. We must press on."

But before they could, a riderless black stallion came careening out of the woods. Drummond recognized the beast as Mad Rob's and spurred his mount into pursuit. After half a mile, he pulled even with the stallion and grasped its reins long enough to yank it to a halt.

The MacLaren's horse was flecked with foam and nearly blown. Otherwise, Lachlan knew he'd never have been able to catch it.

Stewart rode up to him. "Holy God, he's covered with blood."

The horse's flanks were caked with dried splotches, and an open gash sent a rivulet of fresh red down his long leg. Stewart met Drummond's gaze. Neither man had to say it aloud.

Rob MacLaren and his captive had been attacked by a pack of wolves, and the fact that they were no longer on horseback did not bode well.

"We have to press on, Lachlan," Stewart said softly, his tone grim. "I have to know what befell her. Whatever we may find."

"Aye," Drummond agreed, handing off the stallion's reins to one of his men. May as well ring the one bright spot from this damnable turn. Lachlan was getting a prime stud from the deal. "Take Roald with ye, Seamus, and see the beast home to my stable. Tend his hurts if he'll let ye."

His men hurried to loop a pair of ropes over the stallion's neck to insure he couldn't break away from them once he regained his wind. Lachlan didn't have to remind them he'd take the failure out of their hides if they lost this exceptional bit of horseflesh.

That settles the question of going home now, Lachlan thought with resignation.

Alistair Stewart had already turned around toward the woods to continue the search for his daughter. But Lachlan could see he'd lost hope. His shoulders sagged like a man destined for the rack.

❧

"Ow!" Elspeth hopped one-legged toward a fallen log and plopped down on it, holding her velvet-wrapped foot. The increasingly soggy and ragged cloth was no match for thorns. She plucked a long, vicious one from her heel. "I dinna think I can go on like this."

"'Tis no' much farther, lass," Rob said, looking as pale and tired as she felt.

"But I'm hungry and thirsty and I could lie down in the grass right now and sleep for a week," she said, eyeing a flat spot alongside the game trail. Their fitful few hours of rest in the cave wasn't nearly adequate for the events of the long night and longer morning. All their provisions had been lost when Falin bolted.

Elspeth would trade her best brooch for a single swallow of water right now.

"Ye'll sleep soon enough once we get where we're going." He scooped her up and balanced her over one shoulder, letting her head and arms dangle down his back.

"No, wait, put me down!" She pushed herself up with her hands splayed on his back.

"Are ye willing to walk then?" He made no move to put her down.

"I canna. No' a single step."

Rob snorted and started on down the trail. "Then beggars canna be choosers, can they?" He gave her bottom a swat. "Be grateful for small favors."

Elspeth sagged over his shoulder, but it was hard to breathe when her head was hanging down. Little pinpricks of light pressed against the corners of her vision, and she pushed herself back up again.

"Ye really did yourself some damage when ye hit your head on that log," she said when she noticed that Rob's hair was crusted with blood on the back of his head.

"Oh, aye? And I thought the splitting headache was from no' having my morning bowl of *parritch*."

"Do ye think the wolves might come back?" she asked. "Is that why ye insist on pressing on?"

"No. They hunt by night."

He climbed over a thick trunk that had fallen across the path. A low-hanging branch caught in her hair and pulled out several strands.

"Ow!"

If Rob heard her, he gave no sign.

"So long as we have shelter by the time night falls, we should be safe."

"If our destination truly isna far, ye really should stop and rest," she said.

"And ye really should stop talking, lass."

Elspeth heard the weary threat in his tone and decided to heed him.

They left the larger trees of the older forest behind. Rob trudged on through the young, spindly forest, sometimes weaving so she feared he'd topple over.

Then he stopped suddenly, cocking his head to listen.

Something was approaching through the brush, rustling branches and snapping downed twigs underfoot. A big something from the sounds of it.

Elspeth closed her eyes, the better to concentrate, and heard panting coming from farther up the trail. A decidedly wolfish sound.

"I thought ye said wolves hunted only by night."

"Unfortunately, of the two of us, it seems only ye have the honor of always being right. There's no tree big enough to bear your weight nearby," Rob said as he put her down. He stooped and pulled out his boot knife, handing it to her haft first. "If they get past me, dinna let yourself be taken."

Elspeth accepted the knife. Of all the horrors in the world, the fear of being eaten alive by a wild creature turned a body's bowels to water quicker than anything.

Aye, she'd put the blade to her own throat first.

Chapter 8

ELSPETH SHELTERED BEHIND ROB, HER INSIDES QUAKING.
The panting sound was unmistakable now.

Then she heard a sharp whistle and a shouted, "Ho,
Fingal, dinna range so far ahead, laddie."

A thin, shaggy deerhound appeared around an
outcropping of rock.

The set of Rob's shoulders visibly relaxed. He
lowered his knife and chuckled. The hound loped
toward him, teeth bared in a doggie grin.

"Ye know this beast?" Elspeth stiffened as it sniffed
her with thoroughness, Fingal's great head higher than
her waist.

"Aye, and he's meek as a kitten so long as ye pose
no threat to his master." Rob ran a hand over the
deerhound's spine from neck to tail. Then he cupped
his hands around his mouth. "Angus, ye great bear!
Come claim your dog, or we'll fit him with a saddle
and ride him back to your house."

"I wouldna, if I were you," came a gravel-throated
reply. "I gave him leave to eat the last fellow who
tried it."

A man as shaggy as his dog rounded the same rocks. His hair and beard were the color of an old bird's nest, and Elspeth suspected he might be hiding one or two in the tangled mess. As he came nearer, she realized that he topped Rob by half a head, and the MacLaren was a very tall man. His ugly face split in a snaggle-toothed smile that might have terrified her if she hadn't lived through the events of the last few days.

"What are ye doing in the forest instead of waiting for us by your boat?" Rob asked.

"Well, ye're no' there yet, are ye, and ye said ye would be," Angus said. "I thought ye might need some help. Where's Falin?"

"Halfway home, I expect. We ran into a spot of trouble with a wolf pack."

"Ach, I thought I heard the demons early this morning." The big man turned to Elspeth and bowed. "And ye must be the Lady Elspeth. Angus Fletcher, at yer service."

"Ye know me, Mr. Fletcher?"

"Aye, but only by hearsay, ye ken. Robbie said ye'd be making this trip with us, but he didna mention ye were so comely." The big man's hairy ears blushed rosy red. "We've no lasses near so pretty as ye here-abouts. I'd be beholdin' to ye if ye'd call me Angus."

This giant was the first person she'd met since Rob abducted her. Elspeth decided to take a chance.

"Sir…I mean Angus, ye seem a gentle soul. I dinna know what your friend has told ye, but if ye would truly help a lady, then know that I have been taken against my will by Rob MacLaren," she said, taking care to hold the gap in her skirt closed as best she could. "A boon I beg ye, please. Return me to the bosom of my family, and I promise ye'll be rewarded for it."

Angus glanced at Rob and then back at her.

"Weel, Robbie lad, ye're no' a liar. She's a lady, right enough. Talks a fair treat, aye?"

"Talks a lot, ye mean," Rob said sourly. "And she's cast a shoe and needs to be carried. D'ye think ye could manage it, Angus? I'm fair done in just carrying myself."

Without another word, Angus scooped Elspeth up, not slinging her over his shoulder as Rob had, but cradling her in his beefy arms as if she were a bairn.

"Now wait a moment, Mr. Fletcher—"

"Angus," he corrected.

"Angus." There was no point in antagonizing him if she wished to convince him to come to her aid, so she wouldn't complain of the way he carried her. It was certainly better than the undignified way Rob had, slinging her over his shoulder like a sack of meal. "Doing the MacLaren's bidding is no help to me."

"Och, I canna go against Rob. I owe him a debt, ye see."

"My father will see your debt paid if ye help me."

"I owe Robbie for a life, ye see, and no one can pay that debt but me. I know ye've had a miserable time of it, what with the wolves and all," Angus said, "But I expect ye'll sing a different tune, my lady, once we get ye back to my house."

"Oh?" That sounded vaguely threatening. "What's at your house?"

"Weel, since the pair of ye canna have broken your fast, I expect ye're right sharp set. I'll fry up some of the good haggis and see if the hens have left us some eggs."

Just the thought of a hot breakfast made Elspeth's mouth water.

"And while I do that, ye can…weel, not that ye need it, mind"—Mr. Fletcher's cheeks pinked above his beard—"but if ye wish it, I suppose I could heat some water for ye to have a bath."

At the mention of the word "bath," Elspeth decided she could forgive Angus Fletcher anything.

Even refusing to help her get away from Rob MacLaren.

❧

Rob stripped off his filthy clothes on the loch's shore and left them in a pile as he walked to the water's edge. He squatted down and splashed himself all over, sucking a breath over his teeth at the cold.

Normally, he'd have skipped a bath in this weather, but Elspeth was getting clean somewhere inside Angus Fletcher's cluttered, wattle-and-daub two-story home. He didn't want to smell like a boar pit beside her.

The sun was moving steadily across the southern sky. He'd hoped to be sailing across the loch by this time, but they'd missed the narrow inland sea's "tide," according to Angus. His friend knew more about Loch Eireann than any soul alive, so there was nothing to do but wait till the wind and water were more favorable to their cause.

Rob scooped out a dollop of soap from the stone jar Angus had loaned him and smeared his whole body with it. He even gingerly sudsed up his hair, working out the matted blood and hoping not to reopen the gash left when he knocked himself out in that fall against a log.

The savory smell of richly spiced sausages frying wafted out to him.

He turned around to look at the house. Elspeth was behind one of the vellum-covered windows. Did she wonder where he was? If it had been high summer and the windows left uncovered to let in a breeze, would she have peeked out at him as he stood on the shoal, naked as God made him?

He soaped up his groin. Just the thought that Elspeth might spy on him at his bath made part of him happier than it ought to be, considering the temperature.

A cloud covered the sun, and the air cooled even more.

Rob turned and dashed into the loch, the chilly water snatching his breath as he ducked under the waves to rinse off the tallow soap. Then he splashed back out to the shore and rubbed his body briskly with the cloth Angus had lent him.

He sincerely hoped Elspeth wasn't looking now. After a November dip in Loch Eireann, no man was at his best.

"Ye half-wit," he mumbled to himself as he pulled the fresh thigh-length shirt over his head. It was an old one of Fletcher's, so it was a tad long and worn thin in spots, but at least it was clean. "Ye muckle-headed blatherskite!"

Why should he care whether she looked or no'? She was his prisoner, not his sweetheart.

If he muddled that fact, he was destined for trouble.

He wrapped one of his friend's plaids around his

waist and cinched it with a belt. There was plenty left to sling over his shoulder.

And he still had plenty of rage left for Lachlan Drummond. Unfortunately, it was becoming increasingly hard to connect Elspeth Stewart with her betrothed. She was a bonnie lass with more courage than half the men he knew. She certainly showed her quality when the wolves surrounded them. Most lasses—hell, most men—would have shite themselves.

But if his plan for revenge was ever to work, he had to keep thinking of her as Lachlan Drummond's bride.

He suspected he wasn't thinking clearly from lack of sleep. During that brief nap with Elspeth in the cave, Fiona hadn't come to him. He'd merely sunk into a black oblivion. His dreamless slumber hadn't rested him one whit.

The sausages called to him again, a greasy, flavor-ripe summons.

He followed his nose back to Fletcher's house.

Some folk said the Scots race had a miserly streak that ran wide and deep. Angus Fletcher would have argued he was merely thrifty. And because of this, he never threw away anything. His home was crammed to the ceiling with bits and pieces of broken tools, moldering animal hides, and scraps of wood that used to be a chair or an ax handle—things he fully intended to repair someday. A body never knew when something might come in useful.

Rob found his friend squatting by the fire. Plump sausages sizzled in the iron skillet bedded in the low flame. Angus speared them and flipped them over to brown both sides.

"Och, laddie, ye smell almost human again," Angus said with a laugh.

"I dinna think ye've been over concerned about bathing yourself, from the looks of ye." Rob thought it wise to refrain from mentioning that his friend smelled a bit like damp wool.

"I had me bath just last month, thank ye kindly, and won't be due for another again till spring." Angus slanted him a sour look. "Unless I spend a night like the one ye just had."

Rob chuckled. A lifelong bachelor, Angus Fletcher kept his home in an order only he understood. In contrast, his boat, an echo of an old Viking longboat, was as spotless as any goodwife kept her hearth, but Angus was indifferent on the matter of personal cleanliness.

At least when the weather turned cold.

"Water is powerful wet stuff," Angus warned. "Best applied in small doses."

"I'll bear that in mind."

"Aye, and while we're jawing about your mind, I've got to wonder if there's aught in it."

"What d'ye mean?"

"Stealing away a man's bride." Fletcher shook his grizzled head. "Ye told me ye'd be bringing along a Stewart lass, but ye didna tell me she'd be comin' as your prisoner."

Rob filched a bite of sausage from the skillet and popped it in his mouth. It was near to scalding, but the thin skin burst in a rush of flavor that set his tongue dancing.

"Does that mean ye willna help me?"

"No fear of that, lad. Angus Fletcher honors his debts. But if ye want my help, it might make things easier all around if ye tell me all."

"Soon, friend." Rob laid a hand on Fletcher's shoulder. "Where is the lass?"

"Upstairs. Tell her the breakfast is ready."

Rob headed for stairs so steep, going up them was like climbing a ladder. Most folk with such small houses didn't bother with more than one floor, but Angus always complained his feet got cold if he couldn't heat the room beneath his bedchamber. The main level of the house boasted a new slate floor. He'd gotten tired of trying to sweep dirt clean, Angus explained. No matter how hard you packed it, there was always more to sweep. But upstairs, he claimed his wood floors always felt warmer under his bare feet.

Rob's head cleared the ceiling of the main floor, and his eyes adjusted to the dimmer bedchamber. This room was less crowded with things. An oversized string bed, to accommodate his oversized friend, dominated the space. There were a couple trunks and small table that held a ewer and pitcher.

Elspeth was standing with her back to him, next to the table. She poured water from a kettle into the ewer. Steam rose before she added cold water from the pitcher. She dipped a cloth into a basin, unaware that Rob was watching her.

He prayed that happy state would continue.

She was naked as Eve in glory.

Chapter 9

ELSPETH GATHERED UP HER HEAVY HAIR, GAVE IT A twist, and pinned it on the top of her head. A few loose tendrils escaped and curled on her neck.

Rob ached to plant a kiss on the tender skin there. With extreme care, he climbed the last few steps, praying none of them creaked. Then he stepped into his friend's bedchamber, tilting his head to avoid bashing his crown on the sloped ceiling. Cat footed, he moved farther into the room, where the thatch rushed up into a tall peak. He stood in complete silence, willing Elspeth not to turn around.

Not yet.

He longed to trace the indentation of her spine. Her back was smooth and tapered gently to a narrow waist. Then her hips broadened into a sweet bottom shaped like an inverted heart. He longed to run his hands over that glowing skin and palm the globes of her buttocks.

Her legs weren't long, for she wasn't a tall woman, but they were shapely, and her muscles were strong beneath taut skin. He noticed a few scrapes and scratches from her scramble up the tree.

He wanted to kiss each of those small hurts to make them better.

Angus had exaggerated when he offered Elspeth a chance to bathe. He didn't own a hip bath. To him, a basin and kettle qualified. Rob was grateful. He'd never see this much of her if she was half-submerged in a soapy tub.

She lifted one arm gracefully over her head and washed her underarm. Excess water trailed down the side of her body in soapy runnels to the cloth she'd spread on the floor.

Rob didn't dare draw breath. His cock tented his kilt in unrelieved lust.

Then her arms began working before her, and he realized she was soaping the front of her body from breasts to groin. She spread her legs shoulder width to wash her sex.

She seemed to be taking her time over it.

So slippery and wet.

Rob suppressed a groan as his cock twitched at the thought of her damp curls. And her fingers sliding through those intimate folds, all sleek and soft and tender.

He wondered if she ever pleasured herself.

Some night, all alone in her bed, did she ruck up her chemise, lick her finger, and find that little spot that sent delight racing through a woman's veins? Would a virgin merely toy with herself, working herself into unrelieved frenzy because she knew no better? Or would she have learned how to rub herself until the tears came and her insides spasmed?

Oh, to see Elspeth in truth as he envisioned her,

thrashing on sweat-damp bedclothes, her back arched and her body shuddering in release.

The imagined moment made him ache till he thought he'd explode.

Then she bent at the waist to run the soapy cloth down her legs, treating him to a sight of those damp curls and her glistening slit.

There was a tight, wet welcome.

Oh, to swive her till he couldn't see straight. To grasp her hips while her fingers splayed on the floor and plunge himself into her sweet flesh up to the hilt.

Without his conscious volition, a soft curse that was almost an endearment, escaped his lips.

She straightened immediately and turned toward the sound, her eyes wide in the dimness. Then, like a doe surprised by the hunter, she froze.

Her breasts were high and exactly the right size to fill a man's hands. He'd love to explore the crease beneath each one. Her nipples were drawn tight.

Rob could almost taste them, sweet and responsive between his lips.

His gaze raked down past the little goblet of her navel to the triangle of chestnut curls at the apex of her thighs. Such sweet nether lips.

Then he met her gaze again. Her mouth opened softly, but she didn't say a word. Her tongue flicked over the bottom lip.

Was there anything that would convince her to flick it over his cock?

Merciful God, it had been nearly two years since he'd felt a woman's touch, since he'd lost himself in the abundance of feminine softness. Every day of abstinence was now rising to torment his flesh with need.

Lust was no surprise. Present a man who'd not known a woman in a while with the sight of a naked one, and there was no power on earth that could restrain his cock from rising.

But the tenderness in his chest nearly knocked him down. He longed to hold her, to whisper endearments, to kiss away her fears and offer her the protection of his body as well as its need.

"Elspeth," he said reverently, as if her name were a prayer.

That broke the spell. She covered herself, one arm across her breasts, the other hand protectively splayed between her legs.

He continued to look at her, drinking in her exposed skin, all rosy and fresh. It would be like silk under his touch. His hands would know every inch of her.

She snatched up the remains of the velvet skirt and held it before her, but her neat calves and ankles were still bare to his gaze.

"How long have you been there?" she demanded.

"Long enough."

If she was waiting for an apology, she'd wait till the Last Trump sounded.

"Rob, the haggis'll get cold," Angus Fletcher's voice sounded beneath them. "Tell her to hurry."

"The haggis'll get cold," he repeated woodenly. Rob was ravenous, but it wasn't food he wanted.

She swallowed hard, as if she couldn't find her

voice, and clutched the skirt to her body. The uneven hem drew his gaze down to her bare feet and neat pink toes.

Pink.

He frowned.

The pink bit of foolishness along the bottom of the wine velvet was completely gone.

"Part of your skirt is missing."

It was dim in the upper room of Angus Fletcher's house, but Rob noticed she visibly paled.

"Aye, ye cut my skirt when I was trying to get away from that wolf," she said, her voice tight. Then she rushed on, chattering like a magpie. "Do ye no' remember? The skirt is ruined beyond repair, but I thought mayhap to save the fabric. 'Tis too fine a length of velvet to throw away. Angus gave me a skirt that had belonged to his mother. 'Tis hopelessly old-fashioned, but at least 'tis wearable and—"

"No, that's not what I mean," he said, his suspicions making him shove all thought of how tempting she still looked from his mind. "The silk on the bottom of your skirt isna there anymore."

She worried her lip and took a step back. "I used it to tend your wound and—"

"Not all of it. Ye used only a small bit for that." Their tramp over the heath and through the woods might have torn off some of the silk, but not all of it. He closed the distance between them and grasped her shoulders. "What have ye done, wench?"

"Take your hands from me." She twisted out of his grasp, lifted her chin, and met his gaze with defiance. "What do ye think? I did what I could to let my father know where we'd gone. Tell me ye wouldna do the same if ye were taken against your will."

"Ye stubborn, willful…" The fact that he'd braved a wolf pack for her meant nothing to this woman. He grabbed her and held her against his chest. She struggled to free herself, but he'd captured her arms. "If I were another sort of man, ye'd pay dearly for this."

He tried to ignore the softness of her bare back or the way her breasts molded against him. The velvet skirt had slipped during their scuffle, and when he looked down at her, he realized only his shirt separated them.

But he couldn't let his lust temper his judgment. He'd been so sure no one would guess that he'd gone north instead of south, directly to *Caisteal Dubh*. They'd traveled at her footpace for the first half of the night. Then they'd been delayed by the wolves, and he'd been forced to carry her toward morning.

Once Drummond and Elspeth's father picked up their trail, they'd be riding as fast as they dared without overrunning another sign. Rob hadn't put enough miles behind him to keep them from catching up. They might arrive in Angus Fletcher's cove at any moment.

"Angus!" he bellowed. "We have to go. We're about to have company."

"Aye," his friend called back. "But give me a bit to pack the haggis. They're too good to leave."

"Get dressed," Rob told Elspeth as he released her. He settled himself on the end of Angus's long string bed.

"But I can't get dressed while ye watch me!" She pulled the velvet up to cover her breasts once again.

"Obviously, I havena watched ye close enough up to now. 'Tis an error I dinna intend to repeat." He folded his arms over his chest. "Ye dinna wish to continue our journey naked, do ye?"

"Of course not."

"Then I suggest ye hurry."

If she could have shot fire bolts from her eyes, Rob knew he'd be but a pile of smoldering cinders. He smiled at her and almost saw smoke curl out of her ears.

She let the velvet fall to the floor and pulled her chemise over her head. Rob was treated to a quick glimpse of her whole body, quivering with rage. Her nipples flushed a deep rose.

Then, studiously avoiding Rob's gaze, she wiggled into Fletcher's mother's skirt, which was long enough to bunch on the floor at her bare feet. The bodice was designed for a woman with smaller breasts, and it laced in the back. Rob watched her struggle with it for a few moments, enjoying her frustration.

But if they were going to stay ahead of the men who were undoubtedly on their trail, they needed to be gone.

"Turn around, lass." He crossed the room and took her laces in hand.

She fisted her hands at her waist while he worked the leather strips through the eyes and cinched the bodice tight. A quick glance over her shoulder showed him her breasts pushed up and overflowing the old-fashioned bodice.

"There." He tied the laces off and whirled her around to face him.

Rob kissed her hard and thoroughly—a seal of ownership. Until he finished his revenge on Drummond, Elspeth Stewart belonged to him. The sooner she realized that fact, the better she'd fare.

He released her mouth and looked down at her. The loathing he saw in her face made him step back a pace.

"Come." He gripped her wrist and led her to the stairs, indicating she should climb down ahead of him. "And no more tricks. I'd better not catch you losing any bits of your wardrobe again. Or else."

Fury made her eyes glitter.

That was better. Anger he could take. Her disgust made his chest ache.

"Or else what?" she asked through clenched teeth.

"Or I'll make sure you lose all of it."

Chapter 10

As they plodded through the forest, Drummond glanced over his shoulder at Lord Stewart. The man's face was set like stone. He hadn't said a word since they found the last sign of his daughter.

Lachlan didn't blame him.

They'd uncovered a bit of cloth ripped from Elspeth's chemise amid several wolf carcasses. The soiled linen was now tucked into Drummond's sleeve. It was stiff with blood, but he bore it as if he were a knight-errant, wearing the evidence of his lady's favor.

They didn't find any sign of Elspeth's body. Not even drag marks to show she'd been pulled, kicking and screaming, to some other location. Drummond was glad of it. There were some things no father should have to see, and his ally was teetering on the edge of control as things were.

But there was so much blood in the clearing with the dead wolves, it seemed unlikely Elspeth escaped. Especially since only a single set of footprints left the clearing.

Male footprints.

Drummond was coldly furious. This had gone far beyond an annoying inconvenience. Rob MacLaren had upset all his plans. Though Alistair Stewart was united with him now by their supposed shared grief, eventually Elspeth's father would remember he blamed Lachlan's carelessness for allowing the abduction to happen in the first place.

Now that Elspeth was dead, there was no salvaging this disaster. They were just following the trail to its end so they could kill Rob MacLaren.

Slowly, if Lachlan had anything to say about it.

Then he saw something on the game trail that made him hold up his hand to signal a stop to their dreary column. He dismounted and squatted in the dirt before the new set of footprints.

"What is it?" Stewart asked halfheartedly as he dismounted and handed off his reins to his retainer. After sending men back with the MacLaren's stallion, they had only two extra men riding with them.

"Looks like MacLaren met someone here." A big someone judging from the monstrous size of his boot print.

Then Drummond noticed something else that made his heart leap with hope.

"Alistair! Quick! Have a look at this!"

Elspeth's father shrugged off his lethargy and joined Drummond on the path. Lachlan pointed to another imprint, the shallow outline of a small, feminine slipper.

"She's alive," Stewart whispered as if he feared daring to speak it aloud might make it untrue.

Lachlan peered ahead on the trail where two sets of masculine prints led off through the forest.

"Aye, but the men must be carrying her, because that's the only one I see from her."

"She must be injured," Stewart said gruffly, trying unsuccessfully to keep the sob from his voice.

May God strike me blind if I ever become so maudlin over my offspring, Drummond thought. *It's not as if a man can't always sire more.*

"If she is, we'll return the hurts she's suffered a hundredfold," Drummond promised. "But if they are carrying her, that bodes well for us. They must travel slowly. And chances are good that the fellow MacLaren met has a camp or a hovel of some sort nearby. They can't be far ahead."

The men remounted without another word and trotted down the trail, gazes glued to the ground ahead of them in the hope of seeing another slim footprint.

❧

"Hurry, Angus!" Rob said as he shouldered the pack of provisions his friend had prepared. "I dinna know how much longer we have before they find us."

He strode out of the house, dragging Elspeth along by the wrist. "Step lively, girl, or I'll throw ye over my shoulder again."

Angus lumbered after them. "The only trouble with leaving now is we haven't the current with us. It'll make for a nasty start."

"D'ye mean to say it's impossible to sail to Lochearnhead now?"

"No, just slow. We'll have to row till the wind and water changes. And we'll no' be making much headway at that. Then when the current comes about, we must keep our wits about us, ye ken, for that's when the *each uisge* rears his head."

"A water horse?" Elspeth asked, owl-eyed.

"Aye, it came here to Loch Eireann from—"

"Spin your tales later, Fletcher," Rob interrupted. "Now we row."

"Angus, 'tis no' too late for ye to help me." Elspeth dug in her heels and made it difficult for Rob to drag her along. "Ye've been naught but kindness itself to me. My father will be grateful. Honestly, he will."

"Keep quiet, wench." He picked her up by the waist and half-carried, half-walked her toward the shore. She pummeled his arm with her fists.

Angus frowned, and Fingal seemed to sense his master's disapproval. The deerhound bounded alongside Rob, yipping and growling.

"There's no need to be so harsh to the lass, is there?" Angus asked.

"Me, harsh?" Rob said. "Of the two of us, which is trying to do the other damage just now?"

The pounding of distant hooves made all their heads turn. A group of men on horseback broke through the trees, plying their whips.

"'Tis my father!"

"That's why I'm harsh to the lass, Angus. She brought this down on us. Now come on." He scooped a squirming Elspeth up and over his shoulder and ran the rest of the way to the longboat tied up at Angus's dock. Fingal loped after them, his tongue lolling, his mouth lifted in a doggie smile as if pleased to go for a pleasure sail.

"Please, Rob," she begged. "Let me go, and I'll convince them no' to follow ye."

"I said quiet!" He hustled her into the boat, and the deerhound scrambled after. While Angus hoisted the big striped sail, Rob untied the lines. He gave the hull a shove and leaped aboard as the wind caught in the canvas and boat quickened.

The riders drew nearer. Rob counted four of them—Drummond, Stewart, and two retainers. He unshipped the forward set of oars and put his back into the long strokes.

"Father!" Elspeth waved her arms over her head. Fingal barked as though in sympathy.

"Sit, lass, before ye fall," Angus ordered. Rob was mildly irritated that she obeyed his friend without question, perching on one of the bench seats, meek as a dove. The dog settled beside her, obviously deciding she needed his head in her lap. "And ship those oars, Rob."

"But—" Rob began.

"When we've land beneath our feet, I'll be pleased to follow your orders. Now that we're sailing the loch, ye'll answer to me," Angus said pleasantly but firmly. "We canna go the way ye wish for the now. No' if we want to get away quick and clean."

A crossbow bolt thudded into the hull a hand's span north of the waterline, as if to punctuate Angus's point.

"Bloody fool!" Rob glared at the bowman kneeling on the shore. He might have easily hit Elspeth with the bolt. "Get into the cabin," he ordered her.

There wasn't exactly a cabin on board. Angus's boat

was too small for that. Rob meant the portion of the deck covered by a wooden roof. There was room to sit upright beneath the low covering and space to lie on the pallet Angus had prepared, but it was little more than a place to get out of the wind and weather.

But it would still protect Elspeth if there were more crossbow bolts headed their way.

When another bolt tore through the sail, Elspeth obeyed without a word of protest.

Fingal followed but stopped when she disappeared into the enclosed space. Obviously, the cabin was forbidden to deerhounds, but Fingal turned several circles outside the open forward end of the cabin and plopped down to guard his newly chosen favorite person.

"Very well, Angus," Rob said as the boat's prow turned east.

The boat seemed to lift in the water once it fell in line with the prevailing current. The waves divided before the prow like a pair of wings, poised for flight. The men on the shore fell swiftly astern.

"We'll have it your way," Rob said.

"'Tis no' my way," Angus said with a laugh. "'Tis the way of the loch, and ye gainsay that at your peril."

❧

"They're getting away!" Lachlan fitted another bolt to his crossbow.

Stewart put a restraining hand on his shoulder.

"Dinna shoot, Lachlan. I understand how ye feel, but ye canna be sure ye'll no' strike my daughter."

The stripe-sailed craft disappeared around a rocky point jutting into the narrow loch.

"But how can we catch them now?" Drummond gnashed his teeth in frustration. They'd been so close. "This loch flows into the River Earn and then to the Firth of Tay. We can't outrun a river on its way to the sea."

"My daughter's alive," Stewart said with a quick glance skyward that Lachlan recognized as a silent prayer of thanks. "That's enough for now."

"Is that what ye want to go back and tell your wife, Stewart? Our daughter's still in the hands of a madman, my dearest, but she's alive?"

"Beggin' your pardons, my lords," the Stewart retainer spoke up, "but do ye know for certain the MacLaren intended to sail east?"

"We saw him go that way, didn't we?" Drummond said. Stewart's man was altogether too outspoken. If the fellow answered to him, Lachlan would beat that out of him in short order.

"Aye, but will he keep going east?" the man asked.

"How can we know the mind of a madman?" Lachlan demanded. "Of all the stupid—"

"Wait, Lachlan." Stewart held up a hand to signal quiet. "Calum here grew up on the loch. He may know a thing or two about the sailing of it. What are ye thinking, lad?"

"Just that we may wish to bide here a bit," Calum said. "Mad Rob was delayed on the way here, what with the wolves and all. He may have intended to reach this place early enough to sail west."

"Then why did he sail east?" Lachlan said with a sneer.

"This loch is like a little sea. It has a tide of its own that turns every half day or so," Calum explained.

"If the MacLaren means to make for Lochearnhead, they'll have to sail past this point again tonight."

"And why do ye think he means to make for Lochearnhead?" Lachlan demanded.

"The MacLaren told ye to collect yer bride at *Caisteal Dubh*, did he no'? It puzzles me that at every step he's gone in the wrong direction," Calum said, staring at the spot where the boat had disappeared around the point. "But if he means to sail the length of the loch, going west, he'll reach his stronghold much sooner than we could, even if we headed that way this instant."

The Stewart nodded thoughtfully. "That makes sense. Lochearnhead is just a day's ride from *Caisteal Dubh*."

"Even if they do sail past us again, what can we do about it except watch them go by?" Lachlan said. "Ye dinna want me to shoot at them for fear of hitting Elspeth."

"Actually, my lord," Calum said with a grin Lachlan would have loved to knock off his face. "I have a couple ideas we might try."

⁂

Elspeth was weeping. She wasn't being hysterical or obtrusive about it. She was trying to stifle her sobs, but Rob heard them in any case.

He couldn't see her, since the cabin opened forward and he was standing near the bow, but he could imagine her with her hand covering her mouth to muffle a cry, her slim shoulders shaking.

It would have been easier to ignore wailing than those hitched breaths and soft moans.

They pounded at his heart as surely as an opposing army slams a battering ram into a castle gate.

Fingal pointed his nose to the sky and howled.

"Ach, I canna bear it either," Angus said from his place at the tiller. "Can ye no' make her stop, Rob?"

"She's probably just tired," Rob said, sure that wasn't the cause of her weeping. If he admitted she wept because of him, he'd have no way to hide from his guilt. "She passed a long, weary night."

"Aye, and so did ye," Angus said. "Why do ye no' join her? Mayhap it will settle her."

"And mayhap it will set her to keening," Rob said, knuckling his eyes. Angus was right. He, too, had passed a weary night. "A woman is chancier than the weather."

"Aye, there is that."

Angus rummaged in his sporran and came up with a greasy packet. He unwrapped the cloth that held the cooling sarnies. He offered one to Rob, but Rob declined with a wave of his hand. The pallet in the cabin called to him louder than his stomach complained, but he didn't want to share that small space with a weeping woman.

"Weel, in a few hours the tide will turn, and I'll need ye to spell me at the tiller once we come about," Angus said, licking the extra grease from his fingers and helping himself to another sausage. "I think ye should rest in the cabin for a bit."

Rob would sooner face another wolf pack. "The cabin is occupied."

"The lass is a wee thing. She doesna take up much room, ye ken."

A loud sniff came from the cabin.

"I'll make do here." Rob settled himself on the curved hull and leaned against the mast. When he first devised this plan to take revenge on Drummond, he hadn't reckoned on having to deal with the man's bride. Before he met her, Elspeth Stewart was merely a pawn in his game with his enemy. Only a thing, a parcel to be stolen and used in his struggle with Drummond.

Now she was a real person. A real person who was crying her eyes red because of *him*, not because of the fiend she was set to marry. Drummond would undoubtedly break her heart a dozen times once the knot was tied. Instead, she wept on account of Rob's misdeeds.

Truly, there was no justice in the world.

"Ye traveled all night, Rob. Ye'll be no use to me if ye're bone tired," Angus said. "So as captain of this vessel, I order ye to join Lady Elspeth in the cabin."

"I'd sooner wrestle a *kelpie*." Rob knew Angus believed in those malevolent river spirits as thoroughly as he assumed the existence of the water horse.

"I can arrange that," Angus said darkly. "How would ye fancy swimming to Lochearnhead?"

His friend had set his feet, and there was no budging Angus once he'd done that. Unless Rob wanted another dip in the frigid loch, he had to join Elspeth in the little cabin.

He rose and made his way to the prow of the boat like a man destined for the stocks.

Chapter 11

ROB SQUATTED DOWN TO PEER INTO THE CABIN. IT was a neat little space, compared to Angus's cluttered house. There was an inviting pallet and a couple plush wolf pelts to soften the plank floor. A badger-skin pouch hung from a hook on the back wall. Rob guessed that was filled with provisions, since a wine-skin swung near it. A covered chamber pot rested in one corner.

Elspeth was seated on one of the wolf pelts in the other corner with her knees drawn up, her forearms propped across them, and her head bowed down. Her shoulders shook like a lost child.

Guilt made him snort out his breath in self-disgust.

She looked up at him, her eyes and lips swollen with weeping. Her expression of abject misery made his chest constrict. Then she swiped her face with her sleeve, and misery was quickly replaced by cold fury.

He could have kissed her. Tears rendered him defenseless. Wrath was something he understood and could return with little effort.

"What are you doing here?" she hissed.

He crawled into the low space and stretched out on the pallet. "What does it look like?"

"Go away. Haven't ye spied on me enough for one day?"

"I'm no' here to spy." He rolled onto his side and propped himself on one elbow. "'Tis a small boat and I'm tired and this is the only place to rest." Then he smiled at her, because he knew it would annoy her. "But how kind of ye to remind me how pleasant it was to watch ye at your bath. Mayhap I'll see ye again in my dreams."

He lay back down, folded his hands across his chest, and closed his eyes.

"Ye're lucky I havena got a knife, MacLaren," she muttered darkly.

"My thanks once again."

Rob sat back up and pulled out his belt knife and boot knife. Then he flung each of them toward the tall neck at the front of the vessel. The blades dug into the wood and quivered there, well out of her reach.

"Canna have ye using my own weapons against me as I sleep. Now come." He patted the pallet beside him. "Join me."

"No."

"Angus will take it badly." He opened one eye and peered at her. "He's gone to all this trouble of making the place comfy for ye."

"No." Her chest heaved with a deep breath, and her breasts rose, straining against the borrowed bodice.

That tender curve of skin called to him. "Mayhap your bodice is done up too tight for your comfort. I'll be happy to unlace ye."

She was on him in a heartbeat, scratching and kicking. "How dare ye!"

He quickly subdued her, clamping her arms to her sides and wrapping his legs around hers. "Easy, lass. Be mindful of where ye are."

She thrashed and made a sound like a cornered barn cat.

"Everything well, Rob?" Angus called up to them.

"Aye, Angus, fine as frog's hair. I'm just trying to keep my eyes in their sockets." Then he lowered his voice. "Now settle, lass, and I'll let ye go."

He eased his grip when she stopped struggling. She looked up at him, and the anger drained from her features. Then the worst possible thing happened.

Her little face crumpled, and a tear slid from the corner of one eye.

Oh, Lord. Against a woman's tears, there was no defense known to man.

"Now, lass, I've no' brought an ounce of real harm to ye, have I?"

She buried her face in the crook of his neck, and her tears fairly burned his skin.

"Did I no' fight a wolf pack for ye?"

She sobbed on the shoulder of his shirt, leaving a growing wet spot.

"Your father knows ye're alive. That should give him and ye a measure of peace," he said with hope that she'd take comfort from having seen her sire, however briefly.

She wept a fresh torrent instead.

"I promise ye, lass, I'll keep ye safe. No one will harm ye." He grasped at anything he could think of to dry up her tears. "I offer ye the protection of my body and my sword arm for as long as we bide together. And any time ye might have need of them after."

Her whole frame shuddered with a silent sob.

"Please, lass." He stroked her from the crown of her head to the base of her spine. She shivered under his touch, so he didn't do it again. "Elspeth, sweetheart, ye dinna have to cry so."

She quieted and sniffled for a moment. Then she raised herself up and looked down at him, her hazel eyes going dark in the dim cabin.

"I hate ye, Rob MacLaren," she whispered. "I hate ye verra, verra much."

Then she kissed him.

❧

Elspeth pressed her lips to his, damning herself for a light-heeled wanton. But she couldn't be near the man without wanting to taste him.

She'd been all jumbled up since he caught her naked. When his hot gaze ran over her, her insides melted like a dish of butter in the sun.

He'd stolen her from her wedding. Ruined her reputation. Put her parents through the torments of hell, worrying over her. And yet she was drawn to him, and there was no escaping. What was wrong with her?

When she first realized he was there watching her, she couldn't believe it was happening. There she was, bare as an egg, and his intense gaze made her lose the will to move.

His stare had lingered at her breasts. She'd had to bite the insides of her cheeks to keep from covering her nipples with her hands to still the ache. And when his gaze traveled down her body, little flames seemed to lick her skin. When he smiled at her private parts, she caught fire completely.

No wonder her priest always said it was better to marry than to burn, but she never imagined she was about to self-immolate in Lachlan Drummond's arms. No, for some inexplicable reason, her body had chosen to lust after Mad Rob MacLaren.

Rob seemed to think she wept for her lost bridegroom or her parents' pain. She wished she were as dutiful a daughter and bride as he thought her.

Instead, she wept for her lost innocence. She'd have believed herself the model of chaste womanhood, a paragon of self-control all her days if she'd never laid eyes on Rob MacLaren. Now she knew the truth of her own nature.

She was desperately wicked.

And unrepentant to boot. The knowledge grieved her, but she couldn't deny the truth.

Elspeth palmed Rob's cheeks and deepened their kiss. She welcomed his tongue. She gave him her neck to nibble and suckle, loving the rough stubble of his beard as it tickled across her skin. His hands brushed through her hair, stroking and smoothing.

Her laces loosened, and she realized he'd untied her bodice.

She didn't care.

She lifted her arms in surrender to help him slip the bodice over her head without unlacing it completely. Her breasts swung free beneath the thin chemise. A little thrill coursed over her sensitive skin.

Rob rolled her over and pinned her beneath him. The weight of his body on hers was heaven. A ribbon tied at the neck of her chemise held it closed. He caught the end of the bow between his teeth and gave it a tug. The knot unraveled, and the fabric parted to bare one of her breasts.

He stared down at it, clearly fascinated. Her nipple was drawn tight. He circled it with the tip of his finger as his gaze shifted to her face.

Her first instinct was to look away, to shield her wicked thoughts and feelings from his penetrating gaze. But if ever there was a time for truth between a man and a woman, this was that time.

She met his eyes steadily and didn't care whether he saw the abandon and bliss she felt. His face held a cross between the wonder of a boy on Christmas morn and the knowing look of a man who was exquisitely aware of what wicked things he was doing to her. He enslaved her with pleasure, and she had no defense.

Her cheeks heated, and her breath hitched, but she couldn't look away. He might stop, and she didn't think she could bear it if he did.

Instead, she moved. Just a little, so his finger would brush her sensitive tip. A jolt of longing shot through her body from her breast to her womb.

"Merciful God!" she breathed.

"Aye, lass, and 'tis a good thing He is," Rob said with a wicked grin, "for I am no' merciful in the slightest."

As if to prove his point, he lowered his mouth to her breast and licked her taut nipple. She went all soft and liquid inside. Between her legs, she ached in time with the flicks of his tongue.

It was unbearable. It was torment. She prayed it wouldn't end.

His mouth was everywhere. Suckling her breasts, nibbling her neck, and licking at her earlobe, showering her with soft kisses on her jaw, cheeks, eyelids, and temple. When she started to make a noise of unrestrained pleasure, he covered her mouth to catch the sound. Then he kissed her again, a deep drugging kiss that shattered any hope of defense and weakened her last resolve.

He shifted to lie beside her, and she felt the hard evidence of his arousal against her hip.

She'd never seen a man in the altogether before. She assumed their parts were somewhat like stallions, sometimes dangling harmlessly, sometimes a thick, stiff organ designed for rutting. Rob was definitely stiff, and the ridge of him beneath his kilt was thick. She moved against him and enjoyed the way *his* breath hitched for a change.

What would he do if she reached under his kilt to investigate matters further?

But before she could act on her curiosity, he launched a blistering sensual foray.

His hands caressed every bit of her, smoothing over her arms and her belly. She wallowed in the delicious sensations, letting them wash over her like summer rain.

But when his hand slipped under her skirt, she stiffened.

"Easy, lass," he said, nuzzling her neck. "I'll do ye no hurt."

"I expect that's what the Serpent said to Eve," she whispered, her body tensed.

"Have a done aught ye wish I had not?"

She worried her lower lip. What would she take back? His mouth on hers? His hand at her breast?

"No," she admitted.

"I'll no' take anything from ye that ye dinna wish to give," he said softly. "But I would give something to ye, if ye'll allow it. Show ye things about yourself, an' ye let me."

She felt herself tumble into his eyes.

"Aye, Rob." Elspeth swallowed hard. "Show me."

Chapter 12

ROB LOWERED HIS MOUTH TO HERS, TASTING AND teasing. She was so sweet, so fine, he feared he defiled her with just a kiss. But she'd asked for this. Surely this was no sin if the lass wanted him.

Lord knew he wanted her. He'd never thought to ache so for a woman again.

The skin of Elspeth's inner thigh was so soft, so tender, it was all he could do not to toss up her skirt and plant fevered kisses there. But he didn't want to spook her.

The curling hairs on her sex were like silk where his fingertips passed over them. And damp. Her whole body shuddered at his glancing caress.

She was ready for him.

His cock throbbed.

He covered her with his whole hand, holding her hot sex. Her heartbeat throbbed even there. Her thighs tensed, and a soft moan escaped her lips.

"Hush, lass," he whispered. "Ye must be quiet, or Angus will fear I'm hurting ye."

She nodded, her eyes enormous, and pulled his head down to kiss her again.

An excellent way to keep her quiet, he thought as his tongue chased hers in a languid, wet kiss. *Isn't she the canny one?*

He explored her with exquisite slowness. Next time—please God, let there be a next time—he'd lie between her legs and revel in the slick delights of that soft, moist crevice, but for now, his fingers were his eyes.

He parted her, stroking each fold as he went. She quivered under his touch, swollen and sensitive. He found her most responsive spot with ease. The first time he grazed it with his fingertip, she gasped and pulled away from his kiss.

"What is that?" she asked shakily.

"A way for me to give ye joy, lass. Close your eyes and let me."

Unlike with most of his directives, she obeyed this one. He could almost feel her curiosity burning into his questing hand. He pressed a soft kiss on each of her eyelids.

Since he was a lad of about twelve, he'd known what miracles his cock could perform. Still, it didn't surprise him that Elspeth didn't understand much about this part of her body.

Women were kept in ignorance, Fiona had told him. Some were even shackled in chastity belts by wary fathers or jealous husbands. Fiona said...

Guilt burned his soul. He hadn't dreamed of her, hadn't thought of Fiona in days. Why did she invade his mind now?

He looked down at Elspeth. Her brows drew together in agreeable distress as he continued to stroke her. Her mouth went passion slack.

Was he being unfaithful to Fiona's memory by pleasuring Elspeth? The Stewart lass wouldn't even be with him now if not for his wife and what had happened to her. Was he doing this as revenge on Drummond for Fiona? To delight Elspeth? Or to prove to himself that he could still satisfy a woman after such a long stint of abstinence?

His head pounded. It hurt to think so hard.

He decided not to try. Feeling was much easier than thinking.

Rob gave himself over to Elspeth's soft sighs, to her slippery cleft and growing arousal, to the delights of her mouth. A wanting woman had a way of making a man feel grander than a king. He kissed his way down the white column of her throat to her exposed breast.

He nuzzled around her nipple, letting his warm breath tease her. Then when she made a soft sound of distress, he took her taut peak between his lips and devoured her.

Each time he suckled her, his balls clenched, poised for release.

He flicked her nipple with his tongue in rhythm with the movement of his fingers, and she stiffened, back arched, pelvis raised into his hand.

He feared he might come under his kilt.

Then she shattered beneath his touch.

He felt her inner spasms in the soft lips of her sex while her whole body shuddered with the force of her release. Her heart pounded against his hand between her legs.

Rob wondered if a body's soul left it for a moment

when the shimmering glory of bliss became too much for mortal flesh to bear. Was there a place between life and death where souls in the grip of ecstasy mingled together, a joining of spirits separate from the joining of bodies?

If such a place existed, Elspeth was there alone. Rob's body still burned with unrelieved need.

And his head ached with daft thoughts that raced about like herring in a net.

Elspeth lay gasping, her chest rising and falling unevenly as she came back to herself from that shining place. Then she turned her head to look at him with such a trusting smile, Rob cringed inside.

A man who pleasured one woman while another flitted through his mind didn't deserve that kind of trust.

She reached up a hand to palm his cheek.

"I never dreamed."

He removed his hand from between her legs and smoothed down her skirt. Even though he ached to show her more, to finish their coupling and see if they could find that place where souls mingled, he was done. His cock tried to fight him, but his will held firm.

I never dreamed, she says.

Fiona hadn't visited his dreams since he met Elspeth. He wondered if she ever would again.

❧

"Almost, my lord," Calum said, shielding his eyes against the glare of the loch. The crossbow bolt skipped over the waves and sank. The line attached to it floated for a bit before following the bolt down. If they couldn't shoot an arrow into the yew tree on the far side of the loch, they'd never be able to rig a makeshift ferry to catch Mad Rob when he sailed back by. "Only shy by a few bow lengths. Still, a crossbow wasna meant for distance."

Lachlan Drummond pressed his lips together in frustration as he signaled for Calum to pull the bolt back. Thanks to the attached line, at least he hadn't lost any yet. "Ye have something against a crossbow?"

"I've heard my lord say they aren't sporting, not when a bolt can slice through a man's shield like it was butter."

"If a man goes into battle, he ought to go to win. If he's not canny enough to carry the most lethal weapon, he deserves to lose," Lachlan said. He'd heard more than one man complain that a crossbow didn't require the skill or strength of a longbow. The wicked wounds a crossbow left were enough to make it Lachlan's weapon of choice. "A crossbow carries the day more often than not."

Drummond reloaded his bow and shot another bolt. With the same result.

"Pity we're no' in battle, then," Calum said.

"Do ye think ye can do better?"

"I dinna know, but I could try." The Stewart's retainer ran to fetch his longbow.

Drummond and his party had moved from the shore where they last spotted Elspeth and her captor to the rocky point jutting out into Loch Eireann. The body of water was narrow to begin with. From that jutting spit of land, it was no broader than a goodly sized river.

"If we can shoot an arrow with a line attached to it across the loch," Calum had explained, "we can let the line rest below the water level and then pull it taut when the MacLaren comes sailing back by. If we clear the prow instead of sliding under the hull, the line will catch on the mast, and it ought to stop him dead in the water."

"And then what?" Drummond demanded. "Lord Stewart doesn't want us to shoot at him."

"Aye, and he's right. We might hit Lady Elspeth accidently," Calum said. "Instead, we'll build a raft and use the line to ferry ourselves out and board the boat."

The Stewart's man had all the answers, it seemed. So while Alistair Stewart and Drummond's servant dismantled a henhouse for lumber to make a raft—and roasted a pair of chickens over a fire—Lachlan and Calum were trying to secure a line across the water.

Calum sucked in a deep breath, drew back his longbow till his knuckles grazed his ear. Then he pointed the arrow tip at the sky. He released the shaft with a twang of the string, along with his pent-up breath.

Lachlan shaded his eyes with his hand and followed the flight of the long shaft. The line attached to it coiled out with a whipping sound. The arrow found its mark in the big yew on the other side of the loch.

Calum gave the line a stout tug.

"Ye might pull it out!" Drummond warned.

"If it's going to give, better to know now than when we're trying to rescue Lady Elspeth."

Drummond nodded his grudging approval. "This is shaping up to be a good plan. I thank ye."

Calum glanced at him and tied the line off on a nearby boulder. "I didna do it for ye, Lord Drummond. I did it for the lady."

~⁂~

Elspeth no longer felt like a lady. She knew enough about the business of losing a maidenhead to know she still possessed hers, but even so, she wasn't the same.

Rob MacLaren had seen her naked.

Not just without her clothes. He'd glimpsed her soul at its neediest.

She had no language to describe what he'd done to her. She'd had no idea a mortal was capable of such shattering pleasure, no inkling that her body would so thoroughly become his willing ally.

She knew what they were doing was wicked, but she didn't feel soiled till after. When he simply rolled over without saying a word.

Now, judging by his deep, rhythmic breathing, the smug brute was enjoying the sleep of the just.

Elspeth rolled onto her side, giving Rob her back, and pulled her knees up to her chest.

He'd been so tender and giving while he played her body, his touch as sure and exquisite as a bard plucking his harp. How could he be so cold when he was done?

His kisses had brought something to life in her. She no longer felt like a pawn, only one item in a long list of goods to be exchanged. When he touched her intimately, she felt as if he *knew* her.

And she mattered. Not for whatever cattle and agreements came with her. Just for herself.

How could what they'd done together mean so little to him?

She gnawed her lower lip. Maybe that was it. They hadn't done anything together. He did something only to her.

She had certainly kissed him back. Merciful heaven, she'd even kissed him first. But aside from running her hand over his hair, she hadn't touched him.

Maybe she should have reached beneath his kilt after all.

But he knew she was a maiden. How could she be expected to know what a man wants?

She drew a deep breath. When he first abducted her, she'd caught a few glimpses into his heart through the Sight. She'd felt his deep sadness, and it kept her from fearing him as much as she should have.

Now she sensed nothing from him.

Perhaps she'd been listening to her body so intently, it drowned out all the other, less-forceful voices. She'd never been able to call up her Gift at will, but if she concentrated mightily, maybe...

She rolled over and laid a hand lightly on Rob's shoulder. He didn't stir. She closed her eyes, matched the rhythm of his breathing, and tried to empty her mind of the riotous clamoring of her body.

Nothing came to her but the steady roll of the boat and the lap of water on the hull.

No vision flashed behind her eyes, but she remembered suddenly that she'd been given a brief impression when they were in the cave. In her glimpse into

Rob's mind she'd Seen a willowy, red-haired woman. Elspeth didn't know who she was, but she was obviously important to him.

Perhaps that woman was why Rob turned away from her.

Elspeth pulled her hand from his shoulder and rolled over to face away from him again.

"I still hate ye verra, verra much, Rob MacLaren," she whispered. "Dinna think otherwise."

Chapter 13

ROB STRAINED AGAINST THE CORDS AT HIS WRISTS, BUT he couldn't free himself. His arms were outstretched, and for a moment, he wondered if he was being held in a cell beneath Drummond's stronghold. Then he realized he was lying spread-eagled in the middle of a soft feather tick, bound at the wrists and ankles.

It was dark, but there was a storm brewing outside the castle. Occasional lightning flashes showed him that he was in his bedchamber, captive on his bed.

And he was naked.

The door creaked open, and light from the torch in the hall sent a shaft of gold spilling across the rushes on the floor. A woman was silhouetted by the doorway, but since she was lit from behind, her face was in shadow.

She walked in without a word, and the door closed behind her, plunging him into almost total darkness once more.

"Who are ye?" His question circled the room in sibilant echoes.

It also went unanswered for the space of several heartbeats.

Her footfalls rustled across the floor. Once she was beside the bed, she whispered his name.

"Ye dinna know me, Robin?" Her voice was hollow and

bloodless, a reed whistling in the wind. "I am the last wisp of dream when ye first wake. A ghost in the corner of your eye that disappears when ye look at it direct. I am that space between one breath and the next, where all things are possible but none are required."

She was no more than a dark shape, but her form was pleasing, and when lightning brightened the room like day for a blink, he caught a glimpse of her milk-white breasts. The bodice of her gown was cut so low, her taut nipples peeped above it. His cock rose of its own accord.

"Why am I bound?" he asked, struggling against the cords.

"Because ye dinna have the will to free yourself."

"Will ye release me?"

"No," she said softly. "Only ye can do that."

He felt a hand on his shin. He'd expected her touch to be cold and wraithlike, but her palm was warm as a freshly baked bun. Now that he thought on it, she even smelled like fresh bread. His mouth watered. This strange woman wakened hungers of every kind.

Her hand slid up past his knee and circled his groin with maddening nearness.

"Ask what ye will, Robin." Her fingertips teased the small hairs on his scrotum. "In this place, all questions are welcome, though not all are answered. All knots will be untied. One way or another."

One question burned his brain hotter than the others. Even though he feared to ask, he heard himself say, "Am I mad?"

So many named him thus, he had to wonder if there wasn't some truth to it.

"No, not as ye mean it. Ye're only mad in the way all men are."

She kneaded his balls, and his cock twitched in pleasurable agony. He heard the rustle of velvet. When lightning flashed again, he saw she'd shed her gown, but her long hair obscured her features. For a moment, he thought she might be Fiona, but the voice wasn't right.

"Will ye show me your face?"

She laughed. "My face is the last thing most men ask to see when I come to them by night."

Then she lowered her head, and her hair brushed over his cock, a thousand silken fingers. His hands bunched into fists, and every muscle in his body clenched. He was helpless before her. His eyes rolled back in his head as she ran her tongue along his length from base to tip.

Then she took him into her mouth.

The whole world went wet and warm. She lashed him with her tongue. She sucked. She rained kisses on him, drenching him, engulfing him.

He fought the downward pull of his groin.

"I. Must. See. Your. Face," he said through clenched teeth.

"Think ye I canna please ye without that?"

She climbed on top of him and settled herself on his cock, rubbing her wet slit over its length. He fought to keep from spewing his seed over his belly.

He willed himself not to come.

"Your face," he demanded.

Instead, she thrust her breasts toward him, her hard nipples grazing his cheeks, his lips, his closed eyes. He steeled himself not to capture one of them with his mouth.

When she gave up and tilted back, she made sure he slid into her all the way. Bound as he was, he could no more stop that than he could stop breathing.

She was tighter than a fisted glove. And wetter than waterweed.

She began to move. Slowly at first, but then with increasing speed. The pressure on his balls mounted with each stroke. She meant to subdue him with pleasure, drive him to release. She goaded him along like an ox to slaughter.

"Robin," she whispered. "Dinna fight so hard. Give yourself to me."

He shook his head, too incoherent with need for speech.

"Ach, verra well. I see your heart is set on it, and when have I e'er given a man aught but what he most wished?"

She raised herself up on her knees, so only the tip of him remained within her tight grip. She squeezed him once with the tiny muscles of her inner walls, careful not to expel him.

"But which face is it to be, I wonder?" She stretched out a hand and sank her fingers deep into his chest.

Rob sucked a startled breath over his teeth.

Deeper and deeper, she probed. He expected agony as she brushed his beating heart, but he felt only warmth and acceptance in her questing touch.

"There it is," she said softly and pulled her hand back. His flesh closed behind her hand without leaving a mark.

The room brightened, not from lightning but from the woman herself. She glowed like a candle. When she looked down at him, it was with Elspeth's hazel eyes, Elspeth's virginal lips curved in a sensual, knowing smile. The milk-white breasts were Elspeth's, firm and high. The tender triangle of hair covering her sex was Elspeth's rich chestnut.

"Is this the face ye wish for?"

She was everything he wished for. His body raced to the edge of release. He teetered on the precipice, waiting only for her to lower herself onto his cock once again.

"As I thought," she said, the light fading as she leaned

forward and kissed his forehead. "And now, Robin, my love, ye must wake."

He felt himself tumbling into a deep well, but just before he struck the bottom…

Rob jerked himself awake. His cock throbbed beneath his kilt, still primed for release. The sun had long since set, so it was nearly as dark in the small cabin as the bedchamber in his dream. But Rob had always been cat-eyed at night. Strange that he hadn't been in his dream. He could see Elspeth lying beside him right enough, close but not touching. Near enough for him to feel her warmth.

Her mouth was parted in the relaxation of slumber, and her closed eyes made him ache to plant a kiss on them. He willed his body to settle. He forced himself to think of a dog eating its own vomit, a corbie plucking the eye from a corpse on a field of battle, anything to keep from coming in a shuddering rush with her sleeping so innocently beside him.

What if she were to wake and catch his body bucking in release?

He'd been a heartless bastard to turn from her as he did after she'd trusted him to waken her to the joys of the flesh. But he was so confused, he didn't trust himself to speak to her. Didn't know what to say. Not after Fiona had danced in his head while he touched Elspeth.

Double-mindedness was worse than madness. A double-minded man couldn't tell if he was afoot or horseback.

Then the succubus in his dreams! As if he needed a third woman to further muddle the question.

He wanted Elspeth, whether it was wise or not.

He didn't need his dream wraith to tell him that. The fact that she was his prisoner and another man's bride didn't bode well for anything but a fleeting tryst or two between them.

And despite the outcome of his dream, he still loved his wife and feared that he dishonored Fiona's memory every time his eye followed Elspeth about.

The succubus in his dream said he was bound because he didn't have the will to free himself. Even if he had the will, he didn't see any way to break out of this web of his own weaving. Elspeth was still his enemy's bride.

"Rob!" Angus called to him. "Are ye awake?"

Rob silently blessed his friend. A turn at the tiller would give his hands something to do and his head a chance to stop chasing these pointless questions.

"Aye," he said, sitting up and stretching his arms as far as the cramped space allowed. "I'll be there anon."

Elspeth stirred beside him. She sat up and stretched catlike as well. Her breasts were unbound still and strained against the thin fabric of her chemise. He forced himself to look away from those luscious curves, but his gaze sneaked back to them. Her nipples stood out proud under the worn linen.

He started to crawl out of the cabin.

"Wait a moment," Elspeth said. She pulled the leather bodice on over her head and turned her back to him. "I need your help with the laces."

He tried not to think about the way the bodice lifted her breasts and pressed them together till a soft curve spilled over the top. He was totally unsuccessful. He pulled the laces tight and tied them off.

"There you are," he said. Anything to fill the silence between them.

"Here I am." She ran her fingers through her hair to smooth out the tangles.

It only served to remind him how that silken hair had brushed his cock in his dream and then her lips had followed with devastating effect. His body roused to her afresh.

"You're staring at me," she accused.

He looked away, but her image was still burned on the backs of his eyes.

"Ye drag me off with ye, and yet ye seem to be able to forget I exist with amazing speed," she said. "Did it cross your mind that we might have aught to say to one another after what passed between us?"

He shouldn't have turned away from her. He knew that. Not after she let him touch her so trustingly.

He should apologize. He should explain. He had no idea how to begin.

"Well?" she demanded. "Have ye naught to say to me?"

"Rob!"

Praise be to God for Angus Fletcher!

"No' now, Elspeth." Rob scrambled out of the cabin as if his kilt was afire.

Elspeth pulled on her cloak and followed Rob out, but she stayed near the prow. The moon had risen and scattered silver coins across the black water of the loch. Clouds scudded across the sky, so the night was warmer than it might have been for November. She still gathered Rob's cloak at her neck and fastened it with the plain but serviceable brooch.

She pleased Angus by accepting one of his cold sausages wrapped in crumbling bread, and washed it down with some wine that was only days from turning to vinegar.

"The wind shifted whilst ye were resting," he told her. "We've come about with nary a bit of trouble, slick as snot—ach!" He smacked a beefy palm on his forehead. "Ye must forgive me. I'm no' accustomed to conversin' with ladies."

"That's all well and good, Mr. Fletcher."

"Angus," he insisted. Then he leaned down to her and lowered his voice. "And a word in your ear. There's folks as say that Rob MacLaren is balmy, but he's as sane as ye or I, ye ken. O' course, I love the lad like he was my own son. Now, I'm no' saying I agree with everything he's doing, mind, but I understand it."

"I wish I did."

"Reckon he'll explain matters to ye, when he gets it straight in his own mind," Angus said. "But if he ever lifts so much as a finger against ye, weel, the young pup will have to answer to me, ye hear?"

"I thank ye, Mr....Angus," she said as he headed toward the cabin. "Rest well."

Elspeth expected Fletcher's dog to accompany him, but Fingal remained at her side, his shaggy body warm where he leaned against her hip and thigh. She stood still as a figurehead for a few moments, wondering what to do. It was a small boat. She couldn't very well join Mr. Fletcher in the cabin. There was no place to sit in the prow. The only other option was the bench near the stern.

Near Rob.

The deerhound nuzzled her hand and circled around it so she stroked him nose to tail.

Elspeth felt a tug in her heart toward the man at the boat's tiller, but she resisted. He'd already shown her how susceptible she was to his enticements, and how little her surrender meant to him.

"What should I do, Fingal?" She fingered the dog's wiry-haired ears.

The deerhound turned and walked toward the stern of the small vessel as if he understood her question. He plopped his bottom down near enough to Rob that the man could tousle his great shaggy head. Elspeth heard Fingal's tale thumping on the hull.

"That's what ye get when ye ask a dog for advice," she muttered. The furry beast would take affection from anyone. A failing she didn't intend to repeat.

Rob probably hadn't eaten, so she gathered up the badger-skin pouch and the skin of deplorable wine and headed toward the stern. Her priest had always admonished her that treating an enemy with kindness would "heap fiery coals on his head."

She intended to set Rob MacLaren ablaze.

Chapter 14

ALL THE MUSCLES IN ROB'S BODY STIFFENED AS Elspeth headed toward him. She stepped lightly around the cabin and past the mast. Her meek expression didn't fool him a bit. If he'd been a dog, his ruff would've been standing on end in wariness. Fingal, however, stood and wagged his entire body in joy over her approach.

When he devised this plan, he wished he'd considered that Drummond's bride was a living, breathing person. She'd been only a means to an end to him.

No matter what that succubus in his dream had said, perhaps he was mad. His friend Hamish had tried to tell him abducting the Stewart lass was a bad idea, but he wouldn't listen.

"'Tis no' like reiving a herd of cattle, ye ken," Hamish had told him when Rob first came to him with the plan. "A cow is the most biddable creature on God's earth. It'll go wherever it's driven. A woman doesna drive worth a damn."

Truer words were ne'er spoke.

"Have ye eaten?" she asked as she pulled a bannock from the pouch. She offered it to him with a forced smile.

So might a spider smile at a fly.

But it seemed like days since he filched that sarnie from Angus's skillet. His stomach was knocking against his backbone so hard, he couldn't keep his hand from reaching for the crusty bun.

"I thank ye," he said between bites.

If she'd found a way to poison it, he almost didn't care. He wolfed down a couple sausages, giving Fingal a few bites. Surely she wouldn't chance poisoning the dog who'd taken such an obvious liking to her. He upended the wineskin for a deep draught.

"Ugh! This wine's nearly turned." He swiped his mouth with his sleeve, but it didn't help the sour aftertaste.

She seemed to swallow a laugh. "I said as much to Angus, but he seems to be the thrifty sort. Nothing usable must be thrown out."

"Might as well sop this with a sponge and offer it to me on a stick."

"Dinna mock the way Our Lord was offered a drink on the cross," she said with a frown. "Ye're flirting with blasphemy, Rob MacLaren."

If she only knew the half of it. "Blasphemy is but one on the long list of my sins."

"Aye, but it's one the Lord is loath to forgive."

"And not the only one, it seems," he muttered, spitting into the loch to purge his mouth of the vinegary taste. "Ye might have warned me."

"Ye might have warned me as well," she said, her gaze never wavering from his.

They were no longer talking about the wine. The subject had veered into deep water without the slightest hint that an abrupt turn was coming.

How did women do that?

Irritation crept up his neck like a rash.

"I know ye think I owe ye somewhat, but for the life of me, I dinna know what it is," he said, frustration with himself making his voice harsher than he intended. "'Tis no' as if I forced ye, lass."

Her lips pressed into a tight line.

"Well, can ye honestly say anything that passed between us was against your will?" he demanded.

She merely looked at him.

"If ye expect me to be sorry, ye're destined for disappointment."

She didn't say a word, but if glares were arrows, he'd be a dead man.

"And if the opportunity arises for me to do it again, rest assured, lass, I'll no' hesitate."

"Dinna fret, MacLaren." Her tone was sugary as a boiled sweet. "The situation is no' in the least likely to repeat itself."

Elspeth plopped down on the bench and looked out over the dark water, ignoring him completely.

"Well, then," he said uncertainly. "That's settled."

He suspected that was wishful thinking. In the murky world of women, he was always adrift. They always wanted to pry into a man's soul, to find out not only what he thought, but what he felt.

As if a man knew!

When Fiona first asked him how he felt about her, he had said in all honesty, that he didn't have any feelings.

"Of course ye do, daftie man," she had said with a laugh. "Ye just dinna know how to name them."

So Fiona had taught him.

That jumbled-up sensation in his gut every time he saw her was excitement. The warmth in his belly meant he was happy. And when he told her that his chest constricted almost painfully, she had smiled.

"That's love, Rob," she'd said simply. "Ye love me. Your chest knows it. The rest of ye might as well admit it and be done."

He loved her. It was a revelation.

But now that Fiona was gone, he was left to navigate the shoals of his soul alone.

The deerhound left his side, since no more sarnie seemed in the offing, and settled next to Elspeth with his head resting on her knee.

"He likes you," Rob said.

She stroked Fingal's head. "I'm glad someone does."

His chest constricted. *No. That doesn't mean…*

"I like ye," he heard himself say before he thought better of it. "I like ye fine."

Her lips twitched, but she kept herself from smiling. She rolled her eyes at him instead. "Ye have a strange way of showing it."

"Ye too. I havena forgot that ye hate me," Rob said, sensing a way to retrieve the situation. Why had she kissed him after she told him so? "Do ye kiss all the men ye hate?"

Her brows drew together. "I dinna hate ye so much."

"No, 'twas 'verra, verra much,' as I recall."

He nearly jumped out of his skin in surprise when she had kissed him after that. Maybe Elspeth Stewart was as turned about by her feelings as he was bewildered by his.

She wouldn't meet his gaze.

"Why did Angus name his dog Fingal?" she asked.

He recognized her question as a frantic plea to change the subject.

The answer was obvious. Everyone knew Fingal of legend was a giant. Fingal of the Gray Shaggy Fur was too. But Rob decided to let the topic of conversation stray there. The matter of their feelings was fraught with far more peril than a legendary giant or a giant of a dog.

"Angus loves the old tales, ye see," Rob said. "And since Fingal of old is connected with Loch Earn, Angus thought it only fitting to give his hero a flea-bitten, mangy namesake."

Elspeth covered the hound's ears with her hands. "Hush! You'll hurt his feelings."

"Ye tell me ye hate me without batting an eye, but ye're concerned for the dog's feelings?"

"I *like* the dog, MacLaren." She arched a brow at Rob. "Besides, Fingal didna steal me from the altar, did he?"

The hound turned his great head and slurped her cheek with a wet doggie kiss before she could stop him. She hugged Fingal's neck with a laugh.

Rob never thought to envy a dog, but he suddenly wished he could run his lips over that smooth cheek and make her laugh. And feel her arms about his neck.

"Dinna encourage him," he warned. "Or he'll wash the other cheek for ye."

Elspeth wiped her cheek with her sleeve. "What's

the connection with the other Fingal—the hero, I mean—and this loch?"

"Are ye the sort given to vapors?"

"Ye saw me face a wolf pack. Ye know I'm not."

He nodded. "Ye know how to keep your head; that's certain. I'm just saying 'tis best to tell this sort of tale on dry land. 'Tis about the *each uisge*, ye see."

"The water horse?" Moonlight silvered her face, and her eyes sparked with interest. "I love the old tales. Can ye tell it, please?"

If she asked him to walk across the loch with that kind of entreaty in her voice, he'd give it a try.

"I'm no' a bard, ye ken, but I'll do my best." Rob leaned on the tiller to keep the boat sailing down the center of the narrow loch. "The doings I'm about to tell ye of happened long ago, back when the world was young and magical beings were common as…" He searched his memory for a poetic turn of phrase such as a bard might use, but could only come up with one of his own. "Common as bedbugs."

"Common as bedbugs? Ugh!" She shuddered. "Ye speak truly when ye say ye're no' a poet."

"Weel, ye must admit there are few things more common," he said with a shrug. "In any case, young Fingal was walking the heath one day near Loch Tay, where he was wont to roam, carrying a boulder in one hand and an oak trunk in the other. He was set to wander the wide world and wondered what adventure he might find."

"What did he intend to do with the boulder and the trunk?" Chin in hand, Elspeth leaned toward him, clearly interested in the story.

"The boulder was in case he met a foe and needed something to squash him with," Rob explained. "And though Fingal was big enough to step across most streams, he used the tree trunk for vaulting over burns when he found one too wide for him to leap over."

"Makes sense. Go on, then."

"But Fingal didna meet a foe this day. Instead, in a shady glade, he saw a beautiful stallion, strong of haunch and long of limb, with a mane and tail black as..." This time his memory of the last bard he'd heard served him well. "Black as a witch's temper."

"Black as a witch's temper," she repeated. "That's better than 'common as bedbugs.' I have hopes for ye, MacLaren. There may be more poet in ye than ye know."

"My lady does me honor." Rob sketched a mocking bow. "But back to the stallion Fingal found. It looked to be big enough for him to ride. Being a giant, he knew mounts suitable for him were like to be far and few in between, so he decided to catch it, but—"

"But he didna have a rope to catch it with?"

"Who's telling this tale?" Rob demanded. "Ye're getting ahead of me." When she clamped her lips tight, he continued. "So Fingal set down his boulder and his oak trunk and fetched out his rope. For ye see, he *did* have a rope—and a good, stout length it was—tucked away in his sporran. The horse was munching away on the long grass. It seemed to be paying him no mind. As he crept closer—"

"And I dinna expect a giant creeps verra quietly."

"Is this how they tell tales in the Stewart's hall, interrupting the bard at every turn?"

"No indeed," she said. "I wouldn't dream of inter-rupting a *real* bard."

He snorted and started in again on the tale. "So Fingal sneaked up on the horse, verra quietly for a giant of his size. He was almost close enough to toss a loop over its head when it turned and looked at him with eyes that seemed to see into the deepest wrinkle of his soul. 'Ye dinna need a rope, Fingal,' the beast said, lowering its head in a bow to do him honor. 'Aye, I ken who ye are. Who in the glen doesna know so great a hero? Ye can ride me an' ye wish.'"

"Doesn't sound natural for the horse to speak," Elspeth said.

"Oh, it isn't. No' now, in any case. But remember this was a long time ago when such things were common as…as beggars at kirk."

Elspeth sighed. "Still no' much of a poet, are ye?"

"No, I suppose not, but I warned ye I was no' bard," Rob said, glad Elspeth was talking to him at all. Even with her complaints, she seemed to be enjoying the story. Pleasing her was starting to be something he longed to do at every turn, whether it was delighting her body or her sharp wit.

"Go on," she urged. "I'll try not to interrupt again."

"Thank ye. Where was I? Oh! But Fingal thought it seemed odd too. Not that the horse spoke, ye ken, for that was no' something out of the ordinary for those days. But what the horse said gave him pause," Rob said. "He was a mighty big giant, and no horse of any sense would willingly let him ride it."

"Hmmm."

"It was just then that the sun broke through the

clouds, and Fingal saw the stallion's true color," Rob said, enjoying the way Elspeth's eyes had gone round as an owl's. "The horse's dark coat was green as glass."

"And that's how he knew it was the water horse!" Elspeth said triumphantly.

"Aye, that's how he knew," Rob said, deciding he didn't care if she interrupted him so long as she was happy. "'Ye're an *each uisge*,' Fingal cried."

Every time Rob said the hero's name, the deerhound thumped his tail against the hull.

"'Away wi' ye,' quoth Fingal. 'I'll no' have ye threatening the folk who live around Loch Tay,'" Rob said. "So he used his rope for a whip instead and drove the water horse over hill and down dale until they came to Loch Earn. There both giant and beast were so blown, they stopped to rest by common agreement, and the beastie begged him to leave him be. Fingal had run about as far as he cared to, so he suffered the water horse to enter Loch Earn. But he made the *each uisge* promise never to return to Loch Tay."

"And that's how the water horse came to live in Loch Earn," Elspeth finished for him, clapping her hands.

"Ye seem to know quite a bit about water horses," Rob said.

"Oh, aye. Enough to know ye dinna want to ride any strange horse ye might happen upon near a loch," Elspeth said. "Ye may mount such a beast easily enough, but once ye are astride its back, the skin of the water horse becomes sticky. Ye canna leap to safety no matter how hard ye try. Then the *each uisge* runs into the loch and drowns its victims."

Rob laughed to show he didn't believe a word of it. Still, the waves sometimes mounded up on the loch in odd shapes, as if something large and malevolent moved with purpose under the surface.

"Aye, and once they stop kicking," Rob said, "the water horse gobbles them up."

"Hair and bones and all. Everything but the liver," Elspeth said with a shiver of horrified fascination.

"But ye know, the *each uisge* doesna always take the shape of a horse," Rob said. "Sometimes, he poses as a handsome man. Ye'll ken him by the waterweed in his hair."

"Aye, in the old tales they warn of it, but that's only when the water horse is courting," Elspeth supplied. "Sometimes, the beast takes a human maiden for a wife, they say."

"I've heard such things as well," Rob said. "But the water horse is no' a verra good husband."

"No indeed. He's cruel and spiteful, and his wife is kept prisoner till she dies, which didna happen soon enough to suit her in all the stories I've ever heard," Elspeth said. "The water horse is a verra poor husband."

"That's a common enough failing too," Rob said, suddenly serious.

When he didn't say more, Elspeth cocked her head at him. "What's wrong?"

Rob felt suddenly heavier, as if he'd been tossed in the loch and was dragged down by sodden clothes. "I canna throw stones at the water horse, Elspeth."

"What do ye mean?"

"I was a husband," Rob said slowly. "And as it turned out, a verra poor husband indeed."

Chapter 15

"I DIDNA KNOW YE'RE MARRIED."

"I'm not. I said I *was* a husband. My wife died."

Elspeth stroked Fingal's head in silence for a moment, then met Rob's gaze. "D'ye wish to speak of it? Mayhap it will help."

"Women are ever quick to say such, but words dinna change a damned thing." He turned away in self-loathing. "We could talk all night, but Fiona will still be dead."

"I'm sorry for it," she said softly.

"'Tis no' your fault, lass."

Yet he was making her pay for it. He supposed he owed her the truth.

"Did your parents arrange the match?" she asked.

He snorted. As if he'd allow someone else to make that kind of decision for him. "No, my parents are long gone. I've been laird since I was sixteen. Fiona was my choice."

Elspeth sighed. She'd already confessed that her wedding was more a joining of clan interests than two souls. Did she envy Fiona and him their love match?

"Did she bring ye much land and cattle in the marriage?" she asked. "I'm told men value such in a bride."

He shook his head. "Not an inch of earth or a single hoof."

"Then why did ye choose her?"

He shrugged. "I married her because she wouldna live with me in sin."

"Ye can't fault a woman for that."

"No. I wouldna fault Fiona for anything. I simply couldna live without her."

"And yet ye do."

The waves washed along the hull of the boat, filling the silence. Once he'd have fancied he heard Fiona whispering beneath the sound, but now there was only the shushing of the loch against the wood.

Fiona would never speak to him again.

"What I have now isna life, Elspeth," Rob finally said. "'Tis but breathing."

"What—" She stopped herself as if she feared asking something too personal, but because she was a woman, she couldn't bear not to finish the question. "What was your wife like?"

Rob smiled. He rarely spoke of her, but he suspected he should do it more often. Fiona always lifted the darkness of his heart.

"She was…" He finally found a bard tucked in his soul. "Fiona was sunlight on the water. A warm hearth while the wind roars outside. She was—"

"Tall and willowy," Elspeth interrupted, straightening her spine. "And she had long red hair."

"Aye. How did ye know? Did Angus tell ye so?"

She shook her head. "I…guessed."

"Well, then, since ye brought the matter up, aye, she was lovely. And her beauty ran clear to the bone. She was kindness itself."

He could still see her in his mind's eye on the day of their wedding, her cheeks flushed, her green eyes glowing. Then he remembered the last time he saw her, and his chest tightened so he couldn't draw breath.

Once the dark moment passed, he found that his lungs still craved air. "I didna deserve her," he said roughly. "Like the water horse and his bride, I damned her on the day I made her mine."

"What happened?" Elspeth asked so softly, Rob wondered if he heard her only *think* the question.

"Come Christmas, 'twill be two years past. I married her on the day of our Lord's birth, and we celebrated Christmastide in roaring fashion," he said with a melancholy smile. "Then just before Twelfth Night, Fiona wanted to visit some of the outlying crofters with baskets of food, but my friend Hamish had seen a wild boar, a monstrous big fellow, he said, and he wanted me to go after it with him. So I told Fiona the crofters could wait till we had some fresh pork to add to the bounty. But she'd set her heart on going that day."

"'Tis tradition for the laird and his lady to visit the distant crofters before Twelfth Night," Elspeth pointed out. "My father and mother do it each year because their people expect them to provide their feast."

"So Fiona told me," he said. "This was her first Christmastide as my chatelaine, and she wouldna be turned from her duty. We had our first and only row over it. Lord, she was a sight when she was angry."

"Sounds as if she had a right to be," Elspeth said, narrowing her eyes a bit. "At least now I ken ye make a habit of irritating all the women ye know."

Come to think of it, Rob decided, *Elspeth Stewart is fine to look upon when anger bites her cheeks too.*

"Did ye still go hunting?"

Rob nodded. "And we ne'er saw so much as a cloven hoof of that damned boar. But Fiona slipped past the men I'd left to guard her and rode off to see the crofters on her own. While she was out, Lachlan Drummond and some of his cronies came riding by and saw her unescorted."

One of Elspeth's hands crept to her chest, and Rob figured she could guess what was coming.

"Drummond carried her off to his stronghold, and there the coward had his way with her," Rob said, the words more bitter to his tongue than the vinegary wine. "Now d'ye see why I say I was doing ye a favor to steal ye from your wedding?"

Elspeth wisely said nothing.

"Of course, wee Lachlan denied anything untoward. He claimed the abduction was just a bit of Twelfth Night high spirits, but I'm certain the blackguard must have shamed her," Rob said. "'Tis the only thing that explains what happened."

"What?"

"Drummond locked her up in his tower, but she found a way to escape."

"Oh. I'm glad."

"Don't be," Rob said flatly. "Fiona escaped by

throwing herself from the highest tower window onto the cobbles of his bailey."

Elspeth gasped. Rob had never been good at reading what a woman was thinking based on her expressions, but her eyes darted about as if she was searching her memory for something, while distress marred her face.

"You're right," he said as if she'd spoken her thought aloud. "A suicide canna be buried in holy ground. Drummond's priest said she was damned because she knowingly committed a mortal sin, for which she couldna receive absolution."

His shoulders sagged, but he'd started this. He was determined to drive the sorry tale to its bitter end. Unshed tears burned behind his eyes. He swallowed hard, forcing down the ache in his throat. "I dinna even know where she lies."

Elspeth didn't say a word. She simply stood, walked over to him, her step steady in the swaying craft, and put her hands on his shoulders. Then she leaned forward and kissed his cheek.

It was just a simple kiss. No more than the buss of soft lips on the roughness of his cheek, but something inside him splintered.

A sob escaped his throat. The tears he never let himself cry came with no way to stop them. He put an arm around her waist and pulled her close, burying his face in the crook of her soft neck.

He was so ashamed. A man didn't weep. But he couldn't stop his shoulders from shaking with grief.

Elspeth wrapped her arms around him, making small comforting sounds.

"'Twas my fault," he repeated.

"No."

"If I'd gone with her…"

"'Tis done. Hush ye now." Her hands were cool on the feverish skin of his neck.

Rob struggled to regain control over himself, but so many bits and pieces of him were shearing away, he couldn't grasp any of them. The hard lump in his chest melted and reformed several times. The only things that kept him from leaping out of his own skin entirely were Elspeth Stewart's slender arms and soft voice.

She stroked his hair. She hugged him with fierceness. She rocked him, whispering tender things he couldn't quite hear. But his soul understood them and quieted. The ache of loss, the fury of impotent rage, and the guilt flowed out of him, leaving only broken-hearted peace.

Finally, he stilled.

She wiped the last of the salty tears from his cheeks. Then she kissed him again. On the lips this time, firm and sweet. Like a blessing. Like a benediction.

"Ye are no' to blame," she said with conviction.

He didn't have the heart to contradict her, but he didn't believe it for a moment. "After all that, I'm sure ye believe me a madman now."

"'Tis no' madness to weep for someone ye loved." She shook her head. "If ye had no tears, I'd think ye less a man. Never because of them."

"Ye're a strange lass, Elspeth Stewart."

"And ye're a silver-tongued demon." She laughed, obviously trying to lighten his mood. "Dinna think to turn my head with such compliments."

He smiled at her, confused but strangely comforted.

He still grieved for Fiona, but the serrated edge of unexpressed mourning and guilt that threatened to send him spiraling into insanity was gone.

Elspeth returned his smile. He shook his head in wonderment. He'd stolen her from the altar, taken her prisoner, and tormented her body with a wicked lover's touch. And here she was giving him comfort. If he lived to be a hundred, he'd never understand what went on in a woman's head.

Then while he was watching her, her eyes glazed over, and she stared sightlessly over his shoulder.

"Elspeth?"

She gave no sign that she'd heard him.

He let go of the tiller and grasped both her shoulders, but she continued to stare unblinking. He gave her a little shake. She looked at his face then, but he sensed no recognition in her eyes.

"The *each uisge* comes, reaching up from the depths to snag his bride," she said in a voice devoid of all expression. "And a bolt from the dark finds its mark."

"Elspeth!"

Then he was nearly knocked off his feet, thrown forward as the boat stopped dead in the water.

Chapter 16

"WHAT IS IT?" ANGUS CRIED FROM THE CABIN. "What's happened?"

Rob heard him scrambling, but a man as large as Angus didn't move very quickly, even at the best of times. Wakened from a sound sleep, he was like a badger in winter, surly and disoriented, as he banged around in the small space.

"If ye've run my boat aground, Robbie, I'll have your hide!"

"No, we're still in the central channel, but—" Then Rob saw it, the line stretched across the expanse of the water reaching from one shoreline to the other. The long-necked prow of the boat was caught on it, and the stern threatened to come about suddenly.

He'd kept Elspeth from falling when they stopped suddenly, but he released her now and grabbed up the tiller again to right the vessel with the prevailing current. He wished he could have kept hold of her, because she had the dazed expression of a person who isn't seeing clearly. Her otherworldly pronouncements still tied his gut in knots.

"Elspeth, are ye sound, lass?"

She gave herself a small shake and blinked. Then she plopped down on the bench seat as if her legs would no longer support her. Her hands trembled in her lap.

"I'm fine. What's happened?" Her eyes widened. "Oh, no. I had a...Did I say something?"

"Aye, a daft bit about the *each uisge*, but we've no' run afoul of the water horse, I'm thinking. We ran into a snare of sorts." Then he realized the dark shape he'd taken for a small island was moving toward them.

Elspeth followed the direction of his gaze. "'Tis Lachlan," she said woodenly. "He's come for me."

"Well, I'm no' of a mind to let him have ye."

"After what ye've told me, I find myself grateful," she said.

The raft bore down on them. One of the men on board it shouted to another as they used the line to haul themselves across the water. Rob cursed himself for a half-wit. If he'd been on the watch instead of blubbering in Elspeth's arms, he'd have spotted them lurking there in the dark, like a spider waiting for a fly to be caught in its web.

Angus was trying to shove the line down on the prow. If the rope fell beneath the hull, they might sail over it. But the curved neck of Angus's boat was carved with fanciful beasts to ward off the odd water horse, and the line must have caught on one. The weight of the craft and the strength of the current made freeing the vessel difficult.

Rob realized he'd left his knives sticking in the boat's neck. Cutting the line would serve just as well.

"Will ye take the tiller?" he asked Elspeth.

She nodded and moved unsteadily to replace him.

As he fairly leaped toward the prow, Rob realized a minor miracle had just occurred.

Elspeth Stewart had chosen to stay with him of her own accord.

"Pull, damn ye!" Lachlan roared to the man on the raft with him.

After several trials earlier that day, it had been determined that only two could fit on the raft, so Drummond insisted it be he and his retainer.

"I'm her father," Stewart had protested.

"Aye, and I'm the man who will be her husband even after this sorry business is ended," he said. "Ye must allow me a husband's vengeance on Mad Rob."

Alistair Stewart had relented then, tacitly admitting that his daughter was likely no longer pure.

"I understand ye wanting to let your sword drink the man's blood."

But Lachlan had no intention of letting matters progress as far as hand-to-hand combat. He had his crossbow, and he intended to use it.

It was near the darkest part of the night, but Lachlan had already identified the figures on the boat based on their relative size. He was close enough now to see that MacLaren was working his way toward the prow. The other fellow, a monstrous big man, was already there, trying to wrench their boat free. Lachlan sited his bolt on Rob's moving form.

"Rob!" The warning shout came from Elspeth.

The MacLaren ducked, and Drummond's bolt flew harmlessly over his head.

Lachlan glared at the dark form that was his betrothed. How had she seen what was coming so easily? She must be cat-eyed as a witch! She even seemed to be helping her captors by holding the tiller steady.

That was all the proof he needed that Rob MacLaren had taken her. If a man ruts a woman soundly enough, she'll do whatever he demands, biddable as a lamb.

The MacLaren's wife hadn't, of course, but she was a rarity. And to be fair, Lachlan hadn't realized who she was when he and his men first scooped her up. Who could blame them? Ladies didn't wander the countryside unescorted.

By the time he realized her identity, the damage was done. Who'd have thought she'd leap to her death rather than continue to service him? When she fought him just as hard the second time, he should have given Lady MacLaren to his men to pass around instead of leaving her in the tower to think better of her belligerence.

Damned if he'd let Elspeth Stewart behave so willfully.

"Stupid bitch." He'd teach her who her laird was as soon as he got her back. There were few things more enjoyable than reducing a woman to quivering subservience.

He might even get out the shackles and birch switch for his wayward little wife, just to make sure she understood the way of things.

But first he had to get her back. He raised his crossbow and targeted Mad Rob as he reached the prow, but he hadn't reckoned on the pitching loch throwing his aim off. Even aiming a bit high for the distance, the bolt struck wood and quivered in the hull.

"Pull faster," Drummond ordered his man.

The raft drew ever closer to the boat. He might yet have to draw his blade. Then he heard some feral growls and saw a huge deerhound standing with its feet on the gunwale of the small craft. Those slashing teeth were a distraction he didn't need if he was going to have to cross swords in close quarters with the MacLaren.

He loaded his crossbow once more and sited it on the dog's chest. He squeezed the trigger, and the iron shaft flew.

Elspeth cried out and leaped from her place at the tiller, putting herself in the path of the bolt. This one struck true, and she went down. Lachlan couldn't see her any longer because she was below the gunwale. The hound bayed and circled where she fell.

The stern of the boat swung wide, obscuring any possible shot at the men in the prow, and the rope Lachlan's man was hauling on went suddenly slack in his hands. MacLaren had cut the line.

Wind filled the boat's sails. The loch lifted the craft on the waves and propelled it westward too quickly for Drummond to get off another shot.

The last thing he saw was the MacLaren kneeling where Elspeth fell as the other fellow put a hand to the tiller.

Drummond swore under his breath. Elspeth might well be dying, and all on account of a *dog*! Cattle and land and clan alliances be damned. MacLaren had probably done him a sideways favor. If she'd risk herself for a dog, Elspeth Stewart was too half-witted to be the mother of his heir.

"What now, my lord?" Lachlan's man asked, the end of the rope hanging limply.

Drummond took one of his bolts from his quiver and jabbed it into the floor of the raft. Then he cupped his hands around his mouth to shout back to Stewart and Calum, waiting on the shore.

"MacLaren was armed with a crossbow!" Lachlan yelled. "When we got too close, the blackguard shot Elspeth!"

Stewart roared his grief. Lachlan turned to his retainer and spoke in a furious whisper.

"If I hear a word from ye to the contrary, I can only assume ye dinna value your tongue and will no' be surprised when I rid ye of it."

❧

"Elspeth! Oh, Lord, what happened?" Rob took a knee beside her prone form.

"He was…going to shoot Fingal," she said, trying to rise. "But I couldna let—"

"No, dinna talk." Rob eased her back down. "Dinna move either."

He ran his hands over her and encountered warm stickiness on her left thigh. His fingers found the iron shaft and the spreading wetness around it.

Rob swore vehemently then caught himself, swallowing his anger. It would give no comfort to Elspeth if he couldn't remain outwardly calm. But inwardly, he damned Lachlan Drummond and all other cowards with thrice-cursed crossbows to the fires of hell.

"Dinna draw the bolt," Angus warned. "As much as she's bleeding now, there'll be more if ye pull it out."

Rob ripped the fabric of her skirt around the shaft to expose the wound on her thigh. Her skin was pale, except for the dark ribbons of blood.

"I need light," he said, tamping down the rising panic in his gut. "I canna see clear what to do."

"That'll have to wait for dawn," Angus said. "I'll no' have a lit torch on my boat. Fire is a sailor's worst fear."

Rob's worst fear was lying on the curved bottom of Angus's vessel. Elspeth didn't speak, but a small whimper escaped her lips.

"Then put in to shore," he ordered, "and we'll build a fire."

"Look about ye, lad. There's no' a level place to put in anywhere hereabouts," Angus said. Dark sentinels hedging the loch, the highland peaks rose steeply from the water's edge all about. "No' for a goodly ways, and then we must take care to make landfall only on the north side."

"Why?" All Rob could see was delay and disaster.

"The men following ye have someone with them who's knowledgeable about the loch. Else they'd not have waited in ambush for us to sail by that point. They must have suspected ye wished to go west instead of east and had to wait for the current to change," Angus said. "Stands to reason they may try to ride through the passes to greet us at the next level spot on the south shore."

"He's right," Elspeth said, her voice thready.

"One of my father's men, Calum Guthrie, is a lochman. He kens Loch Eireann and the land about it as well as any alive. If he rides with my father, that's what he'll advise."

Rob pulled his shirt over his head and wrapped it around her thigh to stanch the bleeding.

"No, 'tis too cold, Rob," she complained. "Ye'll catch your death."

"Let me worry about that. D'ye think ye can bear for me to move ye? The pallet in the cabin will be more comfortable than the bare hull, I'm thinking."

She nodded, teeth clenched.

He reached under her arms and knees and lifted her as gently as he could. She didn't cry out, but her swift intake of breath cut his heart as sharply as if she'd wailed like the damned.

Before Rob ducked into the cabin to lay her on the pallet, Angus called out, "I'm minded of something."

"What?" Rob stopped, clutching Elspeth to his chest. The hand she splayed on his bare skin was cold.

"There's a wise woman who lives on the loch." Angus crossed himself as protection against the devil. "She's a witch, some say, but they also say she kens a good deal about healing."

"How far?"

"At this rate? A couple hours, and she bides on the north shore."

"Make for her home then."

"Some dinna hold with witches, Rob. Best ye ask Elspeth her wishes on the matter."

While ye can was the unspoken rest of his thought.

Rob looked down at her. Her eyes were closed

and her mouth slack. She was in no condition to make choices.

But Rob was. Perhaps if he was at *Caisteal Dubh*, he might be able to remove the bolt and stanch the bleeding. He could do nothing for her on Angus's swaying vessel.

If the witch demanded his soul in exchange for healing Elspeth, he was ready to swear it away.

"Make for the witch, Angus. If there be a price for turning to white magick, let it be on my head."

Chapter 17

As soon as Rob laid her on the pallet, her breathing went shallow and quick.

"I Saw it," she said, her eyes wide, her brows furrowed. She put a trembling hand to her temple and pressed her palm flat. "I knew the *each uisge* was coming, but I didna warn ye in time."

"Hush, *leannán*." The endearment passed his lips before he realized what he was saying. "Rest yourself. Only a little while," he said softly. He snugged his body tight against hers for warmth, careful to stay on her uninjured side. "Angus knows where we'll find the help ye need."

"Aye, we will." She nodded and closed her eyes. "A bolt in the dark finds its mark."

Those were her very words when she was staring sightlessly over his shoulder, just before they struck the rope snare. He'd feared at the time she'd gone a bit daft, but now the words made sense to Rob's mind. Somehow Elspeth had known the crossbow bolt was coming for her.

And Lachlan Drummond was the *each uisge* she

meant, the cruel water horse come to claim his bride. Elspeth Stewart had the Sight, but her Gift's warning came to her too late to do any good.

"Open your eyes, lass," he urged, palming her cheek. "Talk to me, Elspeth. Ye dinna want to sleep now."

"Aye, I do." He heard pain in her voice. Her skin was clammy and moist. When his hand slid down to her neck, he had to search for the pulse point. Her heart raced, but the beat wasn't very strong.

The deerhound tried to join them in the cabin, creeping in a crouch toward Elspeth, but Rob ordered him out. Fingal whined but wouldn't go far. He lay across the entrance to the cabin with his muzzle resting on his forepaws, his watchful eyes glowing in the dark.

"How long have ye had the gift of Sight?" Rob asked. It was all he could think of to encourage her to talk. If she slipped into sleep, surely the sleep of death was only a short step farther.

"All my life." Her words were slurred. "Oh, my head!"

If her head ached so that she didn't complain of the bolt in her thigh, the pain at her temples must be excruciating.

"But it didna serve me well," she said with a sob in her voice. "I ne'er See what I wish. Only what I'm shown. Sometimes, I dinna even know if the things I See are true."

"What was the first thing ye ever Saw?"

"A boy," she whispered, turning her head this way and that as if she could move away from the pain. "He was playing by a well. He lost his balance and fell into it."

Rob's breath caught. He'd fallen into a well when he was very young. He hadn't seen more than three or four summers. It was his earliest and most vivid memory.

"He was so afraid," she went on, pausing between phrases to take shuddering breaths. "It was so dark and cold, and evil things were crawling on the walls of the well."

The water was so frigid, all the breath had rushed out of his body. Rob couldn't swim, but once he bobbed to the surface, he'd clung to the sides of the well. He'd broken his nails trying to claw his way up the slick rock walls. Worms and creeping things had haunted his dreams for months afterward.

"Did ye see him being pulled out?"

"No," she said sadly. "I ne'er did. The vision ended, and I dinna know if he lived or died."

"He lived," Rob assured her. "And after his father hauled him out, clinging to the bucket and screaming at the top of his lungs, his sire tanned the boy's backside for wandering away from his mother."

"Ye're sure?"

"He had to carry a pillow about with him for a week in order to sit."

Her lips turned up in a slight smile, then a whimper escaped them. Her eyes squeezed shut, and Rob's gut roiled in sympathy for her pain.

Fingal inched his way into the cabin, refusing to go when Rob ordered him away this time. The deerhound crept around Elspeth, careful to avoid the bolt sticking out of her leg, and lay down next to her, resting his head on her shoulder, his wet nose near her ear.

"Well, then, lad, if ye're set on it, ye can help me keep her warm." Rob reached across to pat the dog's head then looked down at Elspeth. She seemed to rest easier with the combined warmth of the man and the dog on either side. "Do ye want some wine for the pain?"

She opened her eyes and met his gaze. "Angus's wine? No thank ye." Then her eyes closed again. "The headache is fading. My leg doesna hurt so much now. I can...hardly feel it...at all."

This time, no matter what he said or did, Elspeth didn't twitch an eyelash.

Rob hadn't had much to say to God since Fiona died. Now he laid his hand between Elspeth's breasts, so he could feel her heart beating, and spoke a few words to the Almighty.

He doubted God answered the prayers of madmen, especially one bound for perdition as he undoubtedly was. But if he was willing to seek out a witch to see Elspeth well, he was willing to ask God to keep her alive long enough to get her to the wisewoman's croft.

❧

"Rob!" Angus's voice dragged him from sleep. "We're almost there."

Exhausted, he'd fallen into slumber with his hand between Elspeth's breasts. Her heart still beat beneath his palm, but it was faint. Dawn was breaking around them, and her skin was so pale, if he hadn't felt her heartbeat and seen the curl of her breath in the frosty air, he'd have thought her dead.

Fingal lifted his head.

"Keep her warm. There's a good lad," Rob told the deerhound before he crawled out of the cabin. He wrapped his plaid about his shoulders against the cold.

"There bides the witch of Loch Eireann." Angus pointed to the small croft coming into view round a rocky point. A few pines rose behind the thatch-roofed cottage, and then the steep Highlands shot up in a wall of rough grass and granite. The place was accessible only by water. If there was a passable way to the wise woman's home through the mountains, he doubted any who didn't have goat's feet could manage it.

Cloven hooves. Well, that's what folk said of the devil's feet, wasn't it?

Angus steered his craft toward the shallows, while Rob stood watch in the prow, eyeing the clear water for any submerged rocks that might splinter the hull of an unwary sailor's vessel. A disreputable-looking skiff was pulled half out of the loch and tied to a large boulder.

Angus made for that spot and eased the prow of his boat alongside the skiff. Rob leaped to dry land and pulled the craft's nose up on the winter-brown grass.

"Wait here," Rob said. "I'll see if she'll help us."

"And if she willna?"

"Then the world will have one less witch."

Though it belonged to one who was reputedly in league with the devil, the farmstead looked remarkably ordinary. Rob strode toward the cottage, a wattle-and-daub construction that listed only slightly. The thatch on the roof was a few years old, but he expected it still turned the rain. There was a cow staring out the open door of a byre. A flock of hens scattered before him. It might have been the home of any of his crofters.

A woman appeared at the door before he reached it. Her iron gray hair was long and flowed over her shoulders like a young girl's. But her face was wrinkled and sunken-cheeked as a winter apple. She wrapped her red shawl more tightly around herself and cast him a wry smile.

"Come to see me, are ye, Mad Rob?"

He stopped dead in his tracks. "Ye know who I am."

"I have eyes," she said. "Ye wear the MacLaren plaid, d'ye no'?"

"Aye, but—" Plenty of men sported the same weave.

"And ears too," she went on. "I listen when folk talk, ye ken. Even though ye're a madman, all the lasses I doctor say as ye're the finest, bravest lad in the Highlands. Well favored, strong of limb. Reckon they didna stretch matters by much." She waved him forward. "Come in then."

He stood his ground. "I have a woman in the boat with a crossbow wound. Can ye help her?"

"How could ye allow that to happen?" she snapped. Her gray brows drew together, and she narrowed her gaze at him. "I canna tell until I see her. Bring Elspeth Stewart in."

He flinched at her foreknowledge.

"Muckle of beauty, little of brains." She shook her head. "Dinna waste time puzzling o'er it. D'ye think ye can steal a bride from the altar and not have the story wing through the Highlands swifter than a eagle's flight?"

She turned and opened the door to the cottage. Then

she cocked her head him, like a robin eyeing the worm she intends to eat for breakfast. "Dinna ye want to know who I am afore ye place your woman in my care?"

Rob grinned. "I have eyes. Ye're the witch of Loch Eireann."

"Cheeky." She frowned at him. "My *Christian* name is Hepzibah Black."

A witch with a Christian name. Rob sprinted back to the boat, feeling as if he'd just had his ears twisted.

Elspeth didn't stir when he lifted her from the pallet. She seemed like nothing in his arms, a disembodied spirit. Her arms hung limply, and unless he supported her head, it lolled.

His chest felt as if someone had placed an anvil on his ribs.

When he ducked to enter the croft, Fingal tried to follow.

"No, ye don't, Master Hound," Hepzibah Black said.

The deerhound thumped his bottom down on the stoop and whined at the doorway.

"He's attached himself to the lass," Angus explained as he followed Rob in. "If ye dinna let him come in, he'll howl and pine and make a horrible racket."

"Verra well." Hepzibah palmed Fingal's muzzle without a hint of fear. "Dinna bother the cat or the bird or I'll turn ye into a rug."

Angus's red brows shot skyward at that, but he said nothing. Fingal accepted the invitation and slinked into the cottage. The hound shot only the quickest of glances at the raven on a roost in the corner and the gray tabby, who eyed him calmly from the chair by the hearth.

"Put the lass on the table," Hepzibah ordered. "And we'll see what's what."

Rob laid Elspeth down carefully. Hepzibah Black took a knife from above her hearth and slit Elspeth's skirt open, baring the length of her leg from groin to ankle.

"No place for modesty in a sick room," the witch said with a shrug.

Then she unwound Rob's shirt from Elspeth's leg. It was matted brown with blood and stuck to her skin in places. She didn't move while Hepzibah peeled it off.

"I have some salts ye'll want to rinse this in afore ye wash it." She handed the shirt to Rob and turned back to Elspeth. She snapped her fingers before the girl's face but got no response.

"The lass is insensible," she said. "That's for the best, but we canna count on her remaining so."

Hepzibah leaned down to examine the bolt. She sniffed at the wound.

"No putrefaction yet. That's all to the good."

She put a hand to the shaft and gave it a slight tug. Elspeth's eyes popped open, and her mouth went wide in a silent scream.

Hepzibah released her hold on the bolt and put a hand to Elspeth's forehead.

"There, there lass," she said in a motherly tone. "'Twill come round right. Ye'll see. Ye'll feel better after I make ye some tea."

"Ye're no' a witch, after all," Angus said, slapping his thigh.

"Of course, I'm no' a witch." Hepzibah rolled her

eyes at him. "But how did ye come to that astounding knowledge?"

"Ye didna shrink from touching iron," he said. "Everyone knows witches canna abide iron on their skin. Burns them something fierce."

"Of all the dunderheaded…a woman has eyes and ears and the wit God gave her, and the eejit thinks her a witch!" She mumbled several things that sounded like spells, or at the least curses, to Rob, before she pointed at Angus. "Ye! Keep her company while Mad Rob helps me."

Angus took Elspeth's hand and began a running one-sided conversation with no discernable topic, while Rob followed Hepzibah into what she called "the still room."

"Put the shirt in that bucket," she ordered.

Rob dropped it into some evil-smelling liquid, which turned blood red and foamed as the shirt sank to the bottom.

"A berry or two of belladonna," she muttered as she gathered herbs from the drying bunches hanging over her head. "And some poppy. A pinch hemlock, I think."

"Ye'll poison her!" Rob said.

"Nay. Well, perhaps. But with luck, I'll send her spirit to bide someplace else while we do what we must," Hepzibah said as she pounded the herbs in a stone crock. "Are ye at all squeamish?"

"What? No."

"I had to ask. Some men faint dead away if they're allowed to see their women lying-in."

"This is no' a lying-in. I've dressed my share of battle wounds," Rob said.

"Aye, but no' on a woman ye fancy, I warrant."

"Who says I fancy her?"

"The worry in your eyes," the witch said. "D'ye no' ever look at yourself when ye peer into the water sometimes? Your face is as easy to read as the signs of the seasons."

Hepzibah scurried back into the main room and returned with a kettle. She poured boiling water over the crushed herbs and set it aside to steep.

"Ye'll kill her with that," Rob said.

"Or the pain will kill her." Hepzibah drew her lips into a tight line. "The problem, ye see, is when a crossbow bolt flies, it turns. When it strikes flesh, it continues to turn. If ye pull it out, the barbs tear the meat afresh, and the wound is ten times worse. We canna draw the bolt."

"Then how—?"

"We must push it through. Straight and even, missing the bone, of course, and any spots that will make the blood gush out."

"She's already lost a lot of blood."

"Aye, but if we draw the bolt, we'll damage so much, she'll likely be a cripple. If we push it through, the wound may close and grow healthy flesh. If she lives, it'll heal cleaner." Hepzibah fixed him with an intense stare. "'Tis no' an easy thing, pushing a bolt through living flesh. Is it in ye to help me?"

"Merciful God," Rob said, not sure it shouldn't count as another prayer. Then he gritted his teeth and nodded.

Chapter 18

"Drink this, dearie," Hepzibah Black said.

"Will it end the pain?" Elspeth asked through clenched teeth. She didn't want to cry out, but she was screaming on the inside. Her whole leg was afire. She put the noxious smelling concoction to her lips and forced herself to take a sip. The old woman had added a healthy dollop of honey to the "tea," but something bitter in the dark cup set Elspeth's teeth on edge.

"It will dull the pain some, but it will no' go away completely," Hepzibah said truthfully. "Ye'll feel a bit drowsy, and if ye wish to sleep, that's all to the good. Dinna fight it."

"But I'll still feel everything?"

Hepzibah had explained in detail what she was going to do though Angus had protested that Elspeth didn't need to know things that might scare her. The wisewoman had argued that truth was necessary, because all truth was God's truth, and they'd need help from every realm of spirit if they would meet success.

Rob hadn't said a word. He just stood beside

Elspeth, propping her upright with an arm around her shoulders. She didn't resist the urge to lean on him.

"Aye, lass. Ye'll still feel, but I canna say ye'll feel pain exactly," Hepzibah said as she tipped the cup up again, encouraging Elspeth to drink. "The important thing is, even if ye do, the tea will help ye forget the pain, and that's almost as good as not having it at all, is it no'?"

Elspeth wanted to argue that not having pain at all was infinitely better than not remembering it. But with each sip of the vile liquid, her brain grew fuzzier and her tongue seemed to grow to twice normal size.

All her limbs felt heavy, and her head became too much for her neck to support.

"Just a wee dram more," the woman said, holding the cup to Elspeth's mouth and massaging her throat to help her swallow. "Good! Now we wait a bit."

The room took a decided tilt, and Elspeth clutched the edges of the table.

"Oh." She put a hand to her head, her movement slow and deliberate, lest she miss her temple and keep going. "I'm dizzy of a sudden. I need to lie flat."

Rob eased her down on the table.

Overhead, the thatch teemed with bright green wiggling things, squirming through the gray dried grasses. Then she blinked hard, and when she looked again, they were gone.

Angus was speaking slowly. She knew because his lips were moving. She watched his words float across the room, lumbering yellowish blobs, but she couldn't hear them.

"I hurt for ye," Fingal told her from the place Hepzibah had assigned the deerhound on the hearth rug. His voice sounded oddly like Rob's. Then the dog stood upright on his hind feet as if he were a man and leaned on the mantel, hooking one ankle over the other.

The red shawl on the witch's shoulders hummed a disjointed tune, and the raven in the corner woke and fixed a one-eyed stare on Elspeth. She knew without the bird saying a word that it didn't like her a bit. But she was sure it could speak if it felt she deserved the effort.

Rob squeezed her hand, and warmth flooded her chest and upper body. She couldn't feel her legs. Either of them. His lips moved, but the blue of his plaid started a high-pitched whine that drowned out his words. He reached over her and tied her to the table. It should have alarmed her, but she was too entranced by the sparks of color trailing his hands to care.

She smelled bread. Hot and yeasty and comforting, it filled her nostrils and made her mouth water.

The wisewoman propped Elspeth's knee up. Rob grasped her ankle. Hepzibah tied a rope around her upper thigh so tight, Elspeth knew it should hurt, but instead she fought the urge to giggle. Then she stopped fighting. Her laughter danced through the air in flashes of light, borne up on grains of dust, sparkling in the sun.

Why had she never noticed how miraculous the world was? How filled with the fire of God? Everything swirled into everything else, all connected, all the same, all different, ever changing, and never changing. She could See back to the beginning and forward to the future at the selfsame time. And all the millions of moments, from deep in the past to those yet to come, stretching forever into the mist of tomorrow, converged in a single beat of her heart.

Angus clamped his beefy paws on either side of her head…to keep it from floating away, she supposed.

"Forgive me, *leannán*," someone said. It might have been Rob. Or maybe it was the dog again.

And suddenly she was cast into hell.

Rob stumbled out of Hepzibah Black's house and down to the loch. Blood was smeared all over his chest and arms. Who knew she still had so much in her? If he didn't wash it off, he feared he'd go mad, finally and completely.

If Elspeth died, he was sure he would.

By rights, that bolt should have found him in the dark. Instead, it had ripped through Elspeth's sweet flesh. He'd have given his mortal soul, and gladly, for the chance to trade places with her.

Why did God make others pay for his sins?

He knelt by the loch and washed himself, praying after a fashion as he did so. God knew he was not the contemplative sort by nature, so he didn't try to dress up his requests with religious-sounding words.

Christ, they say ye be merciful. If ye would prove it, let her wake.

Elspeth Stewart was not a screamer. She'd faced a wolf pack with grim silence, but she had screeched like she was being murdered while he and Hepzibah worked as quickly as they could to push the bolt on through her thigh. Rob had thought it a kindness when she slipped into oblivion. Now that her wound was packed with healing herbs and dressed with bandages soaked in the last of Angus's execrable wine, his gut was all jumbled up because her eyes remained closed.

Let her walk again.

Hepzibah assured him the damage would have been greater had they drawn the bolt out, but it seemed to him that now both sides of her leg were equally offended by the cold iron. Elspeth was young. She should be dancing and skipping, not leaning on a cane like a crone. Or worse.

Let her live.

He could bear anything if that prayer was answered. But she was so pale, her skin practically translucent.

He looked down at his wavering reflection in the water. There was one more request swirling in his brain, but he hesitated to lift it to God. It almost seemed like too much to ask.

Let her forgive me.

He rose and trudged back to the cottage. Only Elspeth Stewart could answer that last prayer.

❧

Elspeth burned with fever for the next three days on Hepzibah Black's straw tick mattress. When her eyelids fluttered open, she didn't seem to see a thing. There was no recognition in her blank stare. When she did speak, she answered Rob's questions in a babbling language no one knew.

"Except the angels," Hepzibah had said.

Or the demons.

Rob still blamed the old woman's poisons for Elspeth's state.

"No," Hepzibah assured him. "The concoction I gave the lass before we worked on her has done its work and already passed. If that was going to harm her, it already would have."

"Then why are ye trying to give her more?" he demanded. Each time Elspeth showed the least responsiveness, Hepzibah forced more fluid down her. Despite her protests to the contrary, Rob wouldn't swear the old woman wasn't a witch.

"This is no' the same mixture as before," Hepzibah said. "'Tis, but sweet basil and *blavers*."

"Blue cornflowers?"

"Aye, pressed down and steeped twice. They'll strengthen her will to return to us," Hepzibah said. "Her spirit wanders now."

Whatever the cause—the witch's brews, the blood loss, or the raging fever—it was obvious that Elspeth teetered on the cusp of life and death, and Rob feared she leaned too close to the edge. He barely left her side.

When she convulsed with chills, he climbed into the bed with her and warmed her with his body. Fingal would have joined them, but Rob threatened to tie him outside if Angus couldn't keep the hound away.

"Dinna be so surly, Rob," his friend had muttered as he stomped outside with his dog. "Ye're not the only one who suffers on the lass's account, ye know."

Maybe not. But Rob was the one responsible for the lass's injuries. If he hadn't stolen her away, she'd be safe now. But she'd be Lachlan Drummond's wife.

He decided a body could learn to live with guilt.

～

The water was delightfully warm. Elspeth let the liquid sluice down her bare body to the cloth she'd spread on the plank floor. She was back in Angus Fletcher's homely bedchamber, thankful to have peeled out of her road-weary clothes.

A creak on the steps made her turn.

Rob was standing there, just looking at her. The hunger in his cobalt eyes made them go even darker.

Her belly clenched and her nipples drew tight as his gaze traveled over her.

"Let me," he said.

Or maybe he only thought it, for his lips didn't move. His voice resounded in her head just the same.

She held the cloth and jar of soap out to him.

He was suddenly beside her without having walked across the room. And she felt his hands on her, smoothing his palms over her. The calluses at the base of his fingers nicked her skin and set it to dancing.

He scooped out a dollop of soap, and his touch glided over her, across her shoulders and neck, around and under her breasts. She draped her arms over his shoulders. He toyed with her nipples, circling them with his thumbs. He made her ache. Then he rolled the needy flesh between his thumb and forefinger, giving a slight tug.

The core of her being throbbed.

He kissed her, and their souls mingled, all tangled up in their shared breath. Rob made love to her mouth with his lips, teeth, and tongue while his hands continued to wash her.

He soaped her ribs, her navel, the mound of her belly. He reached around to stroke the length of her spine.

"Spread your legs."

Again, she couldn't be sure if he'd only thought the command, but she was powerless to disobey. She wanted him to touch her. She ached for it.

He invaded her softly, spreading her gently. The whole world went liquid and warm. He pressed the wet cloth to her and squeezed till the water ran down her legs and puddled under her feet.

She was a river. A loch. A place of deep secrets and hidden magic, but he knew them all. She ached for him to dive into her so she could keep him forever, like the water horse keeps its mate. Greedily, hungrily, because need has no sense of right or wrong.

It just is.

He cast a spell with his fingers, stroking and teasing, working the convoluted charm on her flesh. Marking her as his with each caress. Her insides twisted back on themselves, coiling tighter.

He dropped to his knees before her and found her secret spot. Joy raced in her veins beside the anguish of longing. Bliss called to her, washed over her, bearing her up on its gentle waves, rushing her toward the fall.

Then he stroked harder. Her limbs jerked.

Elspeth's eyes flew open. Her heart pounded between her legs in unrelieved wanting. Her thigh screamed at her, and her body's deep need receded in the face of agony.

She welcomed the pain. Pain meant she was alive.

Biting her lip to hold back a groan, she ran a hand under the coverlet and found a thick bandage on her leg. The bolt was gone, but she couldn't remember anything about how that happened.

She poked about for a memory but couldn't even find the dark hole that time had fallen into.

Dawn was creeping in through thin places in the thatch overhead. The blanket covering her was worn and much patched, but someone had tried to keep her warm and comfortable.

She didn't recognize whose bedchamber she was in, but she knew the man lying beside her with his head on her pillow. And his hand resting on her breast. She couldn't find it in her to be offended by the simple, possessive gesture.

Rob's mouth gaped with the relaxation of sleep, but there were dark circles beneath his eyes.

She felt as if she'd journeyed a long time. Wherever she'd been, he'd obviously stayed with her. A warm knot of tenderness tangled itself in her chest. She smoothed his hair with one hand.

His eyes opened, and he blinked at her with a sleepy, puzzled expression.

"Am I dreaming?" he asked.

"If ye are, I'm having the same dream."

He sat up suddenly. A smile, the first genuine smile she'd ever seen on him, lit his face. "Ye're awake! And in your right mind."

"In my right mind?" she repeated. "That's high praise from a madman."

"Ye canna ken a madman unless ye're a bit daft yourself, they say." He pulled her hand to his lips and pressed a kiss into her palm. "That's two answers, in any case. Ye're going to live. Ye're awake. D'ye think ye can stand?"

"I dinna know," she said as he leaped and ran around the bed to offer her his hands. "It looks as if I'm about to find out."

He pulled back the blankets, and she didn't recognize the shift she was wearing. She ran her fingers over the thin linen and looked askance at him.

"That belongs to Hepzibah Black."

She tossed him a puzzled frown.

"Never mind. Ye dinna remember some things. She said ye might have a hole or two in your memory, but that's a small matter. You're awake now, and it all may come back to ye, though it might be a mercy if some of it did no', she said."

"Who said…what?"

"Dinna fret. It matters no' a bit." Very gently, he lifted her legs and set her feet on the floor beside the bed. Pain streaked up her leg, but she fought back the wince.

"Here, take my hands." He didn't give her a choice and fairly lifted her to her feet. "Aye, ye can stand! Ye'll be walking again afore ye know it."

"D'ye mind if I wait a little longer?" she said as she plopped back down. The pain made her slightly dizzy.

"Oh, aye, I'm a dunderhead." He dropped to one knee before her. "It's just I'm so glad to see ye awake and to see the light shining out of your face."

"And I to see your face." She cupped his cheek. His beard had grown long enough to be a soft pelt.

He covered her hand with his. "I've got to ask ye now before your mind returns to ye entire."

"When ye set yourself to be charming, Rob MacLaren, ye do go all out." She snorted. Evidently he thought her mind faulty, but baring a few gaps in her memory, she felt clearer about everything than ever in her life. "Ask me what ye will."

His smile faded. "I did ye a grave harm, Elspeth Stewart, when I stole ye from your wedding. I put ye in danger and brought this injury upon ye. Do ye think ye can ever forgive me?"

All that he'd told her about his wife and Lachlan Drummond bubbled to the surface of her mind. She should probably wait to hear her betrothed's side of the story, but Rob's was pretty convincing.

And Rob wasn't the one who shot her with a crossbow. That she remembered very clearly.

"Aye, Rob, I forgive ye. But…" She gnawed her lower lip.

"But what?"

"Even if I pardon ye, I dinna think ye'll have any peace until *ye* forgive the one who's wronged ye."

A wall slid down behind his eyes. "Forgive Drummond, ye mean?"

"Aye. There are two sides to every tale, and—"

"This is naught but the poison talking. Hepzibah filled ye with evil humors afore she did her work," he said. "She claims she isna a witch, but I wouldna swear to it. Your mind is no' yet clear."

"No, I've never been so clear." She reached out and caught one of his hands. "It's a truth written in the rocks and trees and the beating of our hearts. Forgive."

"No." He shook off her hand. "Ye canna ask it of me. He took so much…"

Elspeth's heart ached at the enormity of Rob's loss, but she feared for him as well. For his soul.

"Aye, he did."

"And his offense wasna only against me." Rob was pacing now, agitation showing in every muscle and line of his body. "'Twas against Fiona. Tell me ye would forgive one who drove someone ye loved to their death."

Her shoulders sagged. "I suppose I could."

"Then ye're either a saint or a liar." He glared at her.

"At least ye must forgive yourself," she said. "Fiona's death was no' your fault."

Rob wouldn't meet her gaze.

"Bitterness is like death. I see it growing in your heart, Rob, wild as a cankerwort and as hard to root out. Forgive yourself while ye can."

"I'll no' forgive Lachlan Drummond. And I'll no' forgive myself for letting it happen. Never!" Rob strode toward the door. "I'd rather roast in hell."

Chapter 19

DRUMMOND WATCHED HIS GUEST SHOVE FOOD AROUND his trencher without eating a bite. After he reported Elspeth had been shot in the failed attempt to recover her on the loch, Drummond convinced Alistair Stewart there was nothing to be gained by following Mad Rob any longer. Once they returned to his stronghold with the sad news, Elspeth's mother had collapsed, too weak with grief to travel home.

"If I call in my men now," Stewart said as he chased a bit of root vegetable with a crust of barley bread across his trencher, "I can have three hundred ready to march on *Caisteal Dubh* by month's end. How many will ye bring?"

Drummond set down his empty drinking horn. "Ye expect to lay a siege with winter on the wind?"

"We canna arrive at the MacLaren's seat without a show of force at our backs. The only thing a coward like him understands is strength. There's no point in going to him with a handful of fingers."

Lachlan didn't think there was much point in going to *Caisteal Dubh* at all. Elspeth was probably dead.

Mad Rob had likely already consigned her body to the loch.

"What would you have us do if he refuses to give her back? The Dark Castle has never been taken from without," Drummond said. "There have been rumors of a secret way in, but no one has ever found it. All we'll do is shame ourselves before our own men when we must go home empty-handed, or freeze to death camping outside the walls."

"What other choice do we have? Would ye have us do nothing?"

"Ye could send word to the queen." Lachlan leaned toward his ally. "After all, she is your cousin, is she no'? I dinna think she'll approve of one of her ladies-in-waiting being abducted from the altar. The right word in her counselor's ear, and she might well divide MacLaren's land between us to settle the matter."

"No amount of land will settle this."

"Sometimes a man must take the best of a bad bargain," Drummond said, signaling for his servant to top off Lord Stewart's ale. Old Normina toddled forward, but Alistair covered the rim of his horn with his hand and waved her away.

Alistair buried his head in his hands. "Why would the MacLaren shoot Elspeth?"

"I dinna think 'twas his intention. It makes no sense for him to," Drummond said. Stewart had accepted without question his lie about who released the fateful bolt. Lachlan could afford to put a charitable face on the incident. "It was dark, ye ken, but I believe he was aiming at us on the raft, and your daughter put herself in his way."

"Then he must still mean to return her. He said ye could collect her at month's end."

"Since when can the word of a madman be trusted?"

"If he willna give her up, we have no choice but a siege." Stewart pounded his fist on the table in frustration. "Besides, her mother wishes it. She willna give me peace until I do something to bring Elspeth home."

Drummond bit off a hunk of venison and chewed. The haunch was gamey and sorely in need of salt, but his larder was strained by the extended stay of Stewart and his household. And since the marriage ceremony wasn't completed and the union unconsummated, none of the promised dowry had been forthcoming. Yet by virtue of his troth, Lachlan was still obligated to help Stewart retrieve his daughter. Mad Rob probably timed his interruption of the ceremony with that outcome in mind.

"D'ye hear yourself, man?" Lachlan shook his head. "Ye know full well the girl may already be—"

"Dinna say it." Stewart's knuckles turned white as he gripped his meat knife. "Elspeth's yet alive. I ken it in my heart. D'ye no' think a father would sense it if his daughter were no more?"

Stewart wouldn't be so certain if he'd seen Elspeth go down. Even if a crossbow wound didn't kill outright, Drummond knew it could still take a life. A bolt left a gaping hole. It had been too dark to see exactly where Elspeth was struck, but removing a bolt ofttimes did more damage than the initial hit. If loss of blood didn't do for her, then putrefaction almost certainly would.

"No, I'll no' believe she's dead until I see her body with my own eyes," Stewart said, his gaze fixed unseeing at his trencher.

His ally had set his feet, and there'd be no budging him. "Verra well. Since ye wish it, I'll go with ye and yours to *Caisteal Dubh*. And bring my men too. I should be able to muster a hundred and fifty by month's end."

If Lachlan was going to have to play this hand, he might as well go all out. It would serve to cement his tie with the House of Stewart, even though he fully intended to expand his alliances with a new bride from a different clan as soon as decently possible. James Grant's youngest was said to be a beauty.

"Even though our clans are no' yet bound by marriage, we are bound by our common foe," Lachlan said. "For now and all time, may God smite the MacLaren."

He offered his hand to Stewart, and the man clasped it.

"For now and all time, may God smite the MacLaren," Alistair Stewart said. "And may He use us to do it."

❦

It was a full week before Elspeth could walk unassisted, but drinking beef tea and Hepzibah's special brews helped her grow stronger each day.

Angus found a length of green birch and shaped it into a cane for her. She was able to transfer enough of her weight to use the walking stick to get around on her own.

"It'll also come in handy to use as a cudgel if ye

wish to drive a point into Rob's thick skull," Angus said when he presented it to her.

Everyone laughed at the time, but Rob stayed well out of range, in case she should take the suggestion to heart. In fact, he'd barely spoken to her since she asked him to forgive Lachlan Drummond. And himself.

Hepzibah taught her to change the dressing on her thigh herself.

"Once ye leave here, ye'll have to do it, so ye may as well start now," Hepzibah reasoned. When the week passed with no hint of corruption in the wound, the wise woman stitched the seeping openings closed.

"Ye're a fortunate lass, Elspeth Stewart." Hepzibah lit her pipe while she and Elspeth sat on the stoop before her cottage. They were comfortably out of the wind, catching the last bit of the sun's warmth while watching Rob and Angus preparing the boat to continue their journey. "Verra fortunate indeed."

"To be sure, any lass with two holes in her leg is twice blessed."

Hepzibah shot her a sour look. "Ye still have your leg. That's the main thing, but I was talking about the lad."

Elspeth frowned at her.

"Ye've the love of a fine man." Hepzibah nodded toward Rob and followed his movement with her sharp-eyed gaze. "That makes ye fortunate beyond the lot of most."

"Ye're wrong." Elspeth cast a lingering glance at him as he worked, admiring his easy stride, his broad-shouldered strength, his fine, long legs. When he caught her looking at him, she lowered her gaze to her lap. "Rob doesna love me."

Hepzibah took a few quick pulls on her pipe to make it draw well. "Ye wouldna say that if ye'd seen him fretting over ye whilst ye wandered between the worlds."

"He was only feeling guilty, I warrant," Elspeth said. "I wouldna be here, wouldna have been hurt if he didna still love his dead wife."

"I should hope he does still love her." Hepzibah puffed approvingly on her pipe and blew out a trio of smoke rings. "That's all to the good."

Elspeth shook her head, confused. First, Hepzibah said Rob loved her. Then she hoped that he still loved Fiona. "Why is that good?"

"A soul that knows how to love deeply is a rare thing in this world. Rob knows, ye see. And a soul that does, never really forgets how to do it."

"Do it? Love isna something ye *do*," Elspeth said. "'Tis something ye feel, surely."

"Where did ye hear that daft idea?"

"'Tis in all the sonnets and—"

"Sonnets!" Hepzibah's laugh cackled so, Elspeth would have named her a witch if she didn't know better. "What a kettle of goat's piss! Only a dreamer's scribblings."

Elspeth stiffened. She'd been enchanted by the idea of all-consuming courtly love described in her little collection of poetry. Was there anything finer than the adoring praise of a devoted swain?

Maybe the touch of devoted hands, she answered herself.

The memory of the way Rob's touch, Rob's kiss,

had wakened her to something hot and dark and forbidden made her cheeks heat.

"But ye make it sound as if love isna a matter of the heart," Elspeth said.

"Oh, it is that too, ye ken. But ye may feel all ye like and never do a bit about it," Hepzibah said. "If a body willna put feet to the feeling, what good is it?"

Rob laughed at something Angus said, and the rich, deep timbre of his voice made some wild nameless thing inside Elspeth shiver with anticipation.

"He's a fine, braw lad, and it stirs the blood just to look upon him, aye?" Hepzibah's voice sank to a whisper. "But the heart is a fickle beastie, changeable as the loch. There may come a time when the feeling some call love has flown. Then what does a body do?"

Elspeth couldn't imagine her stomach not doing flips each time she caught sight of Rob MacLaren. Not that she loved him, of course, but she couldn't deny there were definite feelings for the man, feelings that showed no sign of abating. But Hepzibah was wise about so many things, she allowed that the old woman might know a bit about this as well.

"Tell me, Hepzibah, what *does* a body do if the feelings go away?" Elspeth asked.

"That's when a soul *decides* to love anyway, with mind and breath and body," Hepzibah said. "Feelings come and go. And come again. But when your soul and your will unite to act, that's when ye know love goes clear to the bone. A body canna forget how to love once it's done that."

Rob started walking back toward the cottage, his

frame casting long shadows on the dead grass. His mouth turned up in a smile when his gaze met Elspeth's.

Hepzibah made a clucking noise with her teeth and tongue. "Whether yon laddie wants to admit it or not, his heart loves again. 'Tis only a matter of time before his soul and body decide to follow."

Chapter 20

ROB INSISTED THEY SAIL AWAY THE NEXT TIME THE loch's tide favored a swift passage to Lochearnhead. Angus fretted that Elspeth shouldn't travel yet, but Hepzibah said she was healing well enough, and sailing was easy on a body. The muscle in Elspeth's thigh still ached, but the pain was manageable.

Besides, Rob scowled each time she limped, so she forced herself to walk as normally as possible. Hepzibah said evidence of her injury made him feel guilty, and that's why his face screwed into such a frown, but Elspeth wasn't so sure.

She bid Hepzibah a tearful farewell and promised to return to visit her next summer.

"Dinna promise what ye canna deliver," Hepzibah said. "Search your Gift. Ye know in your heart we'll no' meet again in this world."

Elspeth's brows shot up.

"Aye, I ken ye have the Sight. I see it on ye, a silver mantle all a-shimmer." The old woman's eyes glistened. "But ye havena decided to take it up in earnest."

"I canna control it. The visions come when they

will and in ways that make little sense. And besides, having the Sight marks me as different."

"Oh, aye, o' course we're all different. God doesna repeat Himself. Surely ye ken that by now." Hepzibah gave her a basket filled with a couple loaves of rye bread and a round of cheese. "Dinna fear what ye dinna understand. Decide to understand it."

Elspeth sneaked a glance at Rob under her lashes. "There's much I dinna understand about a lot of things."

Hepzibah laughed. "Admitting your ignorance is the first step to learning aught. And I'll tell ye a secret. Opening yourself to your Gift is easy. Ye just stay out of its way and accept what comes, even if it makes no sense at the time."

Hepzibah also cast a quick glance at Rob. "Opening your heart to another? Now that takes some doing."

"I dinna think he wants me to try."

The old woman waved her objection away with a bony hand. "Men dinna know what they want half the time. Oh, they're good at recognizing hungers of the body, all sorts, but hungers of the heart go unnoticed ofttimes unless they've a woman to point it out to them."

"Come, lass," Rob called out to her from the deck of Angus's boat. "We're wasting the tide."

"I thank ye." Elspeth folded Hepzibah into a fierce hug. "For everything."

She headed toward the shore, leaning very lightly on the cane, but Rob sprinted toward her and scooped her up. His scowl faded once she was in his arms.

She draped her arms around his neck, enjoying the

added warmth of being so near his body. The westerly wind had taken a bitter turn. "I can walk, ye know."

"Aye, but no' fast enough to suit me," he said gruffly as he carried her and her basket of food the rest of the way.

Rob set her gently into the boat, untied the line, and shoved the prow into the loch. A thin skiff of ice had formed along the shore, but the hull of the boat crackled through it with ease. Rob gave a running leap and landed on the deck beside her, setting the boat rocking wildly.

She wobbled, trying to bear most of her weight on her good leg. Rob caught her in his arms again.

"No' going down, are ye?"

"No, just trying to stay upright while ye bobble us about," she said and pulled away from him. Being treated like an invalid made her hackles rise.

The sail filled with the breath of the loch, and the boat glided into the center of the dark, open water. Hepzibah and her little cottage fell swiftly astern, but Elspeth kept waving until the wisewoman was lost to sight.

"Ye'll be most comfortable in the cabin," Rob said. "Hepzibah gave us an extra blanket for ye. 'Tis spread on the pallet."

She was still wearing his cloak. Even with only his plaid for warmth, he seemed impervious to the growing cold. Not a hint of gooseflesh rippled on his exposed neck. Elspeth almost told him she'd be most comfortable in her own chamber in her father's keep, but she realized that wasn't true.

It made no sense when she examined the bald

facts of the matter, but she honestly didn't want to be anywhere except with Rob MacLaren.

As she ducked into the cabin, she wondered if this was one of those things Hepzibah would say she shouldn't fear, just decide to understand.

Rob commandeered the tiller from his friend instead of joining her in the small space. Her belly spiraled downward with disappointment, but she soon had other company. Angus and Fingal crowded into the cabin with her.

The big man regaled her with tales of the loch as they skimmed over its surface, and his deerhound sidled up to her, sharing his shaggy warmth.

"Poor Fingal," Angus said with a rough pat on the dog's head. "He's grown quite attached to ye, but he'll have to bid farewell to his lady fair soon."

"How soon?"

Angus peered out the open front of the cabin, taking note of passing landmarks. "At this pace, we'll make Lochearnhead by nightfall. Then, come morning, Fingal and me will point our noses home."

"And what will Rob and I do?"

Angus shrugged. "That I dinna ken. I agreed only to this part of the venture. And once I deliver ye safe and sound to Lochearnhead, I'm square with yon laddie." He hitched a thumb over his shoulder in the direction of Rob and the stern.

"If ye dinna mind my asking, what did ye owe Rob for?"

"The daft bugger kept me from being alone in the world. Single-handed, he saved me only nephew from being hanged by the English a few years back."

"Really?" It was a fearful thing for a Scot to fall into the hands of English justice.

"Aye," Angus said. "Young Hamish Murray is the son of my sister and the only family I have left to my name, so the boy's dear to me, ye ken."

Rob was alone in the world, as far as Elspeth knew. His parents were gone, and his wife…Elspeth didn't want to think long about her, lest the willowy, copper-haired Fiona pay her another visit through a vision. She wasn't ready to open herself to some things yet.

"What happened with your nephew?" she asked.

"Seems wee Hamish got himself mixed up with a rough sort down on the border. A bunch of renegade Campbells mostly, and the whole lot were captured for raiding Sassenach farmsteads. O' course, the English said there was raping and killing being done, but I ken my nephew. 'Tis no' his way. 'Tweren't more than cattle thieving. A fine Highland tradition, that."

"Aye," Elspeth agreed with a smile. Even her father had reived a herd or two in his day. "But if he'd been taken by the English, how did Rob save Hamish from hanging?"

"Och, Rob's always been a canny sort," Angus said, tapping his temple. "The night before the hanging, with folk pouring into town from all the countryside around, he went to the magistrate, dressed as a priest come to hear the last confessions of the accused."

Elspeth blinked in surprise. Rob was many things, but priestly wasn't one of them.

"Once he got into Hamish's cell, he pulled a monk's

cassock out from under his robe for my nephew to put on, and a pair of shears. He shaved Hamish's beard and gave my nephew a tonsure on the spot!

"Then he called the guard back and overpowered him. Rob took his keys and released all the other prisoners. Then as the Campbells made a run for it, Rob and Hamish followed them out of the gaol, calling out warnings of an escape to the local constables!

"While the English rounded up the others, Rob and Hamish walked right out the city gates. No one ever gives a second look to a man of God, ye ken. 'Specially not one with a freshly shiny nob like Hamish had! Rob said later that they might as well have stayed to see the hanging, but Hamish wanted to put the English border far behind him."

"Understandable."

"Rob rode that black demon, Falin, home, but he made Hamish walk all the way back to the Highlands, as penance for being daft enough to fall in with Campbells, he said!" Angus laughed. "The plan was madness, but it worked."

"Madness," Elspeth repeated. "Then he's always been known as Mad Rob?"

Angus's face sagged. "No, that was only after Fiona…och, ye ken what happened. He ran a bit wild after that."

Elspeth had seen Rob's blue eyes glinting with madness in the cave after he abducted her. He'd looked right through her when his hand circled her neck, and Elspeth suspected he'd heard voices in his head.

But Rob had been in his right mind ever since then. Perhaps his lunacy was the sort that came and went.

And once Angus and Fingal left them in Lochearnhead, perhaps it would return.

The thought didn't trouble her as much as it ought. If Rob was touched by the malady again, Elspeth would be ready for it. This time, she realized, she was armed with something stronger than madness.

Love.

It surprised her a little when the word bubbled to the surface of her mind, but it didn't scare her.

Love.

Not the "flutter in the belly" sort, though she had to admit her stomach did a jig whenever she looked at Rob MacLaren's handsome face. No, she had the "clear to the bone, willing to do something about it" kind of love.

And if Rob's madness returned, she was prepared to act.

❦

Lochearnhead was a sleepy little village on the west-ernmost end of Loch Eireann. Night had fallen before Rob piloted the craft up to the wharf, but the moon hadn't risen above the mountain called Ben Vorlich yet. The peak rose to the south, a sleek pyramid of granite with no trees spiking its top. A cap of snow glinted on its heights in the starlight.

"Ye surely canna mean to press on in the dark," Angus said as he tied his boat securely to the dock. "Will ye stay on board this night, Rob?"

"No, I bespoke a room over the tavern for the past couple weeks because I wasna certain when we'd arrive," he said as he gathered up his few possessions.

Elspeth was doing the same in the small cabin. Traveling light was easier if a man didn't have a woman in tow. And if he didn't care about her comfort. It made him feel even worse that Elspeth wasn't the sort to complain. At least he could put a roof over her head and a hot meal in her belly this night.

"Paid in advance for the room," Rob said. "It'd be a shame if we didna use it."

Elspeth was saying good-bye to Fingal, and the deerhound responded with loud whines. Angus pulled Rob aside with a quick glance toward the cabin. "Have a care with the lass's reputation."

"Aye, I'll make sure none hear her name or see her face." Rob said, irritated that Angus didn't think he'd protect Elspeth from gossiping tongues. "I didna set out on this course to harm *her*, just her bridegroom."

"No, I believe ye didna, but sometimes the best plans go awry, and this one surely has on several occasions," Angus said with a stern frown. "And besides, there's all kinds of harm."

"I dinna think Drummond will meet us along the road I intend to travel."

"That's no' what I mean," Angus said. "I ken ye can protect her from him. But can ye guard her from yourself? The lass is a maiden, gently bred. Have a care."

"And what d'ye think I am? A ravening beast, I suppose." Rob snorted. "I overheard ye telling Elspeth about Hamish and his brush with English justice. Rape is no' his way, ye said." He crossed his arms over his chest. "Did it occur to ye that it's no' mine either?"

"I just mean—"

"I ken what ye mean. Nothing will happen to the lass that she doesna want. There. Are ye satisfied?"

Without waiting for an answer, Rob turned away and called to Elspeth. She emerged from the cabin and said good-bye to Angus with the same warmhearted-ness with which she'd taken leave of the witch of Loch Eireann. Angus was reduced to blustering to hide his blubbering, and the deerhound didn't even try to disguise his sorrow at seeing her go.

"I'm ready, Rob." She smiled tremulously at him and let him hand her onto the wharf.

Does she just flit through life, collecting hearts as she goes along? Rob wondered. His chest constricted.

Aye, he answered himself. *She does.*

Chapter 21

HALFWAY UP TO THE TAVERN ON THE EDGE OF THE town, Elspeth stumbled. Rob picked her up again.

"Ye dinna have to scoop me up like a bairn every time I wobble a bit," she protested.

"Aye, I do."

"Rob, I—"

"Trust me this once, lass," he said as he tugged the cloak around to hide her face. "'Tis for your own good."

He blustered into the taproom of the tavern, announcing his presence and demanding the room he'd paid for. The tavern patrons had a good laugh, assuming him an overanxious bridegroom with a shy bride in his arms. A man would let a whore walk up to the room behind him, so Rob carried Elspeth on up to the second-story chamber, following the light of the tavern owner's tallow candle. No one would be able to say for certain that it was Elspeth Stewart who spent the night with him above the tavern's common room.

Then Rob went back down to order their supper.

He passed on the mutton, which smelled pretty wooly, and chose the savory venison stew instead. He ordered a skin of wine, a round of cheese, and as a treat, a loaf of real wheat bread instead of coarse barley, along with a dish of thick clotted cream. Mrs. Christie, the tavern owner's wife, promised to bring up their supper tray shortly.

Rob returned to the room, feeling pleased with himself. The tavern was clean and well ordered. After a cave floor, a cramped boat, and a witch's borrowed bed, he was finally providing suitable lodging for a lady of Elspeth's quality.

When he opened the door, she was seated on a straight-backed chair next to the small table that held a pitcher and ewer. The light of a single candle kissed her with a golden glow.

But unlike the time he'd stumbled upon her at Angus's home, she wasn't bathing now. She was fully dressed, with her skirt hitched up to her hip on one side, her stocking sagging to her ankle.

She was untying the length of muslin binding the wound on her thigh.

Her eyes flared at him, and she dropped her skirt to cover herself.

"Ye need to change the dressing, Elspeth. Dinna let me stop ye. In fact, let me help ye." He steeled himself to look at his handiwork. It was his fault an otherwise perfect leg was marred for life.

"I can manage."

"Let me. I want to be sure 'tis healing cleanly." He sank to one knee beside her and uttered a word that rarely passed his lips. "Please."

She met his gaze directly for a moment and then nodded.

Carefully, he drew her skirt back up. He tried very hard to focus on the wrapped section of her thigh, but it was impossible not to notice her tender calf and the tempting crease behind her knee.

He wondered if she was ticklish there.

She'd already started unwrapping the wound, so he continued, reaching around between her legs to remove the muslin strip. His fingertips brushed her inner thigh, that soft skin so near the tempting place between her legs. Her breath hitched on each pass.

"The entry wound looks good," he said once he dropped the soiled cloth into the ewer.

There was no hint of redness around the scab, and he could smell only her warm, healthy scent. Her body was working to repair the damage his plan for revenge had caused. But she would always bear a scar.

He shifted to check the exit wound on her inner thigh. It, too, was healing nicely. He caught a glimpse of shadowy paradise beneath her skirt, just a hint of soft nether lips and silky curls.

He was going to hell without doubt. He should have been concentrating on her injury, but all he could think was how close her delicate womanly parts were to his hands.

"We need to apply the salve Hepzibah gave me."

Her voice pulled him back to the matter at hand. He rummaged in her bag and came up with the small jar. The unguent didn't have a foul odor as most medicines did. There was a hint of bayberry and mint, and when he smoothed the salve over her injury, it glittered silver on her skin.

He lingered a bit over the application, spreading the excess on her uninjured parts, reveling in gliding his fingers over her flesh.

"I can wrap the fresh dressing," she said.

"Once I begin something, I like to finish," Rob said, taking the length of muslin from her.

He brought it around her leg several times, taking care not to bind it too tight, but making sure it was snug enough not to slip down. Her skin was incredibly smooth, unbearably soft. He tortured himself by trailing his fingertips on each pass along her inner thigh.

He noticed a subtle shift in her scent. She was no longer just warm and healthy. There was a definite hint of musk in the air. The whiff of her arousal went straight to his groin.

"There, lass." He tied off the dressing but didn't move his hand from her thigh. "Looks like you'll do."

"Will I?" She was looking down at him, her lips softly parted, her eyes hooded.

His fingers inched closer to her mound. He bent and pressed a kiss on her knee. She didn't protest.

"Elspeth." Her name escaped his lips like a prayer as he slid his hand the rest of the way under her skirt.

"Oh, Rob."

She was damp and tender and swollen. He covered her with his palm, and she throbbed into it with a long sigh. He could feel her heart beating in his hand. Such a knot of caring rose in his chest, he almost couldn't breathe.

His cock stiffened to rock hardness as he stroked

her gently, teasing her curls. Her knees edged farther apart. He kissed along the inside of her leg from her knee to the crease of her inner thigh, hitching her skirt higher with each one. Then when she was totally exposed to his gaze, he covered her mound with open-mouthed kisses.

She made a soft moan and slumped in the chair, edging her bottom closer to the edge of the seat. It was a clear invitation to stay.

He invaded her with his tongue.

Was there anything more miraculous on earth than a woman's pliant wetness?

He was drunk on her scent. He wallowed in her, in every sigh, every moan, every shiver of muscle under taut skin.

Her legs trembled. He wrapped his arms around her hips and drew her closer. He nuzzled the soft lips of her sex, reveling in her obvious need for him.

Her hands smoothed over his head, her fingers tangling in his hair. She twisted and pulled, but he didn't mind. She was too far gone to realize what she was doing.

From a distance, there came a rapping sound.

Elspeth's breath came in short pants as he drove her on, closer and closer to completion. He ached to feel her unravel under his hand.

The rapping grew more insistent.

Her body stiffened as her release drew near.

"I say," a woman shouted on the other side of the door. "D'ye want yer supper or no'?"

Rob roared in frustration. He was on his feet in a heartbeat, stomped to the door, and opened it a crack. The tavern owner's wife balanced a tray on her hip and raised her fist to pound the door again. Mrs. Christie stopped with a flinch when she saw him glaring at her.

"If I dinna answer the first time, ye'll no' knock again." He filled the opening, careful to shield Elspeth from the woman's sharp eyes. "D'ye understand?"

"Aye, my lord." Mrs. Christie was all meekness now. "But the supper?"

"Bring it back in an hour, and be sure it's piping hot," he growled. "And if I dinna answer the first knock, go away and return in another hour."

He slammed the door and turned back to Elspeth.

She hadn't moved. She was still sitting on the chair with her skirt bunched at her waist and her knees sagging apart, her sweet slit glinting all pink and wet at him. The tops of her breasts heaved above her tight bodice with the frustration of being so close to release and yet denied.

She was the most erotic thing he'd ever seen in his life.

He picked her up and carried her to the bed.

"Rob," she said with a sob in her voice.

"Hush, lass. Dinna fret." He laid her down and climbed in beside her, pulling up her hem to bare her again. She was fair all over, beautiful in all her parts. "Once I begin something, I like to finish."

༄

Elspeth felt as if she'd drunk another cup of Hepzibah's mind-altering tea. There was only bliss. Only pleasure.

But there was no sense of unreality this time. Rob's

mouth, Rob's blessed hands on her were more real than anything in her entire life.

Then there was only need. Only aching. Only longing to be filled.

She'd die of wanting, she was sure.

And then she did.

The spasms were so intense her whole body shuddered with the force of her release. Rob covered her mouth with his, and she tasted herself, all salty on his lips. He slipped a finger inside her, drawing out her pleasure. She continued to tighten around him, unable to stop, not wanting to stop, afraid she would stop.

She surrendered control of her body and let him lead her through that dark, hot place. Then once the madness was spent, she finally stilled, jerking only occasionally, like a marionette whose strings had been cut.

She felt wonderful. Even the ache in her thigh had subsided to a distant throb.

His mouth was still near enough for her to nip, to suck his bottom lip. She fisted his hair and pulled him closer for a deep kiss. She suckled his tongue and felt the hard ridge of him against her hip.

She was done wondering what he'd do if she reached under his kilt. Her hand found him, and he groaned into her mouth. She swept his length, clasped her hand around his base, and stroked. She fondled his balls.

Then she pushed against his chest.

"I want to see ye," she told him.

His mouth turned up in a crooked smile, and he rolled onto his back, his hands laced behind his head. "Look your fill then, lass."

"Lie still."

She drew the bottom of his kilt up to his waist, and there it was. Licked by the light of a single candle, a long, thick, glorious rod of maleness lay on Rob's flat belly. And below that in a nest of dark curls, his ballocks were drawn into a taut mound.

He was so fine.

She reached out to touch him, and his cock rose to meet her palm. She drew back in surprise.

"Did ye make it do that?"

"Aye and no." Rob chuckled, and when his belly jiggled, his cock did too. "He has a mind of his own sometimes, ye ken."

"Oh, aye?" She walked her fingers up and down his length and was rewarded by the way a muscle ticked in Rob's cheek. "*He*, is it? Does *he* have a name?"

"Plenty of names, but none fit for polite company."

She stroked him again, enjoying the smoothness and warmth of the skin drawn taut over his granite-hard length. "If he has a mind of his own, he needs a name of his own."

"He's what ye might call single-minded. With only one thought generally, and a verra simple means of expression."

"Then a simple name is needed." She trailed her fingertips around his balls and then traced the line of darker skin that marked the centerline of his scrotum. "What is Rob short for?"

"Robin," he said through clenched teeth.

She found a patch of rougher skin near the head. A pearl of fluid formed at the tip of him when she teased that spot. "Then we'll call him Robin."

"He'll no' answer to it."

"Mayhap he needs training." She grasped him with firmness.

Rob's breath hissed over his teeth. "He's fearsome stubborn. There's only one thing that'll vanquish him."

"What's that?"

He grasped her wrist so she was forced to look at his face instead of his cock. "Ye dinna have any idea what ye're playing with. A good hard swive is all he understands."

She leaned down and kissed Rob's lips, his cheeks, his closed eyes.

"Then that's what we'll have to do."

Chapter 22

ROB SAT UP AND GATHERED HER INTO HIS ARMS. "ELSPETH, *leannán*, I gave ye pleasure because it pleased me to do it. And with no lasting harm to ye. But this is something that, once done, canna be undone. D'ye ken that?"

She palmed his cheek and looked through his deep blue eyes to his troubled soul. She loved this man. She was sure of it. Why would she not offer him the comfort of her body?

"Aye, Rob," she said. "I ken what I'm doing."

"Ye only think ye do."

His voice was drawn and tight. She sensed him struggling with himself. A thrill of power swept over her. Who could have thought she'd bring her captor to such a state of indecision?

"Ye canna say ye dinna want me." She brushed a hand against his groin.

"No, I canna say that."

His eyes went dark and luminous as he looked at her. She peered once more into the well of his soul and was satisfied. He would not see her shamed. She could trust him with anything. Even herself.

"As much as ye want me, Rob, I want ye back."

"Oh, lass—" He interrupted himself to kiss her.

Elspeth realized he'd been holding back in his previous kisses. The longing in this kiss stole her breath. The deep sadness she'd sensed in him the very first time he kissed her returned and threatened to overwhelm her. That time she'd Seen a fleeting image of Fiona MacLaren.

Did Rob think on his lovely redheaded wife while his lips played with hers?

She tried to open herself to her Gift, to move out of its way, as Hepzibah had suggested, so she might discover whether Fiona MacLaren still hovered in his heart. But her senses were so overflowing with Rob, there was no room for her Gift to fill. He crowded out everything else.

She longed to do the same for him, to so fill up his soul there'd be no room for sadness.

But how? She matched him kiss for kiss, and he seemed to enjoy it when she stroked him, but she had no idea how to really please a man.

At her first sight of "Robin," she'd been minded of her father's stallion. Now she wondered if men were like stallions in other ways. One night, Elspeth had sneaked into the stable and hid in the haymow to spy as her father and the groom oversaw the stallion covering a mare in heat.

Elspeth had watched in awe as the horse's huge thing stopped dangling. It grew and stiffened as he sniffed wild-eyed at the mare. Then the stallion climbed atop her, and the mare whinnied her pleasure while he pumped his great thing in and out of her and bit her neck till the blood ran, glistening ribbons down her withers.

She'd rather not be bitten till blood ran, but she could certainly arrange herself for Rob without him having to tell her what to do. She pulled away from his kiss and shifted onto her hands and knees, hoping her thigh wouldn't tremor too much.

"What are ye doing, lass?"

She peered over her shoulder at him. "I'm getting ready for ye. I've seen horses, ye ken."

He almost laughed at her naïveté, but the thought of lifting her skirt and being able to ram himself into her glistening slit from behind robbed him of the power of speech. Oh, to be able to grasp her hips and pound away at her, his balls slapping her thighs.

But that was not how a man takes a virgin. Not one he cared for.

He moved down beside her and lay on his side. "I'll no' say ye're no' a fetching sight from that angle, but people are no' horses."

She settled onto her stomach, resting her chin on her hands. "Then what am I to do? I feel your sadness, Rob, and I want to ease it." She bit her bottom lip. "Are ye thinking of her?"

He didn't ask whom she meant. "I'll no' lie to ye. When I kissed ye just then, Fiona formed in my mind for a heartbeat. She was my wife, and she comes to me unbidden sometimes, but I shoved her away for the now. There's no' enough room in my bed for two women."

Her smile squeezed his heart.

He tucked her hair behind her ear and fingered her soft lobe.

"Then what would ye have me do, Rob?" she asked, rolling to face him. "I want to please ye."

"Just let me take ye, lass, and we'll both be pleased, I promise." He ran a fingertip along the top of her bodice, then he plunged his hand in to cup her breast.

Her eyes closed in bliss. "Aye, take me, then. Steal my lips, my breasts, all that I am." Her eyes opened again. "Steal me away, Rob MacLaren."

❧

Desire was a difficult dance master. The steps for removing unwanted articles of clothing were sometimes bunglesome. Laces snarled in knots. Buttons popped off. Impatience to plant a kiss on needy skin tripped them up more than once, but the reward of seeing each other in glorious nakedness was well worth the slow dance of disrobing.

"Do as I do," Rob had told her. And he began stroking her all over. Elspeth reciprocated, reveling in the shiver of muscle, the hitch of his breath when she touched a spot that gave him pleasure.

They took turns kissing each other, planting their lips on every crease of skin, every indentation and bump. He lingered over her anklebones and toes. She swirled her tongue around his navel.

Finally Elspeth sank back into the feather tick and spread her legs. Rob moved up her body, kissing and teasing, caressing and torturing. He worshipped her breasts, nuzzling and suckling, while she sketched a benediction on his spine with her fingertips.

Then he took her mouth. And as his tongue slid into her, his cock entered her as well.

He didn't thrust or jab. He just filled her. Slowly. Inexorably. Assuaging the aching emptiness.

Her maidenhead shredded in a flash of pain that was gone almost instantly.

The wonder of holding him inside her was too fine, too glorious for words. They fit together with such rightness, a tear tickled across Elspeth's cheek.

And then he began to move.

Elspeth matched his pace, and the dance began in earnest. They found a rhythm, a flow of bodies and hearts and spirits, all intermingled and jumbled together. Did she moan or he? Whose shuddering breath was that? Whose heart was pounding like a drum? It was difficult to tell as they raced toward a distant pinnacle.

She felt her insides clench around him. Once. Twice. Then she retreated from the drop.

"Come, lass," he said hoarsely as he plunged into her. "Come with me."

She launched her soul skyward, and her body followed. He stilled while her inner walls spasmed around him, and then his seed pumped into her. She held him while his body shuddered with the last hot pulses.

The world stopped spinning. Elspeth decided she wouldn't care if she ever moved again.

He was still inside her, the precious connection still intact, but she began to be able to tell her limbs from his. He kissed her neck.

"Are ye pleased, lass?"

She smoothed his hair behind his ear. "Better than pleased. I'm alive now. I didna even realize I wasna before."

They lay in contented silence even after he slid out of her. He shifted to lie beside her so he wouldn't burden her with his weight. She stroked his spine. He drew little circles around her nipples. Then he licked one and blew on it to watch it pucker afresh.

"Are ye no' tired of playing with me yet?" she asked with amusement.

"No," Rob said. "And neither is wee 'Robin.'"

When he rocked against her hip, she felt that he was stone hard again.

"I warned ye he was single-minded."

"And persistent," she said with a laugh. "What's he thinking about now, I wonder?"

"I think he's wondering if horses might no' have a good idea, after all. What do ye think?"

Elspeth kissed him hard and deeply. "I think we ought to find out."

❧

Mrs. Christie rapped loudly on the door, but there was no answer except a rhythmic creaking. She almost pounded again, but she remembered the MacLaren's surly orders from the last time she tried to deliver his supper.

"Verra well, my lord," she muttered as she carried the tray back to the kitchen. "Another hour of rutting may make ye a happy man, but it willna improve this stew nary a bit."

Chapter 23

ROB MEANT TO LEAVE WITH THE FIRST LIGHT, BUT IT was midday before he woke with Elspeth still sleeping warm and soft beside him. He was sated and satisfied, with every knot untied and every coil unkinked. If Fiona had visited his dreams, he had no memory of it in the waking world.

His new arrangement with Elspeth was so pleasant, there was no sense in spoiling matters by living rough. A full day's ride would see them to the gates of *Caisteal Dubh* and a solid roof over their heads. The money he'd put down to save the room at the inn for them had run out, so he paid for another night's lodging. With delight unspeakable, he and Elspeth shut the world out of their little chamber.

The next day dawned drippy, and quickly bloomed into a downpour of freezing rain. Rob counted out more coin for another night and considered himself fortunate. The longer they lingered in Lochearnhead, the longer he could put off what was to come.

As long as he and Elspeth could dally and swive on the soft feather tick and talk of nothing but what pleased them, they could pretend there'd be no piper to pay for this exceedingly pleasant dance.

But Rob knew the piper would present his bill soon. And at Rob's very gates. He climbed the stairs to their chamber, his tread slower than usual.

Elspeth was seated in the middle of their neatly made bed, stitching up the hem of his cloak.

"I dinna know when it was torn." She tied a knot and bit off the thread with her white little teeth. "I probably caught it on something."

"Thank ye. 'Tis a bit long for ye," he said, settling next to her. "I've one at *Caisteal Dubh* that'll be a better fit. And prettier too. As I recall, there's a wee tassel on the hood and a fine copper brooch that goes with it."

She glanced at him from under her lashes before she started on another raveled spot in the wool. "One of your wife's castoffs?"

The question seemed innocent enough, but the hair on the back of his neck sent him a warning. The same warning that tells a wild creature a hunter has an arrow trained on his heart.

"Of course no'." Even *he* knew a man didn't put his dead wife's clothes on another woman. Neither of them would appreciate it. "'Twas my mother's."

He couldn't tell from her expression whether that was an improvement.

All of Fiona's things were scattered with lavender, packed in a trunk, and bundled away to a room in the tower not used for anything else. Whenever he couldn't sleep, he'd wander up there and open the trunk for the chance to imagine he could smell her unique scent over the faded floral.

Sometimes, he actually believed he could.

"Besides," he said, "Fiona was a tall woman. Ye'd no' be able to wear her things. Ye'd be catching the hem with every step."

That was definitely not an improvement. Her brows drew together over her pert nose.

"I expect I come up short in a number of ways," she said tetchily.

"That's no' what I said."

"'Tis what I heard." Her eyes flared at him.

"Ye're angry," he said, confused.

She smirked at him. "Aren't ye the knowledge-able one?"

What had gotten into her? She'd been perfectly pleasant when he left her after a quick but satisfying morning shag, to see to another night's lodging. Perhaps the foul weather accounted for her foul mood.

"I ordered a bath for us," he said in an attempt to brighten her spirits.

"Oh, lovely. Will ye swive me in a hip bath now if I ask ye prettily, my lord?"

That sounded like a good idea to him, but the way she said it made him think her heart wasn't in the venture.

"Elspeth, what's wrong?"

"What's wrong, he says." She jabbed the needle through the unprotected wool with ferocity.

"If ye dinna wish to tell me…" He rather hoped she wouldn't.

The sewing dropped to her lap. "What's to become of us, Rob?"

"Well, tomorrow, if the weather clears, I've arranged for two suitable mounts for us, and we'll ride to *Caisteal Dubh*." It wasn't a difficult journey. Of course, he hadn't reckoned on her injury. "Unless ye think ye'll suffer on horseback with your leg. The way willna allow for a cart, but I could drag a wooden frame—"

"No, ye big ox!" She climbed off the bed and paced the small space, her limp slight. "That's no' what I mean."

He didn't want her to fret over this part of his plan. It was his doing and his fault things had taken an unexpected turn. He'd tend to it.

"Och, I expect your father and your bridegroom are amassing a force, and they'll gather at the gates by month's end, if they aren't there already and—"

"No, that's no' what I mean either."

He looked at her, genuinely puzzled.

"Us, Rob. You and me. What's to become of *us*?"

"Oh." That was a piper he'd hoped to forestall for very much longer. He was more than happy to join his body to hers and create that delicious *us*. What to do once the connection was severed was a riddle he hadn't solved. He wished his body could puzzle it out as easily as it had led him into this silken quagmire.

Her chin quivered, but she straightened herself to her full, if inconsiderable, height. "Dinna tell me ye've taken my maidenhead and it means naught to ye."

"*Leannán*, no, 'tis no' that," he said raking a hand through his hair. Fiona tried to teach him to name his feelings, but he was a difficult student. Give him something solid, a sword, a handclasp, a heart-stopping swive, and the world made perfect sense. Ask him to speak the tangle of his heart, and his tongue cleaved to the roof of his mouth.

"Then, pray, what is it? How many ways have ye taken me, Rob MacLaren?" she said shakily. "And yet no word of love has passed your lips."

"None have passed yours either," he said, hoping to seize a foot of earth in this melee.

"A woman dare no' name her feelings first. It makes her weak. Makes her vulnerable." She fisted her hands at her waist, looking anything but weak or vulnerable.

Unless one counted the excessive shimmer in her eyes.

"Doesna it do the same for a man?"

"No."

"Why in hell not?"

She narrowed her eyes at him. "If ye canna keep a civil tongue in your head, I'll be asking ye to leave."

"I'll do no such thing." He toed off his boots and stretched out on the bed. "I'm paying for the damned room, aren't I?"

"Then I'll leave." She headed for the door.

He cut her off, leaning a long arm over her shoulder to hold the door shut. "Ye'll no' be going anywhere, Elspeth Stewart."

"Oh, that's right." She glared up at him, looking like a cornered cat ready to scratch his eyes out. "I'm Mad Rob's prisoner, just a pawn in your chess game with Lachlan."

"Elspeth." He leaned toward her. She'd never looked more *swiveable* than she did right now, her cheeks painted with ire, her eyes flashing, and the curve of her breasts straining against her bodice. "That may be how things started, but that was before—"

"Aye, before ye began..." Her mouth twitched.

"…Using me…" Tears trembled on her lashes. "As your whore."

She covered her face with both hands and wept.

Oh, Lord, not tears. Let her scream and rage and pound me with her fists, but dinna let her cry.

His gut roiled if she'd punched him in the belly. With the sharp end of a pike.

"I canna believe…I was so wrong…about ye." She sobbed between her words, dragging in deep breaths but never seeming to have enough air.

"I'm the one who's wrong," he said. That was the premise of any woman's argument, wasn't it? If his relationships with women taught him anything, it was that the man was always at fault. "O' course, I canna point to anything I've done wrong in particular, but I'm sure ye'll do that for me once ye've stopped crying."

That made her cry harder.

"Elspeth. *Leannán.*"

"No." She twisted from him and slapped his hand away when he tried to palm her cheek. "Ye havena the right to call me that."

"And ye havena the right to call yourself a whore."

She dropped her hands and glared at him. "That's right. I havena received payment yet. Oh! But ye did promise me your mother's cloak and a shiny copper brooch, so I guess ye do plan to make good your debt!"

Rage boiled in him. "I've never struck a woman in my life, but you tempt me, woman." He spun her around and began unlacing her bodice. It was time to change the tone. "Ye're vexing me sore."

"What are ye doing?" She tried to get away from him, but he held her fast, still unlacing her.

"That should be obvious. What is it ye think we've been doing here, Elspeth?" he said, pulling the leather over her head. Her breasts swung free beneath her thin chemise. People lied, but their bodies never did. "Have we been whoring, ye and I?"

He caught hold of her skirt and yanked at the waist. The horn button popped off and rolled under the bed.

"Rob, stop it."

He picked her up and tossed her onto the bed, grabbing the hem and pulling off her skirt. She fought him every step.

"Is that what it seemed like to ye, when I came inside ye?" he demanded. "Were ye playing a whore's trick when I held ye while ye cried out and shuddered round me?"

He pinned her beneath him. All the anger drained from him as he looked down at her. "It didna seem so common," he said softly. "So mean a thing to me."

She stopped squirming. "What was it like to ye?"

"I'm no' a man of words, ye ken. No' a poet."

"I didna think ye were." She reached up to touch his face, hesitated, then traced her fingertips along his cheek. "But a man doesna need to be poet to speak his feelings plainly. And a woman canna tell what a man feels unless he speaks of it."

Words were just sounds, puffs of air with meaning attached, but Elspeth evidently put a lot of stock in them, so he'd give it his best.

He closed his eyes to compose his thoughts. Looking at her roused his body so, his mind became jumbled. Even with his eyes shut, he could still conjure an image of her, mouth passion-slack, brows tented in pleasurable agony.

His chest constricted, a hard lump of tenderness crowding his ribs.

"When I cover ye, Elspeth, and the glory of your coming is upon ye, 'tis like I hold your soul and ye hold mine." He opened his eyes and met her gaze. "And the brightness of our joining would fair strike me blind, but for the life of me, I canna look away."

Then he frowned down at her. "Does that sound like whoring to ye?"

She shook her head.

"What does it sound like?" he asked.

"Like...trust," she said slowly. "Like...love."

"Well, then." He thought so, but he was no expert when it came to the shadowy realm of emotion. It steadied him to have her confirmation. "There ye have it."

"Have what?"

"Trust and love." He bent to kiss her, but she turned her head at the last moment, and his lips landed on her ear.

"Ye love me, then?"

"I said as much, did I no'?"

She met his gaze squarely. "No, ye didna."

"Then let me speak plainly." He leaned on his elbows and palmed her cheeks. "I love ye, Elspeth Stewart."

Her smile would have lit the queen's hall, brighter than a hundred candles.

He bent to kiss her again but stopped short.

Her eyes flew open. "What's wrong?"

"Ye dinna love me back?"

"Of course I do."

"Then say it," he dared her with a grin. "A man canna tell what a woman feels unless she speaks of it."

Her heart shone in her hazel eyes. "I love ye, Rob MacLaren."

He kissed her, softly and sweetly. Then he cast her a wicked grin. "Prove it."

❦

Mrs. Christie banged on the door to the guest suite. She'd lugged the copper hip bath up the steps with no help at all from that lout of a husband of hers. The water was aboil in the kitchen and ready for her to start the multiple trips it would take to fill the shallow tub.

Good thing the MacLaren was paying them so handsomely.

She rapped the door again before she thought better of it.

The door opened a crack, and she saw Mad Rob's brilliant blue eyes peering out at her. And the rest of him that she could see was naked as Adam.

She hadn't brought in the hip bath yet, so that could only mean the MacLaren and the woman with him were…

Merciful Saint Brigid! And in the middle of the afternoon.

"Mrs. Christie, what did I tell you about knocking on this door?"

"Aye, my lord, I'll leave the tub in the hall and return in an hour to fill it." She turned to pad back down the stairs.

"Mrs. Christie?"

"Aye, my lord?"

"Make that two hours."

Chapter 24

THE RAIN ENDED DURING THE NIGHT, AND THE NEXT morning dawned brisk and clear. It was one of those rare November days in the Highlands, when the sky was robin's egg blue and the sun was more than a cold disc in the southern sky. It was a liar's day, a day that banished all thoughts of the coming winter by aping the appearance of early spring.

Elspeth rode a gentle mare with an easy gait. She was more comfortable on her own mount and figured it was a measure of Rob's trust that he'd given her one. Strange to think that only a few weeks ago, she'd have bolted away from him as fast as she could go. Now she followed behind him along trails only he could see, through passes where the peaks rose around them on all sides, over ridgelines and then back down. They stopped frequently.

"To rest your leg," Rob said.

But Elspeth sensed that he was drawing out the journey for other reasons. That he was reluctant to return to his home with her in tow.

"Are ye ashamed to bring me to *Caisteal Dubh*?" she finally blurted out.

He grimaced at her. "Why would ye say such a thing?"

She wondered whether he was loath to bring another woman into the home where he'd lived with his wife. "Ye dinna seem to be in a hurry to get there."

"Ye're right about that. If we dinna hurry, we'll no' run into an ambush," he said, and she noticed for the first time that his gaze scoured the forest and rock outcroppings as they went. "I'm no' ashamed to bring ye to my home. I only wish it were under different circumstances, ye ken."

"Ye're the one who stole me from the altar," she reminded him.

"And ye'll never let me forget it."

She smiled sweetly at him. "Never in a hundred years."

They topped a rise and looked down into a little valley. There was a castle of gray stones so dark they were almost black. *Caisteal Dubh*, the Dark Castle. It was ringed with a stout curtain wall, and a water-filled moat ran along three sides. A steep granite cliff rose behind it. A highly defensible position. There would be no hostile approach from that direction.

"Looks as if your father and bridegroom willna let me forget it either," Rob said grimly.

Spread out around the other three sides of *Caisteal Dubh*, a host of men were encamped. Pennants emblazoned with Stewart and Drummond colors whipped in the wind. Several parties of men were felling trees to build siege works.

Rob hated to see them waste the lumber. *Caisteal Dubh* had never been taken and wouldn't be on his watch either.

"They're early," Elspeth said. "Ye told them not to come till the end of the month."

"They guessed I wouldna harm ye, but by now, they must also know ye're no' in the castle."

"For all they know, I'm dead." Her hand flew to her mouth. "Merciful God, I hadna thought of that before. Oh, Rob, my poor parents."

"Once we're safe in the castle, I'll go out under a flag of truce and let your father know ye're well. Ye'll have to show yourself on the wall, aye?"

"That'll do, but I dinna think they'll let us ride up to the front gate. How do ye plan on getting in?"

He leaned forward, surveying the array of fighting men amassed before his keep. His people were safe inside, he was sure, but if the army remained long, the land would be scarred. Feeding that many men each day would deplete the nearby game, and if any of his crofters had a private store of grain, he'd bet it was already gone. He had to make sure Elspeth was safe, and then he'd deal with the men at his gate.

"Can ye keep a secret?" he asked.

"Aye."

"Then I'll take ye in *Caisteal Dubh*'s back door."

⁂

They looped around on game trails a bit, and Elspeth almost lost track of which direction the castle lay. Then Rob set his face toward a steep incline. There didn't appear to be any trail worthy of the name making an ascent on it. Only goats might attempt such a rock face. She was certain she'd be unable to drive her mare up it.

"Are we to pass through stone?"

"In a manner of speaking." He swiveled in his saddle and looked back at her. "What I'm about to show you is a way known only to the laird of the castle. My father showed me. Someday, I'll show my son."

"Ye have a child?"

He looked at her intently. "No' yet."

Elspeth's chest ached. For all she knew, she might be bearing Rob's child already. She didn't know whether that would simplify or compound their problem.

"The secret is both a blessing and a curse," he said as he dismounted and tied his horse to a pine. Then he helped her down.

"I've never kenned how a thing can be a blessing and a curse at once."

"'Tis a blessing because should there be a need to enter or leave *Caisteal Dubh* by stealth, as there is for us now, there's a way to do it." His mouth set in a hard, thin line. "But if this secret should become known, 'tis the only way the castle will ever fall."

He took both the horses' reins and led them around a boulder. "Coming?"

She followed. Behind the rock, another cave opened into the steep incline, its dark mouth yawning.

"Ye seem to have a way with the deep places of the earth, Rob MacLaren."

And the deep places in her heart. Though they'd declared their love, it still felt tenuous. Like a rope of two strands that might break if too much weight were put on it.

"Do ye seek out caves wherever ye go?" she asked.

"They seem to seek me. I've stumbled over several in my travels, and all by accident."

"Or by running from those whose herds ye've reived?"

"Aye, ye've the right of it," he admitted with a laugh.

She followed him into the gloom. He handed the horses' reins to her and pulled out his flint. Once a torch was lit and placed in a holder in the rock wall, Elspeth could see this first chamber of the cave was even-floored and dry. It would serve well as a temporary stable. Rob put up some planks to bar the way out and keep their mounts safely in.

"After I see ye settled, I'll come back and tend to these two. If this business with yon armies drags out, I may have to set them loose, but if I do, they're likely to be caught by your bridegroom's men." He patted the mare's neck, and she whickered softly. "Horsemeat is stringy, but it'll feed a multitude."

"Dinna set them free," Elspeth said. "And dinna call Lachlan my bridegroom. I'll no' marry him now."

Rob's eyes glowed at her. "It pleases me to hear it. Come, lass."

He took the torch again and caught up her hand. He led her unerringly through a long tunnel, ignoring the side passages that led off into the dark. She ran her free hand over the side walls. There were tool marks gouged in the stone.

"This was made by human hands."

"Aye. Parts of it," he said. "But the work was done so long ago, the doing of it has fallen out of memory. Some of this cave system has been here since the days of Noah, and others have been improved upon over the years. Like this."

They'd come to a series of stone steps leading up. They were by no means regular in size or height but were obviously the work of man.

"Some of the steps may be wet and slick, aye?" Rob said. "Be careful."

She would have been afraid in the cave if she'd been alone. And the steps looked daunting because of the throb in her leg, but as long as she held Rob's hand, she feared nothing.

Elspeth concentrated so hard on putting her feet aright on each step, she lost track of how long they climbed. Finally the stairs ended, and the cave continued in a fairly level corridor. It was wide enough for them to walk two abreast, and Rob didn't have to duck his head at all.

"I hear voices," she said, and hers echoed several times off the stone around them.

"Aye," he whispered back. "We're close. Ye're hearing the folk who live inside the castle. The sound comes down through cracks and fissures. I expect it might go up as well, so..." He placed a finger on her lips.

She nodded, and they walked on. The voices grew louder and then faded. Finally, they came to a dead stop.

"What is this? There's no way out," she said.

"I was hoping ye'd say that," he said. "It means the entrance might yet be secret, even if someone made it this far." He handed her the torch. "Now we go up."

There was a narrow chimney rising above them. Rob began climbing the walls, placing his hands and feet carefully in finger- and toeholds worn slick from centuries of use. Then he braced himself with one foot on each side of the space and shoved at the seemingly solid roof over his head.

The stone lifted, and he moved it sideways to create an opening wide enough for his shoulders and arms to disappear through.

Faint light showed around him. Then he lifted himself the rest of the way out and disappeared from her sight.

Elspeth was left in the corridor below, holding the torch. The walls seemed to close in on her.

"Rob?"

A rope flopped down before her, and Rob's face reappeared in the opening overhead.

"Put your foot in the loop, snuff out the torch, and I'll pull you up," he said.

She was quick to obey. The thought of remaining in the cave alone a moment longer made her heart pound. The rope bore her up smoothly. When her head cleared the opening, she saw that there was a pulley attached to a very low ceiling. Rob was barely able to sit upright in the short space as he hauled her up.

He tied off the rope and lifted her the rest of the way with a hand under each armpit.

"What is this place?" she whispered.

"We're in the chapel." He slid the slab back into position to cover the opening. "Under the altar."

He peered out through a slit in the altar cloth and then crawled out. Elspeth followed him.

"How could this entrance cause *Caisteal Dubh* to fall?" she asked. "One man could hold this spot against an army."

"Aye, he could," Rob said. "But what if someone was to enter by stealth as we just did, when no one was on guard, and then open the gates?"

"Why not post a guard on the altar all the time?"

"I asked my father the same thing. He said no matter how much ye may trust someone, the human heart is weak and might be corrupted. A secret is best guarded when fewer souls know about it."

"And no one's ever found the way by accident?" she said.

"Who would think to look for something no one knows is there?" he said as he lifted her to her feet. "I think there may have been a priest or two who's been surprised over the years when the laird miraculously appeared under the altar, but never in my lifetime. Or my father's. Or his father's. The secret is well hidden."

"'Tis safe with me," she assured him.

"And ye are safe with me," he said. "Welcome to my home. Come now. There are those who will be glad to see us."

He led her out of the chapel and into the bailey. The sun had set, but the courtyard was lit by countless torches and teemed with life. All his crofters, their bairns, and livestock had been crammed into the space. But instead of quivering in fear over the armed encampment beyond the stout walls, the castle's inhabitants took for granted that the stronghold, which had never fallen, was indeed impregnable. The atmosphere was more like a makeshift fair.

Folks had set up stalls to barter their goods and make more of them. The *Caisteal Dubh* ovens were fired up. But the aroma of freshly baked barley bread didn't quite mask the stench of too many barnyard animals and people in too small an area. Children frisked like colts in a game of tag between the stalls.

The only ominous note was the determined clang of the smith's hammer. At least one soul seemed to realize a conflict was coming and was making preparations.

"The MacLaren!" someone called out. And the cry was taken up immediately as the people realized their laird was suddenly and miraculously in their midst. Rob was surrounded by his awed people, who knew he'd not come in through the barred main gate or any of the other smaller but heavily fortified ones. Men doffed their caps, and women covered their mouths with their aprons.

And narrowed their eyes with suspicion at Elspeth.

So that's the Stewart maiden, she could almost hear them thinking. *The cause of all this trouble.*

Chapter 25

"MY LORD, MY LORD!" A ROUND WOMAN BURST through the crowd and began dogging them across the bailey.

"In a moment, Mrs. Beaton. I'll be with ye directly," Rob said then lowered his voice to Elspeth as they continued toward the smith's determined clanging. "My housekeeper. She's been with us since my mother died. A wee bit tetchy, she is, but a terror with a scrub brush."

"Rob! Ye're alive!" The smith laid aside his hammer and came away from the anvil to enfold Rob in a hug. A great giant of a man with a flaming head of hair, neatly tied back, and a round, smooth-shaven face, he was a younger version of Angus Fletcher. "There's been no word. When ye didna come, we feared the worst. 'Tis glad I am to see ye."

He cast a shy smile in Elspeth's direction. "Ye must be the Lady Elspeth. We didna have time to be properly introduced last time I seen ye, ye being in a hurry and all, and—"

"And ye must be Hamish Murray." When his eyes

rounded with surprise, she whispered, "Ye have the look of your Uncle Angus."

"How long have Drummond and Stewart been here?" Rob asked.

"On the morrow, 'twill be a week."

"Did they parley?"

"Aye, I spoke to them from the walls," Hamish said.

"Their demands?"

"The return of the Lady Elspeth." His massive shoulders cringed. "And yer head."

"Well, I'm no' inclined to give them the first, and assuredly no' the last," Rob said with a snort. "Did ye tell them we were no' here?"

"They seemed to know already," Hamish said. "They said the Clan MacLaren were all prisoners in their own keep till our laird gives up his hostage."

"The first deep freeze will send them scurrying home to their own hearths."

"Ye didna see their faces, Rob." Hamish shook his head. "Foul weather willna turn them from their purpose. Drummond and Stewart are set on this."

"Guess I'll have to talk them out of it, then," Rob said, turning to his housekeeper. "Mrs. Beaton, I believe ye have a room ready as I ordered. Will ye see to the Lady Elspeth's comfort?"

"But, my lord—" the housekeeper began.

"She's to be given the best chamber and every honor due the daughter of a laird, as ordered. D'ye hear me? Now, see to it."

Mrs. Beaton puffed up like a wren fluffing its feathers against the cold. "But, my lord, I have somewhat of great import to say to ye."

"Important or no', whatever it is, it'll have to wait till a time when I've no' got an army at my gate, aye?" He gave Mrs. Beaton his back and turned to Elspeth, taking her hand. "Go with her now, *leannán*, and if ye need aught, all ye have to do is ask."

"Ye'll let my father know I'm well?"

"Aye, and I'll send for ye to show yourself, so he can see ye with his own eyes."

"Tell him...I'm sorry—"

"Hush. Ye've naught to be sorry for," Rob said with a finger to her lips. "'Tis my error. I'll fix it. Go ye now, and I'll see ye at supper."

⁓

Elspeth Stewart has a good deal to account for, Mrs. Beaton thought furiously as she led the way back across the bailey to the laird's keep. *The lass has so witched the laird that he willna even hear her begin to take blame for the way she's thrown him into confusion.*

The laird was cagey about it, but Mrs. Beaton was sure he'd begun to look with favor on her niece Margot before this wild venture. He'd danced with Margot a couple times when the whole castle was trying to make merry to cheer him. Margot's father wasna a laird, but he was a man of stature among the Beatons, rich in cattle and land.

Margot was young and healthy, and her mother had birthed nine live bairns. She came from fertile stock, did Margot. She'd be a good match for the MacLaren.

In fact, Mrs. Beaton's brother-in-law had sent an offer for the MacLaren. He promised a truly princely dowry for Margot, hoping to form an alliance between their clans. And the laird wouldn't even let her tell him about it.

Lord MacLaren's heart was beginning to mend before this scheme to steal Elspeth Stewart took shape in his mind. The timing of the abduction and the laird's obsession with it all smacked of witchery.

And if the Stewart wench witched him once he saw her, she might actually have put the thought to steal her in his head. Through some weird incantation, reaching across the distance to call him to her, like a siren on the rocks. Such things were known to happen.

It was the only explanation for her laird's odd behavior.

And Mrs. Beaton hadn't missed the fact that Elspeth Stewart divined Hamish's name out of thin air. An uncommon skill, that. Some might say unnatural.

Mrs. Beaton glanced back at the Stewart girl. Aye, her father was cousin to Queen Mary, but everyone knew the queen was so tainted by her time on the French throne, she couldn't hardly be named a good Scot except by birth.

Night was falling fast. Elspeth Stewart was looking around at the half-timbered buildings ringing the bailey in *Caisteal Dubh* as she trailed Mrs. Beaton.

No doubt imagining yerself chatelaine here! Well, may God strike me blind before I hand over the keys to the likes of ye!

"Wipe yer feet," Mrs. Beaton said sharply when they entered the Great Hall. The rushes she'd strewn on the flagstone floor a few weeks ago would have to last till spring. As she mounted the steps to ascend to the chamber she knew her laird would want for Lady Elspeth, she noticed the girl limping.

"Have ye damaged yourself?"

"No, 'tis nothing," the Stewart girl said.

Mrs. Beaton led her to the chamber that had stood empty since the laird's mother died. It was a fine chamber once, with a sturdy bed and a heavy trunk for all a lady's things, but disuse had rendered the air stale and the linens musty. She bustled over to the window and pushed it open.

"I'll have the girls air the room now and turn the mattress," Mrs. Beaton said. She ought to have done it before, as the laird ordered, but she'd been so certain this whole scheme would end differently, she neglected preparing the room. "We were no' given notice of yer arrival, ye ken."

"I thank ye," the lady said with every appearance of meekness while she ran her fingertips along the footboard of the bed.

Well, o' course, a body will find dirt if she looks for it.

"I suppose ye'll be wanting the braziers lit to take away the chill," Mrs. Beaton said.

"If it isna too much trouble."

Everything about this lass screamed trouble, but there was no help for it.

"I wonder," the Stewart girl said softly, "if I might have a bath as well. The road was a weary, long way, and I'd like to wash before my father sees me."

Demanding already. "As ye wish, my lady," Mrs. Beaton said. "I'll send a couple girls up to set ye to rights." She turned to go.

"Oh, Mrs. Beaton, one more thing. If I might ask, whose chamber was this?"

"The chatelaine's."

"Fiona's room," she said softly.

"Nay, this room belonged to the laird's lady mother. Young Lady MacLaren and the laird were no' married long, ye ken. She bided with him in his chamber. Verra fond, they were." When she saw the words pained Elspeth Stewart, she felt obliged to repeat and embellish them. "Verra fond beyond the common."

⁂

Later, Mrs. Beaton was checking the store of apples in the cellar, making sure none had gone bad. Only one with a soft spot was all it took to ruin a whole barrel.

"Auntie?" Her niece's voice echoed down into the stone vault.

"Aye, come and ye can help me, Margot. Mind the steps."

Margot was pretty enough, but she needed directions to pull on her own stockings.

The lass came down, her comely face drawn into a frown. "Did ye ken the laird brought her back here?"

"Aye, I settled her in her room, did I no'?"

Margot's green eyes flared. "Oh! Did ye hear what one of the girls who helped her at her bath said?"

"Nay, I didna."

"Something verra odd," Margot said. "It was Nessa who told me."

"I dinna care who it was who said it." Honestly, the girl's head was full of nothing but husks. "What did she *say*?"

"She says Elspeth Stewart has a particularly odd wound on her thigh," Margot's voice dropped to a whisper. "Up fair high too."

"Hmph! I kenned she was limping, but it struck me as a way to gain attention," Mrs. Beaton said under her breath. "A wound, ye say. What sort of wound?"

"Well, it's on both sides of her leg, as if something went clean through it. Just as big coming out as going in, Nessa says."

Margot picked up an apple and crunched into it with her strong young teeth. Mrs. Beaton slanted a disgusted glance at the girl. It wasn't because she didn't have enough teeth left in her head to strain sauced apples. It was because so many gifts were wasted on the young, who didn't have sense to appreciate them.

"Was the flesh around the wound dark? Any red streaks perchance?" Mrs. Beaton asked. That'd fix matters right proper.

"Why?"

"I thought perhaps the wound had gone bad. They do sometimes, ye know."

"Nessa didna say anything about that. What d'ye suppose would make a such wound?" Margot wondered aloud.

Mrs. Beaton had tended men who suffered such wounds in battle from swords or arrows. But she'd never seen the like on a woman. An idea struck her.

"A pitchfork run clear through would make such a mark."

Margot nodded. "I suppose it might do. Just one tine, o' course. But she's a lady and no' likely to be spending her time in a stable. How d'ye think Elspeth Stewart got a pitchfork through her leg?"

"Well, there's a simple explanation, if ye think on it." Mrs. Beaton pursed her lips in satisfaction. "I dinna know for a fact, ye ken, but I'll warrant the devil marks those he traffics with. What better way than with his pitchfork?"

"Elspeth Stewart is in league with the devil?" Margot's eyes grew wide. "D'ye think?"

"Aye, 'tis most likely," Mrs. Beaton said. "Ask Nessa. See what she makes of it."

Margot turned to go, but Mrs. Beaton stopped her with a hand to her arm. "Wear yer best gown to the supper this night. The blue one, aye? And make sure ye tune yer harp. I'm thinkin' ye should sing a bit."

Margot might have the brain of a peewit, but she sang like a lark. A man could forgive a girl for being a bit simple if she had lovely tits and a presentable talent or two. Margot was amply blessed in tits and talent.

As the girl scurried off, Mrs. Beaton pulled a wormy apple out of the barrel. "Ye'll no' be spoiling what I've laid by so careful-like," she muttered.

And Elspeth Stewart wouldn't trouble *Caisteal Dubh* for long either. Given a few days and a few juicy tidbits in the right ears, and Mrs. Beaton would have the entire castle clamoring to send her away.

If they didn't decide to burn her themselves.

Chapter 26

THE BROCADE WAS STIFF AND SMELLED OF CAMPHOR and heather. The style of the gown was woefully old-fashioned, but it was pronounced a good fit by the lady's maids Mrs. Beaton had sent up to attend Elspeth. The tunic and kirtle had belonged to Rob's mother, they told her.

"Lady MacLaren, our laird's lady mother, ye ken, was of a size with ye," the older woman named Aileen told Elspeth. Nessa, the young one who'd helped her with her bath, had skittered out afterward, taking a single bucket of wash water and sending Aileen and Kate to take her place tidying up and seeing Elspeth made ready for supper. "A wee bird of a woman, she was. Not tall and buxom like his wife, the *young* Lady MacLaren. Now there was a fine figure of a woman. What a pair they made!"

Elspeth wondered if Aileen was aware young Lady MacLaren had taken her own life by leaping to her death from a tower room just like the one they were in now. If she were, she didn't seem disposed to speak of it.

Aileen and Kate chattered quietly as they shook out other garments from the trunk. Elspeth ignored them and turned sideways to look at herself in the long sheet of burnished copper.

Her reflection was wavering and distorted, but she didn't think she resembled a bird in the slightest. A copper-and-agate-studded snood gathered her heavy hair in a neat bunch at her nape, and the tunic and kirtle were at least clean and of good quality. She was clearly a lady of rank, albeit in borrowed and old-fashioned finery. It would serve for now.

Eventually, she'd send for her own things.

For she fully intended to stay in *Caisteal Dubh*, no matter how unwelcome Rob's housekeeper or the serving women tried to make her. There was no going home to her parents after this scandal. She wouldn't bring shame to their doorstep.

Elspeth couldn't return to Edinburgh either. She'd be laughed out of Queen Mary's court, sniggered at, and studied covertly with sidelong glances. Or worse, be slapped with a light-heeled reputation no amount of subsequent proper behavior would erase.

And there was certainly no way she'd submit to a loveless marriage with Lachlan Drummond after giving herself heart and body to Rob MacLaren.

There was only one way forward.

Rob hadn't asked her yet, but he'd come to it soon. They must marry. It was the only thing that would serve.

Installing her in the chatelaine's chamber was a good beginning, though it pained her not to share a bed with him. At first, she chafed at not being taken to his chamber, but once she thought the matter through, she saw the right of it. By demanding she be treated with deference, by placing her in his mother's room, Rob had protected her good name. His people might wonder what had passed between them on the long journey from the kirk where she was abducted to *Caisteal Dubh*, but they'd have no hard evidence she wasn't still a pure maid.

It would be best for all concerned if they decided to believe her so.

It was the same sort of outward show of respectability that enabled the English to accept and enjoy the fantasy that their Elizabeth was a virgin queen. At least, that was the tale for the masses.

Privately, her courtiers told a different story. According to the lordlings from England who visited her Scottish cousin Mary's court, Queen Elizabeth had a new favorite so often it was hard to tell who was in and who was out of her special favor without keeping a running tally.

Though they never said so unless they were deep in their cups, and even then, not very loudly.

If Elspeth could maintain a virginal image here in Rob's home, it would make matters less embarrassing for her parents. And easier for his people to accept her as their respected chatelaine once they married.

Because they must marry. That was all there was to it.

Surely he'd see that.

There was a rap on the door, and the serving women who grumbled as they took turns hauling her bathwater away, set down their buckets and stood at rapt attention.

"Come," Elspeth called.

The door opened, and Rob was framed by the opening. Her heart fluttered like a caged bird beating its wings against the wire.

Rob had obviously had a bath and shaved off the stubble of his beard. He was a handsome enough man to turn feminine heads if he were dressed in rags. He'd been a raging madman painted with woad the first time Elspeth saw him, and he still made her breath hitch. Now he was every inch a laird. In full Highland regalia, Rob MacLaren was a sight to tempt even a nun to debauchery.

He smiled at Elspeth, and her insides trembled. The rest of the world faded away in his blinding brightness.

Then she remembered the serving women were hanging on every moment, so she dipped in a formal curtsey. "My lord."

"My lady, will ye honor me by dining at my side this night?" His eyes shone at her.

"Aye, with pleasure."

He offered her his arm. She rested her palm on it lightly and let him escort her from the room. The heat of his body sizzled through the fine lawn of his shirt and into her hand. She tried to give no outward sign, but she was near to bursting into flames from wanting him so.

It felt different, being with him here in his home. As if he were a whole other person, one who still looked like the Rob MacLaren, who fought a wolf pack for her and stole her heart, but this Rob was suddenly weighed down by the cares of his station. He was courtly and correct. She wouldn't have been surprised if he began spouting poetry.

As they walked down the corridor to the stairs, she leaned toward him. "Do ye suppose we'll have barley bannocks and a rind of cheese?"

He laughed at the memory of the first meal he'd offered her. The correct and courtly laird fell by the way, and he was just Rob again. "We're under siege, ye ken, but I think we can do better than that."

Once Rob and Elspeth took their places at a raised table in the Great Hall, he introduced Elspeth with a no-nonsense announcement that she was his honored guest. A ripple of murmurs circled the hall, and none of the faces turned toward her brightened with a smile of welcome.

"My disagreement is with Elspeth Stewart's bridegroom, no' the lady herself. I'll have more than words for any who show her the slightest discourtesy," he said sharply, and the murmurs ceased.

Then he raised his glass, and the people of the Clan MacLaren joined him in a toast to themselves. After a long draught, they all sat down to their trenchers and fell to with a will to welcome home their wandering laird.

But the unfriendly glances in Elspeth's direction didn't cease. They were merely quicker and more stealthy, lest Rob catch one of them at it. Elspeth decided the best course of action was to study her own trencher.

The cooks at *Caisteal Dubh* certainly did better than barley bannocks and a cheese rind.

Elspeth lost count of the courses. There was a cock-a-leekie soup, smoked salmon, savory venison, and haggis. The Forfar bridies, a cunning pasty, must have been one of Rob's favorites, because he wolfed down three of them in quick succession. And lastly, they were presented with a delicious *crannachan*, a concoction of raspberries, honey, oats, and whisky, mixing the sweet with an alcoholic tang.

The menu would have done credit to Queen Mary's table.

But Rob didn't speak to her more than necessary, and then with stilted courtesy. Instead, he leaned toward his friend Hamish, who was seated on his right, and spoke freely.

"I appreciate the welcome," Rob said. "Our larder's been thin during our travels, ye ken, but this seems a bit much seeing as how we've an army at the gate. I'd best have a word with the steward, so we dinna have a repeat on the morrow, or we'll be in want by Hogmanay."

"Och, let yer people rejoice," Hamish said as he refilled his and Rob's drinking horns with some of the oldest and smoothest whisky in *Caisteal Dubh*'s cellar. "They've been thrifty up till yer coming. We've had naught but *parritch* and barley bread and mutton stew. And mighty thin stew at that! But ye're home now. Ye'll end this trouble right enough."

Elspeth tried to attend to her trencher, but she cocked an ear toward Rob's conversation. How was he going to end the hostilities?

"I appreciate your confidence, Hamish, but since I willna meet their demand for my head, I dinna see how I can end the siege quickly."

Hamish nearly spewed drink out his nose. "Och, Rob, I didna mean ye should offer them yer head.

But ye've made yer point with Lord Drummond. 'Tis obvious ye've treated the lass well—something Drummond canna claim when he took yer lady. Ye've shamed the bastard. Just return the Lady Elspeth now, and all will be well."

Elspeth stared into her soup bowl as if her future floated there among the leeks and bits of chicken.

"No, I willna," Rob said. "I'll no' release her to the likes of Lachlan Drummond."

Elspeth's heart sang, but from the corner of her eye, she could tell Hamish wasn't as happy as she with Rob's words.

"If ye dinna, there'll be war."

"No, I'll call for single combat to settle the matter. It's come two years late, but it's come now and welcome," Rob said. "Drummond's days are numbered. He'll no' be able to walk away from a challenge. Perhaps Fiona will rest easier once the deed's done."

Elspeth's heart plummeted. He still intended to kill Lachlan. None of their time together had changed a thing. This was just about revenge for his dead wife.

A young girl with a cascade of golden curls spilling down her back took up a harp and began to sing. Rob seemed to enjoy the music as much as anyone, but Elspeth didn't miss the sly looks the girl cast in his direction when the lyrics spoke of love.

Her song of longing was directed at Rob. Only a blind man would miss it. Elspeth couldn't bear to remain in the hall for another moment. At the end of the third tune, she stood and asked to be excused.

"Ye dinna wish to retire yet." Rob stood and took one of her hands. "The night is young. Margot Beaton is a talented singer, and she knows a hundred songs. Each of them lovelier than the last. I'm certain she'd take a request, if ye have a favorite."

Elspeth didn't think the girl would take a request from anyone but Rob. "I've no ear for music this night."

His brow furrowed. "Are ye unwell?"

"No," she said. "Just verra tired."

He nodded and signaled one of his men. "Light the Lady Elspeth to her chamber, Albus."

Her belly spiraled slowly downward. Rob wasn't going to escort her to her room.

"And stand watch over her door till ye are relieved," he added. The next song was beginning, and Rob's gaze flicked to the pretty minstrel. "See that none enter the Lady Elspeth's chamber...or leave."

If Rob had slapped her, she'd have been less surprised. She wasn't manacled and chained to a wall, but she was definitely his prisoner. It was as if the last few days hadn't happened at all. The air seemed to flee from the hall, and her vision tunneled for a moment. Then she forced herself to breathe, and Rob's face came back into focus.

"Good night, my lady," he said and sketched a courtly bow.

She narrowly resisted the urge to kick his bowed head into next week. If she did, the people of *Caisteal Dubh* would probably tear her to pieces. Instead, she dropped a curtsey. "My lord."

Then she followed Albus and his torch out of the hall and through the dark corridors to her very gilded cage.

Chapter 27

AFTER ALBUS LIT A CANDLE FOR HER OUTSIDE HER chamber, he ushered her in and closed the door. The latch dropped into place behind her with finality.

Elspeth refused help from a serving woman, so Albus called none to aid her. It was better to be alone with her thoughts than be the object of a lady's maid's speculations. The room was cold despite the lit braziers. She could see her breath.

She wiggled quickly out of the borrowed finery and draped it with care on the ornately carved trunk to which it would be returned. Shivering, she slipped on the fresh chemise that Aileen had left draped across the foot of the bed next to a warm bed shawl.

The linen was frail and the lace at the bodice yellowed with age, but it would serve.

She had no desire to climb into the thick feather tick yet, though it looked inviting. The room smelled much sweeter since the linens had been changed and the mattress aired. The window was still propped open slightly, but the glowing braziers weren't keeping up with the cold that rushed in with the fresh air.

Elspeth wrapped a shawl around her shoulders, walked over to the window, and looked out, hugging herself against the breath of winter. Fires from her father's encampment dotted the plain beyond the curtain wall, hundreds of men intent on freeing her from Rob's imprisonment.

Of course, some of the men were Lachlan's, but she wasn't sure why he was even here. He couldn't claim to love her. He didn't even know her. Drummond could have arrayed his fighting men against Rob only out of a sense of insult to his own honor, not hers.

But even after all that had happened, her father was here because he loved her. She was surer of that than of the beating of her own heart. Her longing to see someone she was certain loved her made her chest ache.

Even if Albus would allow her to leave her room, she wondered if she'd be brave enough to slip into the chapel, pry up the flooring under the altar, and steal out through the secret entrance to *Caisteal Dubh* all alone.

Hamish was right. The only way to resolve this crisis short of bloodshed was for her to leave.

Which was why Rob put her under guard, she realized. Just in case she should decide to flee. He wanted the coming fight, and he wouldn't be denied. There wasn't a pinch of forgiveness in him.

"Ye bloody-minded man," she muttered.

She looked into the bailey at the cobbles far below. Her belly clenched at the sheer drop. Fiona MacLaren had willingly taken just such a long fall, never knowing what her action would set in motion.

What misery drove her to that awful choice? Elspeth wondered if Fiona repented that last step as she fell to her death. Did she cry out for mercy as the ground rose to meet her? Or did she fly into eternity with her lips closed and her eyes wide open?

Elspeth's heart pounded. She wouldn't make the same choice. She may have behaved stupidly with Robin MacLaren, but she'd not compound the pain for her parents by adding to their grief. She stepped back from the window and closed the wooden shutters tight, blocking out the night.

Maybe Fiona thought taking her own life was the only way to prove Lachlan Drummond had raped her. Or maybe she couldn't bear to live with the memories of what had happened to her. Or had she gone mad and was incapable of choice?

There was no way to know what had buzzed in her brain at the last. Perhaps that was why Rob was so obsessed with avenging her. He didn't know *why*. Could never know why.

And killing Drummond seemed the only way to still his wife's ghost.

Her head ached. She wondered if that meant she was about to be visited by her Gift or if she was just tired of thinking so hard.

She padded to the big bed, drew back the coverlet, and climbed in. The linens were icy, and there was no one to place heated stones at her feet. She might ask for whatever she pleased, Rob had said, but not if she was no better than a prisoner.

She curled into a tight ball and covered her head, trying to warm the space with her own breath. Between breaths, she heard a soft scraping sound, like stone moving on stone. She peered over the top of the coverlet to see the tapestry on the wall opposite her bed bulge out. The corner lifted, and a figure stepped from behind it, exposing a dark opening in the stone itself.

Her breath hissed over her teeth.

"Hush, *leannán*," came a whisper. "'Tis only me."

She sat upright. "Rob?"

"Who else were ye expecting, lass?" he whispered back. Rob walked toward the bed, peeling off his plaid as he came. "I wasn't sure the doorway from the laird's chamber to this one still worked. It hasna been tried since my father's time, ye ken, but the workmanship was solid, and the lever still moved the stone."

"What are ye doing here?" She lay back down and pulled the covers up to her nose.

His smile flashed white even in the dim light of the braziers. "That should be obvious." He pulled off his boots and stockings, unbelted his kilt, and let it drop to the floor. He stood by the side of her bed in just his thigh-length shirt with his hands fisted on his waist. "I'm come to bed my beloved."

"No," she hissed, mindful of Albus outside her door.

He frowned down at her. "What d'ye mean 'no'?"

"I mean unless ye intend to tie me down, there'll be no bedding, my lord."

"That sounds like a good game. We'll use the cords holding back the bed curtains, aye?" He pulled down the coverlet and climbed in with her. "Ye surprise me, lass. I didna think ye were so adventurous."

"D'ye want me to scream?" she asked, shocked that he didn't seem the least deterred.

"Only if the pleasure is so great ye canna contain yourself," he said, reaching to pull her close. "But I think we might want to be more discreet than that if we can."

She straight-armed him. "Rob, no."

"Ye're serious?"

"As a three-day toothache."

He raised up, sending cold air spilling under the blankets, and looked down at her. "What's wrong?"

"How can ye ask me that?" She wanted to leap out of bed and pace the room, but it was too cold, and his body had brought much-needed warmth to the sheets before he sat back up. Even now, he generated more heat than both the smoking braziers. "Ye sent me up here alone."

"No, I didna. Albus lit your way."

"Ye know what I mean."

"D'ye think it would have been better for your reputation if I'd escorted ye to your chamber?"

Irritation fizzed in her belly. She hated it when he was right. "Ye set a guard over me while ye make merry in your Great Hall with the people who hate me—"

"No one hates ye." He lay back down and pulled the coverlet over both of them up to their chins.

"Ye dinna wish to see the truth, then." She turned and gave him her back. "Your people blame me for the trouble outside the gates. No one wants me here."

His hand was heavy on her shoulder, warm and reassuring. "*I* want ye here."

"As your prisoner," she said, refusing to be comforted.

"No, love."

He stroked her from the tip of her shoulder to the nape of her neck. She fought against the shiver of delight that danced in the wake of his hand.

"Ye are guarded for your own protection," he said.

"As a man protects his hostage, then." She edged away from him, but not too far. He was so warm. "Ye intend to use me so ye can draw Drummond into single combat. So ye can have your bloody revenge."

He snorted like a stallion. "Aye, that's how it began. I'll no' deny it." Then she felt him shift toward her, and his next words were whispered directly into her ear. "But everything's changed now."

He planted a string of baby kisses along her neck and suckled her earlobe. Her body rioted in pleasure.

"Aye, ye're certainly changed," she said, tamping down her reaction to him. "So polite. So correct, ye are. So reserved to me before your people. I hardly recognize ye."

"But I recognize *ye*. And every time I see ye, I ache to hold ye, Elspeth. I want to sling ye over my shoulder and carry ye off again, with a hand up your skirt fondling yer sweet arse as I go," he said huskily, suiting his actions to his words. "But if I dinna treat ye with distant courtesy before others, how would that look, ye think?"

As if we'd become lovers during the course of our journey, she answered him silently. Her bottom warmed under his touch, but she resisted admitting he was probably wise to restrain himself in public.

"I thought ye'd appreciate that I was having a care for your good name," he said.

He continued to stroke her buttocks, pulling up the thin chemise as he did so, till he touched her bare skin. He circled each globe of her bottom then reached between her legs to cup her sex in his palm. Elspeth bit her lip to keep from making a noise of pleasure, but she knew he could tell her body had roused to him. She was moist and warm and swollen, aching for his touch.

"But if ye dinna care one way or the other," he said as he nuzzled her neck, "I'll swive ye on the main table in the Great Hall on the morrow before God and everybody, instead of breaking my fast."

"Ye willna." She wiggled out of his grasp, rolled over, and faced him. He wrapped his arms around her, and she felt his belly jiggle with a suppressed chuckle.

"No, lass, I willna." He claimed her lips with a quick kiss. "But not for lack of wanting to. Only because I couldna bear for anyone else to see ye in the glorious altogether. That's a delight for me alone."

Against her better judgment, a smile curved her lips. "Ye'll no' be seeing much of me now. 'Tis too cold to go about naked."

"Then I'll have to warm ye," he said, pulling the covers over both their heads. Then he climbed atop her, settling between her legs before she even realized she'd spread them. "Skin against skin is the best thing for warming a body."

"Is it now?"

"Aye, let me show ye." He pulled off his shirt and flipped the blankets back long enough to give it a toss to the floor. There was enough light for Elspeth to catch sight of his handsome face, lit with lust and the promise of fevered lovemaking. Then he covered them again, throwing them into almost total darkness.

"I canna see for ye to show me anything," she said.

"Can ye no'? I'm fair cat-eyed in the dark myself,"

he said. "For instance, I can see to untie your chemise right enough."

She felt his fingers working the drawstring knot above her breasts. After it gave, he spread the neck of her bodice wide.

"And I can see your beautiful breasts." He kissed his way down to an aching nipple.

She couldn't suppress the urge to arch herself into his mouth.

"And if sight fails me," he said as he kissed along the valley between her breasts to claim the other one, "my mouth and hands seem to be able to find their way around ye just fine without my eyes to guide them."

He demonstrated his ability by rucking the chemise up and pulling it over her head before she hardly knew that was his aim. Then he settled again, and his warmth and hard maleness chased away her chills. His lips found hers for a long, deep kiss.

"Oh, Rob," she said when she finally came up for air, "ye make it so hard to think."

"Good, I dinna want ye to think." He smoothed her hair back, kissing her temples, her cheeks, her closed eyes.

"But—"

He covered her lips with a finger. "I only want ye to feel."

He trailed his hand down from her mouth, skimming his fingertips over her chin, her throat. He teased her breasts; then he slid off her so he could continue his journey past her ribs to circle her navel in slow strokes.

"And when we're done feeling?" she asked with a

hitch in her voice. It was hard to think past the next time his fingers left her belly to tease the curling hairs at the juncture of her thighs. "Then what?"

"Dinna fret, lass. I have a plan for us."

He stayed to dally in her damp curls, dividing, lifting, stroking each dewy crevice. Her breath shuddered.

"Trust me," he said softly. "'Twill be all right, ye'll see."

"What…?" She tilted herself into his hand's exploration. Sparks of pleasure licked her. "What d'ye wish me to do?"

"Beg," he whispered. "I wish ye to beg, love."

Chapter 28

"DINNA MOVE, LOVE."

Rob hadn't used the bed-curtain cords to tie her, but Elspeth obeyed his order to keep still all the same. Every time she moved, he stopped. She couldn't bear that.

Every fiber of her body, every finger-width of her skin strained toward him, longing for them to join. He'd teased her with his cock's nearness twice, slipping just the tip of him inside her aching emptiness, but he pulled back to torment her more each time. When she moved to stroke him, to entice him back, he gently pushed her hand away, pinioning her spread-eagled.

"This time is for ye, Elspeth." He kissed down her ribs, past her belly, and settled between her splayed legs. "I dinna wish ye to think on anything but your own pleasure."

"What of your pleasure?" she'd asked between gasps as his tongue flogged her intimate places.

He paused, midlick. "Any man who says this didna give him pleasure is a dead man. I love the soft, secret parts of ye, Elspeth, all musky sweet with your dew. And I love that this special bit of ye is only for me."

She was ready to surrender every bit of herself, not just the throbbing mass between her legs. She trembled. She lost control of her limbs. She balled the sheets in her tightly clenched fists. She drew near, teetering on sharp-edged longing. Then as the first contraction pulsed in her nether lips, Rob pulled back.

"Ach, Rob, please!"

He rose and covered her, mouth to mouth, body to body. His full length filled her in one long thrust, and she was once again near the edge of bliss.

"That's all I was waiting for, love," he whispered. "Ye beg so prettily, how can I refuse ye?"

He rocked his hips, and the pressure on her sensitive spot sent her over the edge. Her inner walls spasmed around him in violent embrace. It was as if she was coming unraveled, and the only thing keeping her from unspooling completely was the solid length of his cock. He arched his back, plunging deeper as she continued to pulse.

His kiss swallowed up her cry of completion.

Once she finally stopped throbbing, he began to move slowly. Still aglow from her release, Elspeth fell into rhythm with him. She peppered his neck with kisses. She whispered urgent endearments. She loved every bit of this man with every bit of herself.

And when he came inside her, she held his shuddering frame, still rocking against him, drawing him farther in. He was hers. She would have all of him.

Peace descended like a mantle, draping over them,

SINS OF THE HIGHLANDER

sheltering them. The armies beyond the walls faded from Elspeth's mind. There was no rush. No need. All that mattered was holding each other and protecting their joining for as long as it could last.

"I love ye, lass," Rob whispered as he finally slipped out of her. "Ye ken that, aye?"

"Aye. Ye loved me so well I almost dinna need to hear it, but I'm glad for it all the same," she whispered back. "I love ye, too."

"On the morrow—"

"Let's not waste our time together on such things." She put a finger to his lips. "The morrow will care for itself."

"All right." He rolled to one side and snugged her against him. "What shall we talk of, then?"

"I wasna thinking of talking." She stole away from him and out from under the covers, braving the cold room long enough to retrieve one of the bed-curtain cords. "I was wondering what it will take to make *ye* beg."

❧

The morning dawned gray and mizzling. No hint of the sun's warmth cut through the lowering sky. Rob girded himself in his hardened leather breastplate and strapped on his greaves and forearm guards. He was determined to have his parley with Stewart and Drummond before the heavens burst open and the light rain became a drenching torrent. He mounted the second-best horse in his stable.

He missed Falin. Since the stallion hadn't found his way back to his own stall, Rob feared the worst. He hated to imagine Falin coming to a bad end in a wolf's belly. He preferred thinking the wicked beastie was kicking up his heels, wallowing in his freedom, and rutting every stray mare he found.

Hamish sauntered into the stable and swung his leg up and over a roan gelding.

"Ye dinna have to come with me," Rob said.

"I'm no' likely to let ye go alone, am I?" Hamish said.

"I'll come to no harm under a flag of truce." Rob nudged his mount into a sedate walk across the bailey. Hamish rode alongside as the milling populace parted before them. Rob motioned for the portcullis to be raised, and the drawbridge lowered.

"Ordinarily, I'd agree with ye. Men of honor respect an offer to parley." Hamish hefted the pole with the white flag fluttering at the top, and clomped across the bridge behind Rob. "But that means ye must trust Lachlan Drummond to be honorable. I've no' got that much trust in me. Ye might have signaled from the safety of the walls and given Stewart and Drummond safe conduct."

"No, I need to be seen making this offer of peace," Rob said. "By both sides."

But only one person seeing him do this really mattered to him. He knew Elspeth watched him from the battlements of *Caisteal Dubh*, though he resisted turning to look at her. She needed to see that he was trying to settle this impasse, that he wished to make peace with her father.

But damned if he'd make peace with her former bridegroom.

"This canna be. 'Tis a trick," Lachlan said, narrowing his eyes at the approaching pair of horsemen. The colors of the caparison on one of the mounts declared its rider was the MacLaren himself. "Mad Rob wasna inside the castle when we parleyed last week. And not a soul has entered or left while we bided here."

"That's as may be, but they come under a flag of truce," Stewart said, pulling on his heavy gloves. "The riders halted beyond the range of their archers and within the reach of ours. 'Tis a gesture of good faith. Whoever it is on that horse may have news of Elspeth, at least. I'm willing to hear what they have to say. " He shot a cold glare at Drummond. "Come or stay, as ye will. 'Tis of no consequence to me what ye do."

In the time they'd been encamped before the castle walls, squabbles between their men had strained the relationship between the two lairds. Drummond watched his ally stalk toward the groom who led the Stewart's horse from the picket lines. If Stewart's daughter was dead, their alliance was on shaky ground at best. It was time to mend the damage. Lachlan signaled for his horse to be brought as well.

But he didn't hurry. The riders from the castle were the ones who wanted to parley, not he. He would have been just as happy to mount up and ride back to his own stronghold for the rest of the winter.

Once there, he'd be able to plan and find someone from *Caisteal Dubh* with a grudge against his laird deep enough that he might be bribed into opening the gates for Lachlan's assault come spring.

The Dark Castle had never been taken from

without. No one had tried to take it from within, but Lachlan was willing to be the first.

But Stewart would brook no delay in settling this question. If Drummond could have left him there in the mud and still kept his agreements with Stewart intact, he'd have been gone in a heartbeat.

When Alistair saw that Lachlan was making ready to join him, he reined in his mount and waited just beyond the first ranks of men. Lachlan knew all eyes were trained on them as he caught up to Stewart and they rode to meet the delegation from the castle.

He straightened his spine. Men respected strength, so he always tried to project it.

But *his* men also appreciated guile. Cunning was strength of a sort, after all. Lachlan wasn't about to disappoint them.

❦

"Well, Robbie," Hamish said as Stewart and Drummond approached at a trot. "Ye're about to get yer wish. Dinna say I didna warn ye."

Rob raised a hand in greeting and also to show that he was unarmed.

Alistair Stewart's eyes flared with recognition as they drew closer. Lachlan's shifted from Rob to the castle and back, clearly reasoning that there were more ways into the stronghold than met the eye.

"Where's my daughter?" Stewart demanded.

"Straight to the point. I respect that," Rob said. "Your daughter is safe and well."

"Ye'll pardon me if we're disinclined to take the word of a madman," Lachlan said.

Rob reached into his saddlebag. His opponents' hands shot to the hilts of their swords. They hadn't come unarmed to parley.

"One moment, and ye'll be able to see for yourself," he promised Elspeth's father. He drew out a pair of glass discs and attached them at either end of a leather cylinder. His grandfather had brought the strange ocular device home from the Crusades, and it was one of Rob's most prized possessions. He always called it his "Grandsire's Eye." He handed it to Stewart. "Look at the rightmost turret. Elspeth is there."

Lord Stewart brought the glass to his eye and scanned the battlements for a few heartbeats. A smile burst over his face. "I wish to speak with her."

"That I cannot allow," Rob said. "But you have my word she is being well treated. No harm will come to her while she bides in my care."

"So ye willna kill her as ye threatened?" Lachlan asked with a sneer.

Rob ignored him and spoke directly to Elspeth's father. "Your daughter has naught to fear from me."

Stewart's gaze flicked to Drummond. "We've been told she was injured."

"Aye, she was," Rob said with a glare at Drummond. "But no' by me."

"All this talk is a waste of time," Drummond said. "Ye've heard our demands, aye?"

"Aye," Rob said calmly. "Ye wish the return of Elspeth Stewart, which I'm prepared to consider. My head is no' negotiable."

"All I want is my daughter," Stewart said.

"Then you and I can come to an accord," Rob

said, deciding he liked Elspeth's father. "I'm prepared to release the lady to ye, Lord Stewart, on the condition that her betrothal to Lachlan Drummond be sundered immediately."

"Ye canna do that," Lachlan thundered. "There have been agreements made, moneys paid."

"Unmake them. Return the money," Rob said. "I'll no' release the Lady Elspeth if there's the slightest chance she'll be forced into marriage with ye. Ye may lay a siege on *Caisteal Dubh* till Our Lord comes again, but I willna budge. On that matter, ye have my solemn promise."

Stewart didn't speak, but Rob could see he was considering the offer seriously.

"And once she is free, Lord Stewart, I ask your leave to court her and marry her," Rob said.

"So that's what ye're about!" Lachlan all but pounced. "Ye wish to increase yer herds and lands by yoking yourself to the House of Stewart."

Rob shook his head and turned back to Elspeth's father. "I ask no dowry. I'll pay whatever bride price ye name, my lord. My men will answer your call should ye find yourself in need of MacLaren swords, with no return promise of aid. All I want from you is your daughter to be my wife. That's riches enough for any man."

"*If* I accept your terms, and I'm no' saying I do, ye must accept mine as well, MacLaren," Elspeth's father said. "While I might give consent to ye courting her, I'll no' force Elspeth to marry anyone. It didna work the first time. If she willna have ye, there's an end to it, aye?"

"Agreed." Rob's chest burned with triumph. Elspeth would be his. He was certain of it.

Lachlan Drummond's face was turning an unhealthy shade of scarlet.

"And as for the second of your demands, I'll make it part of my own," Rob said, turning to Drummond. "Ye may have my head, Lachlan, if ye're man enough to take it. Before I release the Lady Elspeth to her father's keeping, ye and I will meet in single combat."

"Why should I agree to that when we have your castle surrounded?" Lachlan said. "Your people willna be satisfied to stay inside the walls come spring when there's planting to be done."

"Spring's a long ways off," Rob said. "D'ye really intend to pass Christmastide in a cold siege instead of warm by your own hearth? I'd warrant a coward such as yourself would prefer that."

Drummond drew his sword in one smooth motion.

"Peace!" Stewart thundered, drawing his own and crossing it over Lachlan's. "We are under a flag of truce, and the man is unarmed."

"He insulted me!"

"Then accept his challenge," Stewart said.

"Can ye no' see what he's doing?" Lachlan returned his sword to its sheath sullenly. "He only made this offer to divide us."

"If so, he's done a good job of it," Hamish muttered under his breath.

"Ye'll have your answer on the morrow, MacLaren," Lord Stewart said as he returned Rob's glass device. "I thank ye for your care of my daughter. I trust it will continue, whatever our decision."

Rob nodded solemnly.

The Stewart reined his horse around and rode off the field. Lachlan glared at Rob.

"If we meet in battle, ye should know I give no quarter," Drummond said.

"And I was set to show ye mercy," Rob answered pleasantly; then his face went hard as winter oak. "The same mercy ye showed my wife."

Chapter 29

"Ye canna mean to consider this lunatic's proposal!" Lachlan slammed his fist on the ornate travel table positioned in the center of Stewart's pavilion. The large tent was furnished as comfortably as if it were a room in his keep, complete with a camp bed, a wash stand, and a wolf-pelt rug. Drummond's camp was far more spartan than his wealthier ally's. "We had an agreement!"

Stewart's eyes glittered dangerously at him. "And I'm of a mind to alter that agreement." He returned his attention to the stack of missives that had come by courier earlier that day, as if he were totally unconcerned by Lachlan's outburst. At least one of the messages bore the royal seal. "So far, there's no evidence MacLaren has harmed my daughter. She looked healthy, clean, and well fed. She even smiled a time or two while I looked at her. Why should I not consider what he had to say?"

"He admits she was injured. The bastard shot her with a crossbow bolt." Lachlan paced the perimeter of the tent. "I saw him do it with my own eyes."

"Aye, so ye say." Stewart looked up from his missives only briefly. "He denies it."

"Are ye calling me a liar?"

"I'm saying it was dark, and the eye can play tricks." Lachlan dragged a hand over his face. "Ye're distraught, so I'll let that go for the sake of our bonds."

"What puzzles me is why ye dinna wish to fight the MacLaren," Stewart said, laying aside the stack of correspondence. "I've a feeling if the tables were turned and ye had stolen his bride at the altar, heaven and earth couldna turn him from taking up his sword against ye."

"I dinna know why ye hold the MacLaren's actions up to be admired and repeated. He broke the sanctity of a kirk, for Christ's sake! He stole your daughter. Probably stole her maidenhead as well. The man's no' exactly sane."

"He seemed perfectly sane to me, and you will keep your scurrilous assumptions to yourself. There's no evidence he's harmed Elspeth in *any* way. It appears she's been accorded every respect." Stewart rose to his feet and stared at Lachlan until he was forced to look away. Then Stewart took his seat once more and picked up another oilskin packet, breaking the seal with his dirk.

"But he demanded we sever our alliance."

"And if ye kill the MacLaren in single combat, perhaps we'd renew it. Ye can take him surely," Stewart said. "All in all, his demands dinna seem unreasonable."

Stewart would think that. He wasn't risking his neck in single combat with the bloody MacLaren. Lachlan had the reputation of being a wicked swordsman, and it was well deserved in his younger days. But drink and soft living had caused him to lose a step or two, more than might be expected of a man who should be in his prime. Sometimes, his hand shook uncontrollably when he took up a blade, one of the reasons he'd shifted to the crossbow as his weapon of choice. Now he fought only men he was certain he could kill. Whether by superior swordsmanship or by cunning.

He didn't feel confident either would help him best Rob MacLaren.

"What do ye intend on the morrow, Stewart?"

"I havena decided." Alistair Stewart sent him a withering glance. "Ye'll know when I give my answer to the MacLaren, but if I were you, I'd polish up my swordplay. Now will ye leave me in peace? I've been gone from home too long, and there's a great deal here that requires my attention."

Lachlan shoved out of the tent flap and stomped toward his encampment. Matters were spiraling out of control. He had to get a grip on them again. His body servant had lit the lamp inside his tent and stood by ready to serve, but it would take too long for him to pour wine into a horn. Lachlan lifted the wineskin from its peg and upended it into his mouth in a long stream of red.

"Leave me," he growled and swiped his mouth on his sleeve.

The fellow, whose name Lachlan couldn't even remember, bowed and started to sidle out.

"No, wait." An idea suddenly rushed into him. "Send Randall to me."

Randall was the best marksman under Lachlan's

command. He was wicked enough with a long bow, but deadly accurate with a crossbow. And best of all, he owed Lachlan more fealty than was common, since he'd killed a man and Drummond had covered the deed for him by accusing and executing someone else for the crime. Randall was bound to serve the House of Drummond by an oath he dared not break.

When the man appeared, Lachlan didn't acknowledge his presence for about ten heartbeats. He was still poking at his idea to see if he could detect any flaws. He found none.

"I want you to leave camp this night."

"Where am I bound, my lord?"

"I want ye to find a place to hide near the castle walls, a snug spot from which ye can shoot a bolt far enough to reach the place where we held parley this day."

"Ye mean for me to kill the MacLaren by stealth?"

"No," Drummond said with a sly smile. "On my signal, I want you to plant your bolt in the heart of Alistair Stewart."

After a few more instructions, the man left, ready to make his way to a place of concealment. On the morrow, because of the direction of the bolt's path, it would seem as if one of MacLaren's men broke the truce and killed Stewart. After that, Stewart's men would never let MacLaren or his second reach the safety of their castle. They'd be torn to pieces before their own walls.

If there were men worthy of the name inside the castle, they'd not suffer their laird to be cut down before their eyes. The Clan MacLaren would throw open the gates and flood out to meet the angry Stewarts. Lachlan would quietly lead the Clan Drummond from the field.

And when the dust settled and the bodies were collected, there'd be two clans in want of leadership, weakened and broken. And they'd both be beholden to him for keeping his head and negotiating a peace settlement between them, a settlement that would include fealty and yearly tributes to be paid to the Clan Drummond.

Lachlan might be laird in all but name of three clans by the time the moon rose twice.

❧

Elspeth felt better about attending supper this night. Rob's people had been friendlier to her all day—all but Mrs. Beaton and her niece Margot. When Elspeth stood at the battlements, folk talked of her bringing their laird luck in his negotiations. And since he returned to the castle unharmed, she was considered *good* luck.

Rob had come to escort her down to the Great Hall again, and she was greeted warmly by several people who'd glared at her the night before as they took their place of honor. Rob looked so handsome, she could scarcely tear her eyes from him. Though he didn't share what he'd discussed with her father, he assured her she'd be happy about it once he was able to tell her.

"At least, I hope ye'll be happy," he'd said, stealing a quick kiss in a dark corridor on their way down to the evening meal.

She didn't think she could cram in much more happiness than she felt now. If only she didn't have this niggling headache. It was like a claw at the base of her skull, and nothing she did could shake it.

She took a sip of wine, hoping that might ease the discomfort. Then one of the serving girls lit another candle at the end of their table, and suddenly her vision tunneled and Elspeth was sucked into the flame.

Brightness burned the backs of her eyes. Then the light dimmed, and she could see.

Oh, God! The battle scene. Not again.

Hundreds of bodies littered the field, bleeding into winter-brown grass. Corbies cried and circled overhead, waiting. Women culled items of value from the fallen or searched, weeping, for dead loved ones. A large carrion bird swooped down, impatient for the upright humans to clear the heath so the corbies could feast on the bodies that remained.

Elspeth wandered through the glen of death, looking for something. She knew not what. The only thing that made it possible for her to put one foot before another was her certainty that she had Seen this battle before. This was all but a vision, as insubstantial as a dream and over as quickly.

Someone groaned, a dying man among the dead. Another bleated piteously for his mother. Whose son was he? She couldn't see his face.

No, he didn't have a face.

She jerked her gaze away. It started to rain, heaven weeping for the fallen.

Oh, Merciful God! This vision was different. She saw something she recognized—a scrap of Stewart plaid. She ran toward it. Her father stared unblinking into the dripping sky. A crossbow bolt protruded from his chest. She sank down beside him, rocking in agony. A soft keening escaped her throat.

Then a shout drew her gaze. A rabble had surrounded a single man. He fought like a demon, slashing and turning, but there were too many. A blade cut him, and he roared in agony. They closed in like wolves around a wounded buck. As he went down, he turned toward her, and she saw his face for a blink before they hacked him to pieces.

Rob!

The blades fell like scythes on wheat.

Someone started wailing, a wordless cry with no end.

Elspeth had no idea the screams came from her. Even once the mists of Sight faded and she was back in the Great Hall of *Caisteal Dubh*, she couldn't make herself stop.

Mrs. Beaton and Nessa followed Rob when he carried a shrieking Elspeth up the long stairs, away from the shocked faces in the Great Hall. While he paced outside the room, Elspeth calmed a bit, crying out only at intervals as portions of the vision seeped back into her in stark clarity.

The serving women stripped her of her evening finery and put her back into her chemise for bed, murmuring softly to each other but not to Elspeth. She wasn't offended. Their words were only muffled sounds, garbled and wavering, as if they spoke underwater. She didn't know if she could have answered them intelligibly anyway.

Mrs. Beaton sent Nessa for a steaming cup of willow-bark tea, and supervised while Elspeth drank it. Only then did Elspeth's heaving sobs finally subside into sniffles. Rob burst into the room, despite his housekeeper's protest, refusing to be kept out a moment longer.

"Hush, *leannán*," Rob crooned, stroking her brow. They were the first words that made sense to Elspeth's mind. "There's no need for tears." He turned to the servants standing by Elspeth's bedside. "Leave us."

"But, my lord, 'tis not seemly for ye to—" Mrs. Beaton began.

"And it's no' seemly for ye to question your laird," Rob fired back at her. "If ye canna obey a simple command, mayhap ye need to seek employment elsewhere."

"As ye wish, my lord," Mrs. Beaton said, tight-lipped. The serving girl, Nessa, followed her out of the chamber. When the door was open, Elspeth caught sight of Albus's long, worried face in the corridor. He'd taken up his post as her guard once more. Her heart was eased by his presence this time.

Elspeth thought she heard the brush of a corbie's wing making a low pass over the room. She grasped Rob's shirt and pulled him close. "Rob?"

"Aye, love, I'm here. There's naught to fear. None will harm ye, no' while I breathe."

"Oh, but they'll harm ye," she sobbed.

"Whist, now, no one's going to harm me." He cradled her head on his chest. "Where d'ye get such notions?"

She sat up straight. "Because I've Seen it."

In halting words, she started to recount the details of her horrifying vision.

"I told ye I have the Sight. My Gift visited me this night, and if ye leave the castle, if ye meet Lachlan on the field of battle..." Her voice faltered.

"Then I'll kill the blackguard."

"Ye'll die, Rob. Ye'll die horribly, and I willna be able to bear it." She pounded a fist on his chest once. "And so will my father."

Hot tears scalded her cheeks, and she fought for breath.

"But ye're wrong, *leannán*. In your vision, ye see many men dead on a field of battle. But there won't be any battle," he said, stroking her softly. "On the morrow, I'll meet Drummond in single combat. Your father will be in no danger. This vision isna a true one."

"All my visions are true," she said woodenly. He might not be planning a battle, but one would overtake him nonetheless. The knowledge pressed against her chest, heavy as an anvil. If Rob parleyed with Drummond again, he and her father would die.

Unless she did something about it.

Chapter 30

"Father Kester, might I have a word with ye?" Mrs. Beaton cornered the young priest at his evening prayers before the altar of the chapel. Father Kester rose, crossed himself elaborately, and walked toward her. Bookish and long-winded, he didn't even have a pleasant voice for singing the mass. Mrs. Beaton had thought him a young fool when he first came.

Now she'd see if he could be a useful young fool.

"Of course, Mrs. Beaton. I live to serve the souls here," he said. "But please be brief. I was heading to my pallet. We who keep the canonical hours dinna get much sleep, ye ken. What's this about?"

"Well, I'm usually not one to carry tales, but some troubling matters have come to my attention."

"Troubling? In what manner?"

"In a spiritual manner, Father, else I'd not have come to ye," she said primly. "I greatly fear an evil has come upon the people of Clan MacLaren."

"Whist, ye needn't fear." He patted her shoulder as if he were very much older and wiser than she, though he was young enough to be her grandson.

A sanctimonious, half-witted grandson. "My studies have prepared me to deal with every wile the devil may use to lure us into sin."

"Indeed? And did they prepare ye to recognize and try a witch?"

His sandy brows shot skyward. Prosecuting a witch, especially if she could be proved to be consorting with the devil in the most lurid fashion, won a certain notoriety for the priest who successfully convicted and punished her. Father Kester was the ambitious sort.

"And who d'ye think might be wandering such a grave path of error within these walls?" he asked.

Unfortunately, his ambition was far greater than his intellect. Mrs. Beaton restrained herself from rolling her eyes. "Were ye no' in the Great Hall at supper this night?"

"Ye mean the Lady Elspeth?"

"Aye, she was possessed of Satan himself, I'll warrant."

"Hmmm. I was at the other end of the hall when all the commotion started, and our laird spirited her out of the hall verra quickly," he said, tapping his teeth with a long fingernail. "I just thought the young woman had seen a mouse. There've been plenty of them of late." He shuddered. "Nasty wee beasties."

Mrs. Beaton bristled at the slight to her house-keeping skills. "Well, she didna see a mouse, but she was seeing something else right enough, or so she claimed. The devil was showing her a battle, she said. The last battle, I'm thinking, and Elspeth Stewart was shrieking encouragement to his evil horde."

"Ye're certain of these things?"

"Certain as I'm standing here. I helped put her to bed whilst she raved," she said. "Did ye no' wonder how the MacLaren won his way back into the castle without coming through one of the locked gates?"

"No, I simply thanked God for granting us a miracle."

Simple is right. "I'm thinking another power might be responsible for his sudden appearance among us, and the devil used Elspeth Stewart to spirit our laird back into his stronghold. Witches can fly, ye ken."

"I've heard of such things." Father Kester narrowed his eyes. "I'd need proof, o' course."

"Oh, aye, there's proof and more. Much more, and several who can bear witness to her unholy bent, and…" Mrs. Beaton lowered her voice to a whisper. "There's an unusual mark upon her person, high up on her…well, best we not speak here where anyone might stumble on our counsels."

"Will ye step into my private chamber?"

Mrs. Beaton nodded and followed him to his spartan little cell. She'd see the way cleared for her niece to become the lady of this place or know the reason why. By the time she was done with Father Kester, he'd be ready to light the fagots beneath Elspeth Stewart's feet with his own hand.

"T'would be best for the sake of my good name that ye be seen leaving my chamber verra soon," Elspeth said. "Albus is watching outside the door and forming his own conclusions. Besides, your people need to see ye in the Great Hall. Ye dinna realize how much heart they draw from ye."

Rob argued for a bit but finally gave in. "I'll check on ye later then," he said.

"I usually sleep like the dead after a visit from my Gift," she warned.

He kissed her cheek. "Verra well. I'll no' disturb ye." Then a rogue's smile tilted his lips. "But if ye wake in the night and wish to disturb *me*, slip under the tapestry and come to my chamber."

"I might do that," she said, wishing it could be so.

"I'll just stay till ye're asleep, then," Rob said and would not be dissuaded. He pulled a chair next to her bedside to keep watch over her.

Elspeth closed her eyes, intending to feign sleep. But she was skimming the surface of slumber in truth, almost ready to sink into oblivion, when she heard the door latch lift and fall back into place. She forced an eye open.

Rob was gone.

Even though her head still pounded, she dragged herself from bed. With haste, she donned the skirt and leather bodice she'd worn when she and Rob arrived at *Caisteal Dubh*. She needed the broad skirt if she was to ride astride, assuming the horses hadn't been turned out of the cave. Then she rifled through Lady MacLaren's clothes trunk and found the warm cloak Rob had mentioned. As he described it, the cloak had a hood with a wee tassel and a fine copper brooch.

She plumped a pair of pillows and arranged them to mock a sleeping form. After she pocketed the tinderbox, she blew out the candle Rob had left burning. Then she slipped under the tapestry.

It was the first time she'd been in Rob's chamber.

The room was smaller than the one he'd assigned to her, the furnishings less ornate and more masculine. But there was a fireplace on the outer wall for heat instead of braziers. And the ceiling soared clear to the distant thatch on the top of the turret.

The massive bed looked soft and inviting.

What would Rob do if he found her snuggled between his sheets when he returned after supper? A number of wicked possibilities sprang to mind, and her body felt hot and achy at the mere thought.

This is the chamber where he bedded his wife, she realized suddenly.

The fact that he invited Elspeth to join him in this very bed must mean the madness that drove him at first was fading. His wife's ghost troubled him less and less. Elspeth wished she could stay and love away that last bit of bitterness and anger and grief from his heart.

But the only way to show Rob she loved him was to leave as quickly as possible. It was all she could think to do to stop her vision from coming to pass.

She lifted the latch and peered into the corridor. The space was empty, since Albus was around the curve of the wall, guarding her chamber. With extreme care, she pushed the door open and padded out and down the steps, running her fingertips along the stone walls to keep her bearings, since she didn't dare a candle.

On the ground floor, she skirted the Great Hall and stepped into the bailey. Keeping to the shadows, she worked her way around the half-timbered buildings to the chapel.

Candles burned in the nave. She picked one up and

carried it with her into the sanctuary. Stone angels stared down at her from the tops of columns before the ceiling soared in a high arch. No one seemed to be about, so she hurried to the altar and slipped beneath the cloth.

I have to find a way to move the stone.

Lifting her candle, she studied the underside of the altar. Next to the hidden pulley and rope, she found a stout metal bar fastened to the underside of the altar. It seemed to be part of the construction, but the bar slid out from its fastenings easily.

Then she felt for the seam in the stone and wedged the sharp end of the bar into it. The stone lifted enough for her to slip her fingertips underneath it. She raised it another couple inches and then slid the flagstone off the opening with a grunt of effort.

And heard the sudden patter of footsteps. She pinched off the candle and froze in the darkness, ears pricked as the steps came nearer.

"There doesn't seem to be anyone here," someone whispered.

"I'm sure I heard something," another voice said.

"This old chapel has many voices. Ye should hear the way the wind plays tricks on me sometimes."

"Or mayhap the devil's trying to spy on our meeting."

"They do say the Prince of Darkness favors the hour of shadows. Perhaps we should speak more later. In daylight. And no' here, ye ken," the first voice said. "A witch knows where her enemies may be found."

A witch? What on earth are they talking about?

"Verra wise, verra wise," the second voice said, but something about the hissed tone made Elspeth suspect the person speaking wasn't sincere. "I'll see ye on the morrow, then. After the laird parleys with the Stewart and Drummond again. Then we'll see what's what. Good even, Father."

"God send ye rest."

Two pairs of footfalls moved away from the sanctuary, heading in different directions, judging by sound. Elspeth waited until silence reigned for the count of thirty before she twitched so much as an eyelash.

Then she uncoiled the rope attached to the underside of the altar and let it drop into the dark opening. She swung her legs over the edge. She could see nothing below.

Something inside her shivered, and not with cold.

'Tis only a dark space. Nothing to fear, she thought sternly as she started to lower herself. Then her grip on the rope slipped, and she slid the rest of the way down, burning her palms. She landed in a heap at the bottom. Her thigh screamed in pain, and she suspected such rough treatment would have it bleeding again.

Elspeth didn't move for the space of several heartbeats. She strained to listen for any sound that indicated her descent was heard from above. Or attracted attention from anything that might lurk below.

Finally, she stood and felt for the torch. She'd simply dropped it after she stubbed it out when she and Rob used this secret way to enter the castle. It wasn't there. Then she remembered that there were wall notches at the entrance to the cave. If Rob used the torch when he saw to the horses, he'd have replaced it in a holder on the wall when he was done.

Darkness-blind, she swept her fingertips over the rock walls and found the torch. After only a few tries with the flint, she managed a spark which caught, and the torch burned brightly. The smell of pitch and sulfur almost covered the mousy staleness of the underground space.

Then Elspeth retraced her way out. She crept down the long steps, mindful of the slick spots and listening to the steady drip of water through the rocks. She walked softly through the corridor with dark passages leading off at intervals. Once or twice in the corner of her eye, she thought she saw the gleam of feral eyes in the dark, but when she turned her head, they were gone.

Her heart pounded in her throat. She heard the scritching of wee claws on rock and held the torch aloft, banishing the shadows. The temptation to run snatched at her skirts, but she forced herself to keep to a steady walk. She never caught sight of any creeping thing, but she sensed movement in the shadows on all sides.

When she smelled warm dung and hay and heard the soft whicker of the horses ahead, she nearly wept with relief. Rob had been back to see to their care. There was water in their trough and fodder in the manger.

The soft starlight stealing into the opening of the cave was enough for her to see to saddle the mare, so she stubbed out the torch and replaced it in the wall notch. When she led the mare out, the gelding tried to follow, but she pushed him back and reblocked the exit.

"No, my fine lad," she said softly. "There's nothing for ye abroad in the world but misery. Stay with my Rob, now. He may need ye."

As she mounted and rode in the direction of her father's encampment, tears gathered in her eyes. She swiped them away.

He wasn't her Rob. Not really. And he might not ever be.

Chapter 31

ELSPETH WANDERED THE GAME TRAILS, USING THE snow-kissed peak of Ben Vorlick as a touchstone to keep her bearings, always turning the mare's head east toward the fighting men arrayed against her lover. It was still dark when she stumbled onto the outer edges of the armed encampment. Fortunately, the guard standing night watch was a Stewart man and recognized her when she responded to his challenge.

"If it had been one of Drummond's men, they mighta thought ye was another camp follower come to—Oh! Begging your pardon, my lady. O' course, ye're not…oh, bugger!" the poor man stammered. Elspeth suspected the man's ears were bright red, but it was too dark to be sure. "I shouldna ought to've said that."

"No matter. Dinna think on it," she said. "Take me to my father, and all will be well."

Even though dawn was another hour away, her father wasn't asleep. Alistair Stewart's tent glowed with the light of a single lamp. The guards at the entrance didn't try to stop Elspeth from pushing the flap aside.

Her father was sitting at his camp desk, a stack of missives on either side of him. But he wasn't working. His face was buried in his hands. Elspeth suspected he wept. Or prayed.

"Father."

He looked up, and the dark splotches under his eyes made her heart ache. Drawn and haggard, he'd aged a decade since she'd seen him last. Then his face lit in a disbelieving smile.

"If I'm dreaming, may I never wake," he said softly as he rose to his feet.

She rushed to his waiting arms. "Ye're no' dreaming, Father. I suspect ye've no' been asleep often enough of late for that."

He rocked her in a great hug, which she returned just as fiercely. She knew she was blessed to have the affection of her parents when so many were distant with their offspring. Being the last bairn born to the House of Stewart was probably to blame for the way they doted on her, but she'd not complain, whatever the reason. She leaned into her father's love, but it didn't begin to fill the gaping hole where Rob should be.

Would Rob hate her when he realized she'd tricked him and run back to her father?

"How did ye manage to escape?"

The last thing she wanted was to divulge the secret of the back door into the castle. Rob had trusted her with it. She couldn't betray him.

"That's no' important," she said. "I'm here now, and I want to go home. Please, Father, take me home. Let's go now."

"There'll be time enough for that." He held her at

arm's length. "Tell me what happened to ye. Did the man force...did he hurt ye, daughter?"

She shook her head, knowing her father asked if she was yet a maiden. She hoped heaven would forgive her small lie to spare his sensibilities. "The MacLaren did me no hurt."

Rob gave her only unspeakable bliss and the love she'd always longed for.

Her father released her and motioned for her to sit. She sank gratefully onto his clothes trunk. "Then your marriage to Lachlan Drummond can go forward."

"No. I'll no' marry the Drummond. No' after what I've learned of him." Elspeth told him about Rob's claim that Lachlan had raped his wife and driven her to her death.

"I've heard this rumor. Drummond denies it."

"But I believe the MacLaren," Elspeth said. "Lachlan Drummond is no' the man ye think he is. Ye canna make me wed him. Please dinna try."

"I'm your father, lass." His voice held a hard edge. "If I say ye'll wed him, ye will."

Elspeth tried to control the tremors that threatened to take her, but failed. She'd been reluctant to wed before, but her parents had coaxed her into it with gentleness. Always indulgent, her father didn't seem the sort to force her into a match.

"Lord Drummond and I have made some solemn agreements, and..." Alistair Stewart must have noticed the way she shivered. He poured a horn of wine and pressed it into her shaking hands. "All right, daughter. I'll see what I can do."

Elspeth grasped his hand and pressed a kiss on it,

relief making her slightly light-headed. "Thank ye, Father. Now, I know ye dinna approve of the Sight, but I must tell ye I've had a visit from my Gift."

Stewart shook his head. "Oh, lass—"

"Please listen. I've had this same vision half-a-dozen times but never understood why I was shown it. Now its meaning has finally become clear to me. Believe me when I tell ye, ye're in mortal danger." She set down the drinking horn, heedless that it bobbled and overturned. The red wine spilled, pooling like a bloodstain on the camp carpet. Elspeth dropped to her knees before her father. "If ever ye bore me the slightest filial love, call your lieutenants to ye. Ye must strike the camp and be ready to ride at first light."

༄

"The siege is lifted! They're leaving," Hamish called down from the battlements.

Rob sprinted across the bailey, strapping on his sword and buckler as he went. Hamish's summons had been so urgent he hadn't even taken time to check on Elspeth before he threw on his clothing and bolted out of his chamber. He'd peeked under the tapestry last night and saw her still form in the bed. After her terrifying outburst in the Great Hall, he'd decided to let her sleep undisturbed.

"Come see for yourself!" Hamish shouted and looked through Rob's "Grandsire's Eye" again. "Stewart has struck his colors. He's withdrawing."

Rob climbed the steps to the ramparts, taking them two at a time.

"Wait! Who's that with him?" Hamish said, still peering through the system of lenses. "A woman!"

"Wherever there's an army, there are always camp followers," Rob said, snatching the looking device from him and bringing it to his eye.

"That's no camp follower," Hamish said. "That's a noblewoman."

Rob recognized the hooded cloak, and his gut sank with foreboding. The woman reined in her mount and turned to look back at the castle. Her face came into sharp focus in the center of his wavering lens.

"Elspeth," Rob whispered.

"Aye, I thought as much, but I didna wish to say so until ye'd had a chance to see for yerself," Hamish said with a heavy sigh. "All that unholy racket she made at supper must have been a ruse to lessen our watchfulness of her. But she didna slip out any of the gates. We're locked down tight as a tick. How the devil did she manage to escape?"

Rob knew, but he couldn't say. He'd trusted her with the secret known only to the lairds of the castle, and she'd used the secret passage. Now she was riding off behind her father on the mare Rob had bought for her in Lochearnhead.

"Elspeth!" he shouted. His voice echoed back from the surrounding peaks. She didn't turn to look this time.

Rob handed the Grandsire's Eye back to Hamish. Then he raced down the steps to the bailey, bellowing for his groom to saddle a horse for him.

"What are ye doing?" Hamish dogged his steps. "Stewart may be leaving, but Drummond's men are still out there. If ye set foot outside the castle walls without a flag of truce, they'll cut ye down in a heartbeat."

"Then get me a white flag."

A glossy bay was led from the stables with just a simple saddle on its back. Rob was glad the lad had realized there wasn't time to adorn the horse with the MacLaren's showy accoutrements.

"Ye're no' thinking clear," Hamish said, blocking the way. "With the Stewart leaving, Drummond willna honor a truce. And the man willna give ye the fair fight ye deserve now that ye no longer have anything he wants," He lowered his voice so only Rob could hear. "Think, Rob. Ye're no' a man who can do as he pleases. Ye have a whole clan depending on ye. If the lass wished to stay with ye, she'd still be here. Ye canna risk yer life to go after her like a lovesick pup."

"Ye presume too much on our friendship." Rob glowered at him. "Get out of my way."

When Hamish didn't move, Rob threw a punch. His fist landed on his friend's jaw with a bone-crunching thud. Hamish might be built like an oak, but his jaw had always been brittle as Frankish glass. He reeled and staggered out of the way.

Rob started to mount the horse, but someone clubbed him from behind, knocking him solidly at the base of the skull with a blunt object. He dropped to his knees.

Pinpoints of light burst in his brain, and Rob's vision tunneled. Before he winked out completely, he heard Hamish say, "Now look what ye made me do, Rob. I broke yer Grandsire's Eye on yer thick skull."

❧

Mrs. Beaton bustled into the chapel, looking for Father Kester.

At first she'd thought it a good thing that Elspeth Stewart had taken herself out of *Caisteal Dubh* by some nefarious means. But now it was evident that the witch had sunk her claws into the laird's soul so deep, he could barely be restrained from following her to his doom.

Hamish had carried the unconscious MacLaren up to his chamber, and Mrs. Beaton had left Margot to sit with him. After Hamish left, Mrs. Beaton strapped the laird to the bed to prevent his escape. Margot was under instructions to spoon in the tea laced with henbane whenever he stirred. With any luck at all, the MacLaren could be kept in drug-induced oblivion for days.

Long enough for Mrs. Beaton to see Elspeth Stewart was gone for good.

Mrs. Beaton's gaze swept the sanctuary. The priest was nowhere to be seen.

"Father Kester!" she called again, her tone strident with irritation.

The priest appeared from the sacristy and walked toward her, folding his hands into the capacious sleeves of his robe. "Peace, Mrs. Beaton. This is the House of God. He's no' pleased by the sound of a voice raised in anger."

"Aye, and I'll warrant He'll no' be pleased if ye let a witch escape His justice either."

"But Providence has protected us. She's gone. Elspeth Stewart is no longer within our walls."

"Aye, but she still troubles the House of MacLaren. Even now our laird raves on his bed, half out of his mind with her curses." *And henbane.* "Ye must follow the witch and see this thing through to its divine end if there's ever to be peace in this place."

Father Kester frowned. "I was watching from the ramparts with everyone else. She's under the Stewart's protection now. Even if Lady Elspeth *is* a witch, it's up to Alistair Stewart's priest to convince him to give her up for judgment."

That wasn't likely to happen. It was a rare father who would surrender his own child to the flames.

"Mayhap ye noticed that she's no longer in Drummond's good graces," Mrs. Beaton said. "I've no doubt there's a marriage that willna go forward."

"How d'ye know this?"

Didn't the man have eyes? "If there was still going to be a wedding, Drummond would have been riding beside his betrothed, would he no'? Instead, he and his men hung back and left the field only after the last Stewart man had quit. There's no love lost there, or I'm mistook."

"Hmmm," Father Kester said.

Honestly, would she have to put every single thought into the man's head for him?

"Dinna ye see? Ye must go to Lord Drummond," she said with urgency. "Tell him the Almighty calls him to hold a witch trial for Elspeth Stewart, and see if he'll no' jump at the chance to aid ye in your righteous cause."

"We'll need witnesses," Father Kester said doubtfully.

"And we'll have them. Leave that to me." Mrs.

Beaton had half-a-dozen serving girls she'd brought with her from Beaton lands when she took this position. They owed her their living. She could twist them into giving whatever testimony was wanted. "Go ye now, and I'll be but half a day behind with all the proof ye'll need."

❧

Travel was a muckle of trouble. From the moment the castle gates closed behind him, Father Kester felt the sky lowering on him. The world was too big, too wild a place for a man of peace to take comfort in it.

Give him the tranquility of a monastery, the quiet of a scriptorium, the diligent hum of scholarly pursuits, and he was a happy man. Instead, Father Kester bounced along on his mule, sure the beast was trying to step in every hole along the way.

He was more surprised than anything when he overtook the rear of the Drummond column, which was traveling at the pace of their wagons and baggage. A man of the cloth was welcomed most everywhere, but he was further surprised when he was hustled into Lord Drummond's tent after he made his first request to speak with the laird. Evidently, anything related to Elspeth Stewart was of keen interest to the Drummond.

While Father Kester laid out his case for the witchery of Elspeth Stewart, Lord Drummond listened with the intensity of a fox eyeing a rabbit hole. When he was finished, silence descended for the space of several "Our Fathers." Finally, the laird rose from his chair and paced for the length of a few "Hail Marys."

Father Kester began to fear Lord Drummond harbored tender feelings for the lass and might do him hurt to silence him.

"Ye're certain ye can convict her?" Drummond asked, his voice like the whisper of snakeskin through dry leaves.

"With or without her confession, aye," Father Kester said. "There is enough evidence."

"Ye'll no' shrink from burning her?"

"'Thou shalt not suffer a witch to live,'" he quoted. "I'm a man inclined to mercy, but I must please God rather than myself."

After he was ushered from the presence of the laird with the injunction not to speak of his purpose to anyone until Lord Drummond gave him the sign, he began to wonder what might happen after the trial.

Perhaps Father Kester would be given charge of a monastery. A group of monks would be so much easier to manage than a castle full of sinners. Being able to pick and choose who would copy scripture all day and who was fit only to weed the turnips would be a lovely post indeed.

Chapter 32

THE SECOND DAY ON THE ROAD, LIGHT SNOW BEGAN TO fall. The wet flakes didn't stick, but they turned the paths into a churning morass of mud. Elspeth and her father rode at the head of the Stewart column, but their pace was slowed by those at their heels. She was surprised when Lord Drummond picked his way around the Stewart fighting men to catch up to them.

"Since Lady Stewart is still awaiting us at my stronghold, I assume ye'll be going there to collect her before ye return to your own land," Lachlan said, pointedly ignoring Elspeth as if she wasn't riding alongside her father.

That was fine with her. She hoped never to speak to the man again.

"No doubt she'll be thrilled to see the Lady Elspeth safe and sound," he continued.

Elspeth didn't meet his gaze, but she watched him from the corner of her eye as if he were a hound she wasn't sure was quite safe.

"We'll no' be imposing on your hospitality longer than necessary, Drummond," her father said.

"Ye're welcome to stay under my roof as long as you like, of course, but frankly, I'm thinking your men would welcome returning to their own hearths as soon as may be," Lachlan said. "The way divides just up ahead, and if they take the right fork, your fighting men can be on Stewart land in another day's ride and by their own fires in two."

"I am aware of it," Stewart said stonily.

Lachlan looked pointedly at the leaden sky. "The air smells of snow."

Elspeth's father nodded.

Lachlan bid them a pleasant good day and turned back to join his own force. Once he was gone, Elspeth's father called his second in command to join them. He gave orders for his men to turn aside and make for Stewart land at the coming fork in the road.

"Pick a contingent of ten to remain with us as a guard, and lead the rest home," her father said. "Winter's hard upon us. I would not have my men away from their women and children when the snow flies in earnest."

Once the man left to do his laird's bidding, Elspeth screwed up her courage.

"Father, ye know I'd not question your judgment, but I have to wonder if it's wise for us to be so few when we must return to Lord Drummond's stronghold."

"Whether or no' our clans are bound by a marriage, the man is still our neighbor. We must find a way to live in peace with him," he said softly so as not to be overheard by any other ears. "Besides, if his intentions are ill, Lord Drummond has just reminded me that he holds my wife."

Elspeth gasped. She hadn't considered that. If Drummond was still intent on wedding her, threatening her mother was one thing that would make her yield.

"But if his intentions are good, he was asking me not to flood his keep with my men. They might be trapped there by heavy snows for a long while and so deplete his larder," her father said. "No man wishes to admit baldly that he canna support so many mouths. By turning my men aside, I save Drummond's dignity and earn his gratitude."

"Is every conversation such a chess game between the pair of ye?"

"More often than not," he admitted. "It comes with leadership. Ye never really know when a man's 'yea' means 'yea.'"

Rob MacLaren was as much a Scottish laird as Drummond or her father, but she had yet to see him engage in such crafty plans that someone had to decipher what his words meant. Even his abduction of her was straightforward, his goal of single combat with Drummond the stated outcome from the beginning.

An uncomplicated man with a boatload of stubbornness might be trying at times, but his lack of guile was restful to her spirit.

Her chest ached from missing him so. She wondered what he'd done when he realized she was gone. He was probably furious that she'd used the secret passage. Perhaps that was why he hadn't come after her. Of course, it would be folly in the extreme to brave two armies to reach her, but part of her wished he'd try it.

Surely he'd come for her at her father's stronghold.

Unless he believed she'd left him because she still intended to wed Lord Drummond. Her heart sank with hopelessness.

"Sometimes, ye must give a man trust in order for him to behave in a trustworthy manner," her father said, interrupting her despairing thoughts. "I withdrew from the MacLaren field without his leave. Ye have spurned Drummond as husband, and yet he's behaved with courtesy toward us both. I can afford to give the man a sop now."

They plodded on side by side. The horses' hooves made such loud sucking noises in the mud Elspeth almost missed her father's soft "I hope."

❧

Elspeth enjoyed a tearful reunion with her mother, but their joy was short lived. Before they could speak ten words to each other, there was a scuffle and a clash of blades outside their door. Drummond and a dozen armed men broke into their guest chamber. Elspeth's father's sword was out of its scabbard in a blink.

"What is the meaning of this outrage?" he demanded.

"Sheath your blade, friend. The quarrel is no' with you," Lachlan said smoothly. A priest peeked around the doorjamb and then scuttled in behind Drummond. "We war no' against flesh and blood but against the powers of darkness itself."

Stewart's sword didn't lower one jot. "What nonsense is this?"

"Tell him, Father," Drummond said to the priest.

The priest glanced at Elspeth's father then hastily averted his eyes. Instead they fastened on her. "Elspeth

Stewart, ye stand accused of the sin of witchcraft, of consorting with the devil and leading others into the grave errors of sorcery and magic. Ye must answer for yer crimes. Arrest her."

"By God, ye will not!" her father bellowed and slashed at the men who tried to approach.

"Stewart, your men are dead. Ye canna hold out against so many," Lachlan said. "If your daughter is innocent, I promise she will come to no hurt."

The accusation of witchcraft was as good as a conviction, and everyone in the room knew it. Her father didn't back down, flailing away at all comers.

"Father, no!" she shouted. "I will surrender, Lachlan. Call off your men."

"I forbid it, Elspeth," her father said.

"Ye have naught to say in the matter." She broke free of her mother's arms and ran to stand before the priest.

"Disobedient to parents," the priest muttered, and she realized she'd given him another bit of evidence against her.

"Drummond," her father said as his sword clattered to the floor, "I'm begging ye. Dinna do this thing."

"The trial will commence as soon as the witnesses arrive. Tomorrow probably, Father Kester assures me," Lachlan said. "For your own safety, ye and Lady Stewart will remain under guard in this chamber. Once the court's decision is reached, ye'll be free to go."

"And what of Elspeth?" her mother sobbed.

"I've a chamber in the tower for her for now," Lachlan said. "'Tis quite comfortable, with a window that opens onto the bailey." He marched her out of the room and then hissed into her ear, "Ye'll have a good view of the stains left on the cobbles by MacLaren's wife."

❧

He hadn't seen her in so long, it took Rob a moment to realize who it was that appeared overhead in the thatch. Fiona wavered before his eyes and then sank slowly to the floor, her long gown fluttering in a nonexistent breeze. She halted her descent before the tips of her bare feet brushed the cold flagstone.

Fiona drew near his bedside. She smiled, and the room brightened around her.

"Lazing in bed when ye're needed elsewhere." She reached out to cup his cheek, and for the first time in all his lovely dreams of her, Rob couldn't feel her fingertips. "What are ye doing, my daftie man?"

"Daftie man," he repeated, though he realized his lips hadn't moved. "Ye always called me so. Ye must have known I'd come to this. D'ye ken they say I'm mad in truth now? Mad or witched."

"Aye, but ye're no' mad. Nor witched either," she said. "The one caring for ye now has slipped a net o'er your mind. She spoons it in each time ye wake."

He turned his head and saw Margot Beaton as though through a thick mist. The lass was propped in a chair, her head lolling to one side, her mouth gaping in sleep. A cup balanced on her lap.

"Aye, that's it," Fiona said when he frowned at the cup. "Dinna accept another drop. There's one who needs ye, and ye'll be no use to her wandering among the poppies."

"Who needs me?" He wouldn't stir a muscle for Margot Beaton, whatever her need.

Fiona settled a hip on his bedside, but the feather tick didn't sink an inch under her weight. "Elspeth Stewart, of course."

"Ye know of her?"

She smiled sadly. "Aye, Rob, I know she has your heart in her keeping as I used to."

"Ye still do," he said.

"I know that too, but there is a great divide between us. I canna hold on to ye anymore. I must let ye go." She leaned down to kiss his forehead. Her lips were light as angel's breath on his skin. "And ye must let me go."

He knew she was right, but his chest still constricted.

"Aye, that's love," she said, still naming his feelings for him. "That willna end, though all else does. Dinna feel sad, Rob. 'Tis the way of things."

She began to float away, and he strained against his bonds to reach for her.

"Even if ye were unbound, ye canna hold me here longer," Fiona said. "Ye must wake, Rob. Ye must hie yourself to Drummond's stronghold before it's too late."

"Too late? Elspeth isna there. She left with her father. What's happened?"

"Wake, Rob." Fiona hovered near the ceiling then began to pass through the thatch as if it weren't there. She faded completely from his sight, but her voice whispered into his ear as if she rested her head on the pillow beside him. "Open your eyes, love, but this time, truly see."

He came to full wakefulness, but he didn't open his eyes immediately. Instead, he slitted his eyelids and checked his surroundings. He was in his own bed. Margot Beaton was sitting in the chair exactly as he'd dreamed her, complete with the foul cup in her lap.

His tongue felt too large and thick for his mouth. He tried to move his arms and legs and found that he was bound as tightly as in his dream. His stomach was queasy, and his bladder ached to be relieved.

He opened his eyes completely, wincing at the light even though the room was shuttered.

"Ha...Hamish," he said, shocked at the disembodied sound of his own voice.

Margot snorted and woke. She skittered to his side. "My lord, be at peace."

She tried to spoon some of the tea into his mouth, but he spat it back out.

"Hamish," he repeated.

"Now, my lord, ye mustn't excite yourself." The spoon wavered before him again, beckoning him to oblivion.

"Pish," he said.

She flinched.

"I haf to pish." He formed the words carefully, but they still came out slurred. "Call Hamish."

"My lord, I was ordered to—"

"I gif oders here," he roared, and her eyes rounded. "Unbine me, or when I free mysel', I'll eat yer liffer for supper."

Sometimes being thought mad was a good thing. Margot leaped to do his bidding. She unstrapped him and then scuttled away to find Hamish. Rob rose from the bed shakily and stalked to the chamber pot, hoping to piss the rest of drug-laden tea out of his body.

He threw open the shutters and inhaled the snow-fresh air. Then he began pacing the room, trying his body for signs of weakness. He seemed to be in possession of all his limbs. His head felt clearer, but there was an aching knot on the back of his skull. His tongue still felt oversized.

Hamish rapped once and then came in. He folded his arms over his barrel chest and curled his lip. "Ye're no' any the prettier for three days' rest."

A yellowish bruise purpled his friend's jaw. "Look who'z talkin'."

Three days. Rob pulled a shirt out of his trunk and drew it on over his nakedness. He put a hand to the back of his head. "Pounds like a…hammer."

"Good. Is it knocking any sense into ye?"

"Aye, but I havena changed…toward Elspeth." His tongue was settling. The slur faded. "She had a notion that there'd be a battle if she stayed. Ye canna deny she broke the siege. And now she needs me."

"Ye'll be wanting me to come with ye," Hamish said matter-of-factly.

"Aye, I'll need your help."

"And ye'll have it, so long as ye dinna plan on getting yourself killed."

"I try to avoid that whenever I can," Rob said as he wrapped a kilt around his loins. He chose a length of fabric that had belonged to his mother's clan, a soft brown and tan weave. It would probably be wise not to announce his presence with a MacLaren plaid, since he intended to beard Lachlan Drummond in his own den. "But I'll have your promise that ye'll no' clout me on the head again."

Hamish grinned at him. "If ye promise ye'll no' deserve it."

Chapter 33

IN THE CHAMBER FROM WHICH FIONA MACLAREN had leaped to her death, Elspeth spent a sleepless night. No doubt that was Lachlan's hope. Perhaps he also hoped she'd make a similar choice to end her own life.

Very few who were accused of witchcraft were acquitted. She could hardly be blamed for wanting to escape burning, but Elspeth purposed in her heart not to follow Fiona's path.

It wasn't that she feared damnation if she chose suicide. She didn't believe God was as vindictive as His creatures. Wherever Fiona's spirit now bided, Elspeth didn't think the manner of her death had anything to do with it.

But losing his wife to suicide had disordered Rob's mind. If Elspeth were to make the same choice…She feared what another similar loss might do to him more than she feared the flames.

Normina, the silent serving woman, appeared with a breakfast tray. Elspeth's stomach roiled so, she couldn't touch a mouthful. Normina helped her with her hair and made her as presentable as possible under the circumstances. Then she was left alone.

Elspeth knelt at the little private altar near the window and prayed. In silence, she started pleading for her life but found her prayers drifting away from herself and her straits. Her thoughts turned to Rob and her parents and how her trial would affect them. As she prayed for those she loved, a curious peace descended on her, and her fear lessened to a manageable level.

Still, the rap on the door made her flinch. Lachlan Drummond entered the room before she could rise.

"Praying, Elspeth? A very touching scene," he said. "Might turn the judge's heart to be kindly disposed toward you. Pity only I saw you kneeling."

She rose with all the dignity she could muster. "It's what God sees that matters."

Then she walked past him to the guards who were waiting outside her door to escort her to trial.

The court was assembled in the Dining Hall, the largest room in Drummond's stronghold, to accommodate all the onlookers crowding the space. The many tables had been cleared away, but the benches lining the walls were crammed with Lachlan's retainers.

The dais at one end of the room was dominated by a man in a rich surplice. He was seated behind a table draped with velvet embroidered with liturgical symbols. Elspeth recognized him as the priest who tried to conduct her interrupted wedding. He owed his living to Lachlan Drummond. She could expect no leniency from him.

Below the judge, Father Kester, the priest who'd accused her, was seated beside Mrs. Beaton and a couple of the serving girls from *Caisteal Dubh*. If they were gathered here this quickly, it could only mean this accusation had been made with plenty of advance planning.

Her parents were nowhere to be seen.

Neither was Rob, though she could hardly expect him here in Drummond's stronghold.

Elspeth was ushered to a straight-backed chair directly before the judge's seat.

Mrs. Beaton was the first to be sworn to truthfulness and made to testify.

"Elspeth Stewart, by means of sorcery most foul, did bewitch my Lord MacLaren into stealing her away from her wedding to Lord Drummond," she said.

The judge nodded. "I myself was present at the time, and it did seem an act of lunacy. Is the MacLaren here to confirm that he was acting under compulsion?"

"No, Father," Mrs. Beaton said. "He is confined to his bed with an unnatural sickness. It came upon him suddenlike the morning after Elspeth Stewart left *Caisteal Dubh*. She witched him again, I'll warrant."

Elspeth's hand flew involuntarily to her chest. Rob was sick. If he was ill enough to be bedridden, he wouldn't have led his men in battle. Her vision of his and her father's deaths couldn't have come true. She'd fled for no reason.

Mrs. Beaton glared at her. "No doubt she cursed him to keep him from testifying against her here."

A chorus of murmurs and nods greeted this pronouncement.

"Is there any other evidence of witchcraft to which you can attest?" the judge asked.

"I heard her call Hamish Murray's name *before* she was introduced to him, which could only have been because a demon whispered the name into her ear," Mrs. Beaton said. "And Nessa and the other girls tell me she bears the wound of the devil's pitchfork upon her body. And the devil always marks those who consort with him."

"Ye've no' seen the mark yourself?" the judge asked.

"Weel, no, but if ye make her strip off her clothes," Mrs. Beaton said with a practical shrug, "I expect we'll find it's there."

This suggestion was greeted by lewd calls of encouragement from the men gathered. The judge rapped his gavel for order.

"Lady Elspeth, do ye admit to the mark, or do ye wish to disrobe to disprove Mrs. Beaton's assertion?"

Elspeth stood, her face hot with embarrassment. "I have a pair of scars from a recent crossbow wound. 'Tis no mark of the devil."

"Such is the devil's deceit that she might not even recognize the mark for what it is. It would have to be examined in this court in order for a determination of its origin to be made," Father Kester piped up.

"Duly noted," the judge said.

"The scar is in…an indelicate place, Father," Elspeth said, sure the tips of her ears must be scarlet. If she was going to prove her innocence, she had to maintain the dignity of a noblewoman. Most women convicted of witchcraft were commoners. Her rank and birth were her best defense.

"If ye willna allow the mark to be examined, we must assume Mrs. Beaton is correct and ye have been in unholy congress with Satan," the judge said.

"That's no' true," Elspeth said.

"There's a simple way to prove whether or no' she's had sexual union with the Dark One," Father Kester said. "Lady Elspeth is unmarried. A midwife can examine her to determine if she's yet a virgin."

The judge nodded. "An excellent suggestion, and a determination about the nature of the mark upon her body might be made at the same time."

"I've served as a midwife on many occasions," Mrs. Beaton offered.

"In the interests of impartiality, we will find a different midwife, one with no association to this case," the judge said. "Are ye willing to submit to examination, Lady Elspeth?"

She hadn't intended to sit, but her knees gave way beneath her. A midwife would immediately know she was not a virgin. "No, Father," she said softly. "There is no need."

The room erupted with laughter and vulgar specu-lations. The judge once again rapped for silence, but he didn't admonish the crowd this time.

"The court will draw its own conclusions, then, my lady," he said.

A soft titter escaped Mrs. Beaton's lips, and the judge silenced her with a glare. "Is there anything else you wish to add to these proceedings?"

"Aye, Father," Mrs. Beaton said, composing her features quickly into such a somber expression, she reminded Elspeth of a blooded hound. "Elspeth Stewart was possessed of the devil in the Great Hall of *Caisteal Dubh*. She began spewing nonsense about death and destruction and prophesying evil upon all around her, till our laird lifted her up and carried her from the hall."

Father Kester stood. "I can confirm that. I was in there when it happened."

"And what's more," Mrs. Beaton continued, "through her dark arts, Elspeth Stewart did spirit Lord MacLaren into *Caisteal Dubh* and herself out again. A locked fortress, mind ye, without passing through any gate or opening made by human hands."

"I saw her fly right over the castle walls," Nessa piped up, and the other serving girls chimed in their support of the claim. One had seen her backlit by the full moon. Another watched while Elspeth mounted a broom and circled the castle turrets. Each of them shouted out a more fantastic variation on Elspeth's abilities than the next.

The judge pounded his gavel for order. "In good time, ye'll each be sworn and given a chance to unburden yourselves," he told the nearly hysterical girls. "Mrs. Beaton, proceed."

The day droned on. One lie after another was gleefully reported and embellished.

Elspeth's back hurt. She stopped listening to the testimony after a while, her thoughts drifting back to Rob. If she could fly, why would she still be here? She'd have soared over the Highlands to be at his side and tend him through his illness, as he'd tended her. Part of her wished she really was a witch.

Finally the judge invited her to speak in her own defense. She swore to tell the truth and took the more comfortable witness seat, facing the assembled onlookers. She composed her hands in her lap, hoping no one could see them trembling.

"Father, allow me to address Mrs. Beaton's testimony first," she said. "I was able to call Hamish Murray's name because I'd met his uncle, Angus Fletcher, whom he favors greatly. Has anyone here ever noticed that family members sometimes resemble each other, and you can name their kinsmen with a glance? That is how I was able to guess at Hamish's name, not through magic of any means."

A few heads nodded and she took heart.

"It has been suggested that I submit to an examination to determine my purity," Elspeth said, willing her voice not to shake. "Since I am bound to tell the truth, I will admit that I am no longer a maiden."

Grunts of disapproval greeted this admission.

"Unchastity is a sin," she continued, "but one which may be forgiven. My lover was no devil. He is as human as I."

"His name," the judge said stonily. "So we may confirm your story."

Elspeth's lips clamped shut. So often in witch trials, the aim of the court was to get the accused to name their cohorts. If she named Rob, he'd be the next one condemned.

"I cannot give you his name."

"That's because she likely didna see his true face." Father Kester stood and shook his finger at her to punctuate his remark. "The Prince of Darkness took a man's form when he stole into her chamber and took carnal knowledge of her body!"

The judge nodded but motioned for him to sit.

"Everyone knows how an incubus does his evil work, Father Kester. There's no need to go into lurid detail." Then he turned to Elspeth. "Proceed."

"My wound, which I canna show ye for modesty's sake, came from a crossbow. The bolt was shot by Lord Drummond." There was a name she didn't mind bringing to the judge's attention.

Drummond stood. "Ridiculous! Why would I shoot my betrothed?"

"I dinna think ye meant to," Elspeth said. "Ye were aiming at a dog at the time."

She heard several suppressed snorts.

"Pray, be seated if it please ye, my Lord Drummond. Ye are not required to give testimony unless ye wish." The judge turned back to Elspeth. "A crossbow bolt results in a wicked injury. Since ye survived it, ye must have had help. And whoever it was, they most likely had knowledge of the dark arts to affect such a healing. For the sake of your eternal soul, ye must give us their names."

Hepzibah Black already had the whispered reputation of being a witch. If she were named in a witch trial, even her home's remote location wouldn't protect her.

"If I gave ye names, I would be repaying their kindness sorely."

"Doing so might earn ye a bit of clemency." When she refrained from answering, the judge narrowed his eyes at her. "Upon your head, so be it. Continue."

She swallowed hard. "Mrs. Beaton has testified that she saw me prophecy. In truth, I do possess the Gift of Sight. She witnessed the expression of that Gift."

"Such things have been known to be," the judge said solemnly. "Men of faith have been visited by visions from God, but the devil is prone to imitate the Almighty's gifts. Demonstrate your ability that we may judge from whence this Sight of yours comes."

"I canna control its coming or going. I am shown that which I am meant to See. No more."

"And what did ye See?"

"A great battle, Father."

"And did this vision prove true?" the judge asked.

"No, but—"

"Sounds like the wiles of the devil to me," Father Kester said.

Elspeth resisted the urge to glare at him. He might claim she was trying to give him the Evil Eye.

"Finally, I freely confess that I canna fly," she said. "Though I've wished I could several times during this trial."

This time unrestrained laughter ringed the hall, and several faces actually seemed friendly toward her. The judge's wasn't one of them.

"Perhaps we should adjourn this court and repair to a high tower," he said. "If ye are given a push off, we'll see whether or no' ye're telling the truth right enough."

She sucked her breath over her teeth. The judge was serious. "The truth is, if ye do that, ye'll see me plummet to my death."

"Which would lead to an acquittal," the judge said, bringing his circular argument to its logical conclusion.

"*And* my death," she reminded him.

"There are things worse than death, my child,"

he assured her. "Your soul would at least be clean before God."

Mrs. Beaton leaned over and whispered in Father Kester's ear. He nodded and stood.

"If I may, I have one question for the accused." Father Kester cast a wolf's smile at her. "If ye are no' willing to do as the judge suggests and offer us concrete proof that ye canna fly, will ye at least explain how ye were able to make Lord MacLaren and yourself appear suddenly inside a locked fortress?" Mrs. Beaton nudged him with her elbow. "And how ye were able to leave undetected the same way?"

Elspeth's knuckles whitened on her lap. She couldn't divulge the secret of the back entrance to *Caisteal Dubh*. It would mean betraying Rob. She'd rather take a leap from the tower.

At last, she understood Fiona. And the judge was right. There were things worse than death.

"I canna tell ye," she said.

The judge rapped his gavel three times. "Then it is the judgment of this court that Elspeth Stewart is guilty of consorting with the Evil One. The accused will stand while I pronounce sentence."

The air fled from her lungs, but she managed to rise to her feet.

"All sin is an affront to God, but the sin of witchcraft is especially heinous and requires purification by fire," the judge said with a self-righteous gleam in his eyes. "In two days' time at the setting of the sun, before God and a company of assembled witnesses, ye shall receive your purification."

Chapter 34

WORD OF ELSPETH STEWART'S WITCH TRIAL SPREAD over the Highlands on swift, dark wings. Folk left their hearths, braving the possibility of being caught in snow, for the chance to watch her burn. Those who witnessed the witch burning would retell the story all winter long. Their flagon would remain full, and they'd never have to buy a drop of their own ale. Rob and Hamish fell in with a merry party on their way to Drummond's castle.

"Why didna Lord Stewart lead a party of men against Lord Drummond to free his daughter before it came to this?" Rob asked the fellow who seemed to be leading the group they'd met along the road. The man had provided a steady stream of details about the trial, seemed to know a good deal about the particulars, and wasn't afraid to share his knowledge. No doubt honing his storytelling skills for later use.

"Because the Stewart's being held by the Drummond till the burning's over. He canna send word for help," the fellow said. His few teeth were yellow as gourds. "They say Lord Drummond has posted guards on all the roads to stop any wearing Stewart plaid, just in case."

Rob digested this bad news in silence. He hadn't wanted to delay his coming long enough to raise a force from *Caisteal Dubh*, but he'd hoped to join with Elspeth's father and his men. Hamish had brought the new hand-held cannon he'd recently forged, but even with a fearsome weapon, two men wouldn't be enough to project much power.

"The Lady Elspeth's been the devil's consort, they say," Yellow-teeth said to no one in particular. "D'ye suppose they'll lead her to the stake bare breasted? That's what they do, ye ken, when a witch admits to swiving the devil."

Rob gritted his teeth. He was the only devil who'd swived Elspeth Stewart. Imagining slicing Yellow-teeth's head from his shoulders gave him grim satisfaction. Unfortunately, it wouldn't help Elspeth one bit.

"Never seen a noblewoman's tits before," Yellow-teeth said, blissfully unaware of how close he was to decapitation. "Ought to be a fair treat."

To remove himself from further temptation to do murder, Rob dug his heels into his horse's flanks and left the party of burning-goers behind. As they neared Drummond's stronghold, the roads became almost impassible. Carts carrying whole families were stuck in the mud. Using game trails, Rob and Hamish picked their way around the mess.

When they reached the open gate, Rob flipped up the hood on his cloak and pulled it closer around his face. There was nothing on his person that marked him as the laird of the Clan MacLaren. Even his horse was of ordinary quality, not worth a second glance, as he and Hamish rode into Lachlan Drummond's stronghold with the rest of the crowd.

Everyone was required to leave their blades and bows in a pile outside the gate. Hamish kept the hand cannon, which was bound up in his cloak and strapped to the back of his saddle.

Rob gave up his longbow and dirk, but beneath his cloak, he bore the solid weight of a claymore strapped to his back in a shoulder baldric. He kept his boot knife. If he had to fight his way back out, at least he'd be armed with the means to do so.

The atmosphere was more like a fair than a burning. Enterprising merchants had set up stalls ringing the bailey to sell foodstuffs and other goods. Children scampered between the stalls, light-fingered urchins lifting a sweetmeat or two. Everyone seemed in high spirits.

But at the far end of the bailey, Rob saw the stake, already ringed with fagots. A path had been marked with ropes, leading from the stake to the tallest tower at the opposite end of the courtyard. Elspeth would walk that way to her death. His gaze swept up the tower.

A small figure stood at an unshuttered window. A woman. Her long brown hair fluttered in the breeze like a banner. The distance was too great for him to make out her features, but he knew instantly who she was.

"Oh, God. Elspeth," he whispered. "Dinna jump, lass."

Drummond had placed her in the tower chamber with that hope in mind, Rob was sure. He held his breath until she stepped away from the window and out of his sight. His relief was short lived.

What was one man, or even two, against so many?

"I thought I could…I dinna see what's to be done," Rob said, suddenly bone weary. They'd ridden without stopping, except to rest the horses, in order to make it here in time. Now he realized what Hamish had probably known all along but was too good a friend to say.

It was all for naught. There was no help coming from any quarter. All they could do was watch Elspeth die.

But he didn't have to let her burn. A desperate plan formed in his mind. If Rob could find a longbow and stake out a position with a clear shot, he'd have one chance to put a shaft in Elspeth's heart before the flames reached her. Then he'd bury his boot knife in his own chest. It would be a small matter. His heart would already be dead.

"I can keep her from suffering," he said woodenly, "but…I canna save her."

"Come, Rob," Hamish said, his rumbling voice soft with pity. "Let's see to stabling the horses; then we'll see what's what."

When they reached the stables, Rob heard a ruckus at the rear of the structure. A pair of grooms was trying to move a black stallion into the far stall, but the horse wasn't having any of it.

"Come, ye big bastard!" one of the men shouted, raising a whip to the beast, which only infuriated it more. "If ye dinna mind, they'll burn ye next, I shouldn't wonder."

The horse lashed out with its rear hooves, and one of the grooms sailed over the rail into the next stall.

A grim smile spread over Rob's face as he tied up

his biddable gelding. "That's my Falin, or the black devil has a twin," he said to Hamish. Having that stallion under him would be worth ten men at his back. "Either way, I need your help. I have an idea."

⁂

The sun balanced on the Highland peaks for a heartbeat and then began to sink behind them. Elspeth sat perfectly still while Normina ran the boar-bristled brush through her hair. She'd decided to wear it unbound, falling past her hips.

"Once the hair catches, it goes fast, they say," Normina had advised, tight lipped.

If Elspeth had to burn, she wanted it fast. And besides, it was the only decision left to her. She'd been given a clean chemise to wear, and all her other things were taken from her. She'd walk on bare feet across the bailey's cobbles to her death.

She wouldn't let herself think of Rob. Whenever she did, the desire to live was so great, she felt as if her heart would leap from her chest. It hurt too much. If life was going to be ripped from her by violent means, it would hurt less if she weaned herself from earth first. And the dearest thing on earth, the man she loved.

"I've been tending to the needs of your parents, my lady. They send ye a message by me," Normina said as she laid down the brush. "Lord and Lady Stewart say to tell ye they know ye are guiltless and they will see ye in heaven."

Tears gathered at the corners of Elspeth's eyes, but she blinked them back. "I thank ye."

"Have ye a message for them?"

A heavy knock sounded on her door. The guard had come for her. Elspeth squared her shoulders. "Tell them…tell them I was unafraid."

God had forgiven her so many things. Surely He'd forgive one more small lie.

⁂

She never thought so many people could fit into Drummond's stronghold. On the other side of the ropes, they stood ten deep, chest to back, all jostling for a better view of her in her thin chemise. Their angry shouts were a wall of sound. Her hands were bound before her, but even if they were free, she wouldn't have been able to stop her ears against their roar.

She tried not to look around, focusing instead on the long tassel dangling from the back of the judge's surplice. It swung back and forth as he led the way before her, bearing aloft a gilt cross.

Cold lanced the bottoms of her bare feet and shot up her shins. It didn't matter. She'd wish for cold soon enough.

One foot in front of the other. That was all she had to do. The last task. She must walk across the bailey with her head held high.

The first rotten bit of cabbage that struck came as a surprise. These were the people who would have owed her fealty if her wedding to Lachlan hadn't been interrupted. Now all they offered her was scorn.

She hoped her parents were being held some place where they couldn't see what was happening.

Then suddenly the walk was ended. They reached the stake. Lachlan Drummond was there, waiting for her with a death's head grin on his face. She looked away. Her hands were jerked over her head, and a leather strap was run from her wrists through the iron loop at the top of the pole. Elspeth had the eerie sense of watching herself from outside her own body, a poor puppet whose strings were so tight her arms couldn't be lowered.

The crowd quieted to listen to the judge drone on about something. Elspeth heard only the pennants overhead, snapping in the breeze, and in a distant meadow, the mournful call of a rain crow. There'd be a fine, soft rain this night, maybe a hint of snow, and the world would wake with hoarfrost painting every tree and bush and blade. The winter-brown grass would crackle under her boots. She closed her eyes. She could hear it crunching beneath her tread. Then those sounds faded, and all she heard was the rush of her own blood, pounding in her ears.

Torches were lit as the light faded. Several guards held them nearby, waiting for something. Someone lifted a little boy up and propped him on their shoulders. He was a beautiful child, with a mop of poorly cut hair and the brown eyes of a roe deer.

Elspeth smiled at him. She and Rob might have had a dozen just like him.

Oh, Rob. Oh, God! I want to live.

A tear slid down her cheek as the guards lit the branches at her feet and stepped back lest they be engulfed once the flames took hold. Smoke curled around her.

Then Elspeth was visited by her Gift.

A loud boom followed by a puff of smoke drew

every eye to the battlements near the gate. Hamish stood there, holding a hand cannon. His first volley struck the slate roof of the Great Hall. The crowd scattered as bits of the slate slid off, peppering them with shards.

A wild battle cry echoed throughout the bailey. "Mad Rob" MacLaren was riding down the center aisle of the kirk astride that black devil horse of his. Its hooves threw sparks off the cobbles.

Fire licked at her feet, and she cried out in agony.

No, she wasn't having a vision. Rob really was bearing down on her, laying about with his claymore. The stunned crowd gave way, scrambling to stay out of reach of his blade. He reined Falin to a stop before her.

The hand cannon boomed again.

In one smooth stroke, Rob slashed the strap binding her wrists and pulled her up onto the stallion's back behind him. Rob beat back a trio of guards with several wicked swipes of the claymore. Drummond stood behind them, shouting orders, but no one wanted to dare Rob's blade.

Then he wheeled Falin around, and they bolted back down the roped-off path, while people shouted and scattered before them. Elspeth peered around Rob to see that Hamish really was on the ramparts. He was working the wheel that raised the heavy portcullis and lowered the drawbridge.

They were almost there. Rob crooned an oath to the stallion, and Falin laid his ears back and stretched his neck out to give them more speed.

Then one of the guards whacked Hamish over the

head with the butt end of a pike, and the big man went down. The chain raising the portcullis rattled back down, and the gate dropped into place with a thud, trapping them inside Drummond's stronghold.

Rob reined Falin to a stop and turned back to face the mob. Elspeth laid her head against his back, thanking God she was able to touch him once more. They might be torn to pieces, but at least they'd die together.

"Drummond!" Rob bellowed, and the crowd quieted before him. "Ye have no right to burn this woman. Elspeth Stewart is a noblewoman, and as such, she's entitled to *wager de battel*!"

"He is correct, my lord," the judge said to Drummond. "If the lady has a champion, she may challenge the ruling of the court with trial by combat."

"She has a champion," Rob shouted and slid off the stallion's back. "Stay on Falin," he ordered her quietly, thrusting the reins in her hands. "If any come near ye, he'll kick them into the next world."

Then he strode forward as the crowd parted before him. "I will prove upon my body that the Lady Elspeth is innocent of the crimes of which she's accused." His deep voice rang against every stone in the castle. "Who will meet my challenge?"

No one spoke up. The judge turned to Lord Drummond. "God will favor the right, my lord. Have no fear to take up the sword in defense of the truth."

"Aye, wee Lachlan," Rob said, cocking his head at his adversary. "Defend the truth, if ye be a man."

"I'll defend the truth, right enough, and ye'll be a *dead* man, MacLaren," Drummond said, his dark eyes blazing. He drew his sword, roared his defiance, and ran toward Rob. The crowd stumbled back to clear a space for the arcs of the blades.

Rob and Lachlan met in the center of the bailey with a clash of blades and the rasp of steel on steel.

Chapter 35

ELSPETH DUG HER FINGERS INTO FALIN'S MANE AND urged him to stand still. The stallion's ears pricked forward, his hooves restive. Blades flashing, tartans swirling, the combatants circled each other, looking for weakness. When Falin snorted, the people standing near them gave way. His reputation as a horse with a wicked temper, whom no one could ride, preceded him.

Several people made the sign against Evil. Of course, a witch could ride the devil's horse, they seemed to say. But in truth, they had more to fear from Falin's sharp hooves than any malevolent spirit.

Even though she was a good distance away, since Elspeth was on the stallion's back, she saw every stroke and parry of the fight. She almost wished she could not. Lachlan's blade whistled over Rob's ducked head, missing him by a hair's breadth. For the life of her, she couldn't look away.

At first, the populace cheered for their laird, but as the fight wore on, boiling in tight circles, the people quieted. The only sound was the clang of steel on steel and grunts of exertion from Rob and Lachlan. They were strong men, seasoned warriors and canny in the way of the blade. Lachlan had a stone of weight on Rob, but Rob was younger by several years.

It didn't seem to matter. They both fought like men possessed. Three lives hung in the balance. Theirs and hers.

Elspeth couldn't swallow for the lump in her throat. She struggled for each breath, not realizing she was holding it as Rob's blade sang.

"Ye have no heir," Lachlan said between gasping breaths. "Once I kill ye, I'll take your lands before your people have time enough to rally in their own defense."

"No one has ever taken *Caisteal Dubh*," Rob said between clenched teeth. He leaped to avoid a blow that would have taken his legs off at the knees.

"No one's ever known for sure if there was a secret entrance, but there must be one. I dinna believe Elspeth flew over your walls," Lachlan said, feinting right and then swinging around to strike from the left. Rob barely had time to meet his blade. "She'll tell me where it is."

"I willna," she whispered, not wanting to distract Rob. That's what Lachlan was trying to do with his gasping words.

Rob parried Lachlan's shoulder–jarring blow and answered with one of his own.

"Elspeth wouldn't tell to save her own neck, but I hold her parents, ye ken." Lachlan leered at him with an evil grin. "Think ye she'll keep silent while I take them apart once ye're gone?"

Rob roared and rained a hailstorm of blows, which Lachlan managed to parry while giving ground. Then in one sickening moment, Drummond caught the tip of his blade in the hilt of Rob's and twisted Rob's sword from his hand.

The claymore flipped end over end, landing directly in front of Elspeth and Falin, point buried in the crack between two cobbles. The stallion reared, but Elspeth kept her seat and managed to quiet him after a few quick turns and kicks.

When Falin settled, Elspeth saw that Rob was unarmed, on his knees far enough from his lost sword that a single lunge would not bring him close enough to snatch it. Lachlan circled, toying with him. He bloodied him in half-a-dozen places. The crowd urged their laird to finish his enemy.

"Oh, God!" she prayed. "Not like this." Then Elspeth lifted her voice. "Stop, for the love of Christ, I beg ye! I waive my right to *wager de battel*! Ye dinna need to kill him. I'll return to the stake of my own free will."

"In good time, my dear," Lachlan said. "In good time. But first, we'll settle the question of your guilt once and for all."

He lifted his sword in preparation for the strike that would take Rob's head from his body. But as the blow fell, Rob dropped and rolled toward his sword. In one smooth motion, he drew the claymore from the cobbles and drove the blade between Lachlan's ribs clear to the hilt.

A collective gasp ringed the bailey. The crowd watched in stunned silence.

For a moment, the two men were locked in a death embrace, Lachlan clutching at Rob, Rob gripping

Lachlan's sword wrist like a hound at a boar's throat. He gave the claymore a twist. Drummond's sword clattered to the cobbles. Rob yanked out his blade. A spurt of red spewed out like a fountain as Lachlan sank to rise no more.

Rob squared his shoulders and walked over to kneel before the judge. "Father, ye have a verdict."

"By dint of trial by combat," the judge said in a quavering voice of disbelief, "Elspeth Stewart is found innocent of witchcraft. She is free to go."

Accommodating as a whore, the crowd roared its approval. They'd come for a spectacle, and by God, they got one. It didn't matter one whit that it wasn't the one they'd expected.

Rob stood. "Lachlan Drummond died without an heir. Release Lord Stewart. He and I will meet with the leaders of the Clan Drummond to help ye choose a new laird."

The cheers that greeted this proved Lachlan Drummond's passing would not be mourned overmuch.

Then Rob walked toward Elspeth, the crowd scrambling out of his way like sheep giving a wolf a wide berth. He held a hand up to Elspeth.

"And as laird of the Clan MacLaren, I'm choosing a new lady." His eyes shone with love. "If she'll have me."

"With all my heart." She accepted his hand as he helped her dismount. He swung her into an embrace and deep kiss.

The fickle crowd roared with as much enjoyment over this display as they had for the combat that led to the death of their laird.

Later that evening, Rob and Elspeth were reunited with her parents, and they feasted in Lachlan Drummond's hall with Osgar Drummond, the good man named to succeed him. Osgar's first act was to expel Father Kester, Mrs. Beaton, and the other false witnesses from his keep. Rob and Elspeth's father admonished them never to show their faces on MacLaren or Stewart land again either, lest the lairds be in a less merciful mood.

As the evening wore down and wine flowed freely, the old serving woman, Normina, leaned to whisper in Rob's ear.

"I ken where she lies, my lord."

Rob's head turned sharply toward the woman, but his hand gripped Elspeth's more tightly.

"Yer lady wife," Normina said. "A kindly lady, she was. If ye wish, I can show ye where she rests."

"Go, Rob," Elspeth whispered. "Ye should go."

He brought her hand to his lips and placed a kiss on her knuckles. "If ye come with me."

They said their good nights to their host and donned heavy cloaks to follow Normina into the night.

They slipped out of the castle by a small gate and tramped toward a copse of trees. Snow-kissed air washed down from the surrounding peaks, but there was a break in the clouds, and the moon shone on their path with silver light.

Normina led them to a massive fir. Protected from bitter winds by the giant tree, a cairn of granite stones lay in the leeward side. Frost glittered on the mound, bedecking Fiona MacLaren's grave with pinpoints of light.

"She deserved better, my lord," Normina said softly. "So I tend her resting place. In the spring, I'll plant heather and holly, so even once I'm gone, she'll still have flowers."

Rob nodded his thanks as Normina withdrew, his heart too full for words, his gut all a-jumble. If Fiona was there, she'd be able to tell him what he was feeling.

"I'll leave ye for a bit," Elspeth said softly and started to pull her hand from his.

"No, stay. I want ye here," he said. "'Tis fitting. Fiona was the first woman I ever loved." He turned to Elspeth and cupped her cheek. Her hazel eyes sparkled up at him. "Ye are the last. And I'll love ye, Elspeth Stewart, with my whole heart till I'm dust. Longer, if such things be."

He lowered his mouth to kiss her, savoring her sweetness mixed with the salt of a tear. He thought it was hers but couldn't be sure. The last hint of madness sizzled out of him. He was no longer driven, no longer tormented. He felt only peace and love and longing for more of Elspeth Stewart. She was the woman who filled his heart. Filled his bed. And, God willing, would fill his hall with rosy-cheeked bairns.

And from that place, where only love bides, Fiona MacLaren looked on and smiled.

Here's a sneak peek at

LORD OF FIRE AND ICE

by Connie Mason with Mia Marlowe

KATLA WISHED BRANDR WOULDN'T KEEP TURNING those deep, amber eyes on her. They made it hard for her to think.

"I'm not sure what you're fit for," she said, willing herself not to betray how his hard body affected her. The son of Ulf had the frame of a warrior, honed to lean fitness. His muscles stood out beneath smooth skin marred by only a few battle scars.

Katla's bed had been cold for three years. She didn't miss having a husband countermand her decisions, but she sorely missed the feel of a man's body. Brandr Ulfson made her remember that longing in exquisite detail.

She set her mouth in a tight line. It was a man's world. A woman had to be strong when dealing with a male, even one wearing the iron collar of a thrall, lest he run roughshod over her.

"Have you any skills besides wenching and drinking?"

"I'm a fighter by trade." His mouth turned up in a

lazy, sensual smile. "Obviously drinking isn't one of my strengths. At least, not when someone taints the mead. But don't discount wenching. I know how to please a woman. My bed skills are yours for the asking."

Her cheeks flushed with irritation that he'd divined the direction of her thoughts. Why shouldn't a widow enjoy a bed slave so long as she kept herself from bearing?

She gave herself a slight shake. This new thrall was nothing but the son of Ulf. She had to keep thinking of him as such.

"I accepted you as my thrall to exact revenge for my husband's death," she snapped. She'd sworn to avenge Osvald and this was her first chance to make good on her vow. She'd humble him so abjectly his name would become a byword throughout the North, a warning to all men who fell into the hands of a vengeful woman. "Keep your lewd suggestions to yourself."

Brandr Ulfson eyed her with boldness so she felt obliged to return the favor. Usually, a bald head made her look away. Only freemen let their hair and beards grow long. But by shearing Brandr's locks, her brothers had accentuated his strong, even features. A man had to be breathtakingly handsome to still be so appealing after he'd endured the shame of being shorn.

She knelt beside him and stretched out her hand to run a palm over his head, down his neck, and around his firm jawline. In a few days, he'd be prickly with new hair growth—fine blond hair judging from the pale curls licking his brown nipples—but for now, the bare skin on his head and face was begging to be touched.

She straightened her spine.

"Letting you demonstrate your bed skills doesn't sound like revenge," she said. "It sounds like you're trying to trick me into pleasuring a thrall."

"If we shared a bed, it would be about *your* pleasure." His amber eyes darkened to sable. "Not mine."

"So bedding me wouldn't please you?"

"I didn't say that. I'm sure it would please me. Very much. But my aim would be your delight."

Her breath caught and she couldn't move. He gave her a thorough look, starting with her mouth, lingering at her breasts, which tingled under his direct gaze, and traveling down her loins and limbs.

"You're a beautiful woman, Katla. And you've missed a man's touch."

"I haven't missed yours," she snapped. "And you will address me as 'mistress' or 'my lady.' You may not use my name, thrall."

She turned and rummaged through her clothes trunk for the oldest, coarsest tunic she could find. She hoped it would be big enough to fit him, but for now, she'd be satisfied with draping the undyed fabric across his groin.

"Varangians are supposed to value honor above all," she said. "Before I loose your bonds, will you swear upon your honor to obey me and not to run away?"

"I won't run. Your brothers took me by guile and womanish potions, but they took me. As long as your commands do not conflict with my honor, I so swear to obey you," he said. "May Thor strike me blind if I do not."

"If the god doesn't, I will," she promised as she cut the bindings on his wrists.

He worked the knot at his ankles as soon as his hands were free. Then he stood to pull the rough tunic over his head.

Katla took a step back from him. The tunic was snug across his broad chest and struck him mid-thigh, leaving his well-muscled legs exposed. At least his disturbing maleness was covered.

"Now what, *princess*?" He managed to make the title he gifted her with sound like a curse.

She had to show this man his place and quickly. "I saved you from the gelding knife this night. You will show your appreciation by kissing my foot."

She lifted her nightshift to ankle height and presented one to him, toes pointed.

That should wipe the smug expression from his face.

He shrugged, bent over and grabbed her ankle. Then he yanked her upside down. Her bottom took a glancing blow on the floor before she found herself hanging precariously, her foot level with his mouth when he stood back upright.

It happened so quickly, surprise forced all the air from Katla's lungs. Her nightshift billowed down to bunch at her armpits, exposing her to him. When she tried to kick free, he grasped her other ankle as well. Her fingertips splayed on the slate floor to steady herself.

She clamped her lips shut to keep from crying out. There were a dozen strong men snoring on the other side of the door. They'd all rush to her aid, but she'd die before she let anyone catch her in this undignified position.

He planted a wet kiss on her instep and then

lowered her to the floor. She managed not to land on her head; her right shoulder took most of her weight before she rolled to lie flat on her back on the cold slate.

He glared down at her and bared his teeth in a wolf's smile. "Want me to kiss anything else, princess?"

Coming July 2012

The Highlander's Sword

by Amanda Forester

A quiet, flame-haired beauty
with secrets of her own...

Lady Aila Graham is destined for the convent, until her brother's death leaves her an heiress. Soon she is caught between a hastily arranged marriage with a Highland warrior, the Abbot's insistence that she take her vows, the Scottish Laird who kidnaps her, and the traitor from within who betrays them all.

She's nothing he expected and
everything he really needs...

Padyn MacLaren, a battled-hardened knight, returns home to the Highlands after years of fighting the English in France. MacLaren bears the physical scars of battle, but it is the deeper wounds of betrayal that have rocked his faith. Arriving with only a band of war-weary knights, MacLaren finds his land pillaged and his clan scattered. Determined to restore his clan, he sees Aila's fortune as the answer to his problems...but maybe it's the woman herself.

---

*"Plenty of intrigue keeps the reader cheering
all the way."*—Publishers Weekly

For more Amanda Forester, visit:

www.sourcebooks.com

The Highlander's Heart

by Amanda Forester

She's nobody's prisoner

Lady Isabelle Tynsdale's flight over the Scottish border would have been the perfect escape, if only she hadn't run straight into the arms of a gorgeous Highland laird. Whether his plan is ransom or seduction, her only hope is to outwit him, or she'll lose herself entirely...

And he's nobody's fool

Laird David Campbell thought Lady Isabelle was going to be easy to handle and profitable too. He never imagined he'd have such a hard time keeping one enticing English countess out of trouble. And out of his heart...

"An engrossing, enthralling, and totally riveting read. Outstanding!"—Jackie Ivie, national bestselling author of *A Knight and White Satin*

For more Amanda Forester, visit:

www.sourcebooks.com

True Highland Spirit

by Amanda Forester

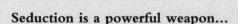

Seduction is a powerful weapon...

Morrigan McNab is a Highland lady, robbed of her birthright and with no choice but to fight alongside her brothers to protect their impoverished clan. When she encounters Sir Jacques Dragonet, she discovers her fiercest opponent...

Sir Jacques Dragonet is a Noble Knight of the Hospitaller Order, willing to give his life to defend Scotland from the English. He can't stop himself from admiring the beautiful Highland lass who wields her weapons as well as he can and endangers his heart even more than his life...

Now they're racing each other to find a priceless relic. No matter who wins this heated rivalry, both will lose unless they can find a way to share the spoils.

"A masterful storyteller, Amanda Forester brings new excitement to Scottish medieval romance!"—Gerri Russell, award-winning author of *To Tempt a Knight*

For more Amanda Forester, visit:

www.sourcebooks.com

Highland Hellcat

by Mary Wine

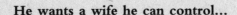

He wants a wife he can control...

Connor Lindsey is a Highland laird, but his clan's loyalty is hard won and he takes nothing for granted. He'll do whatever it takes to find a virtuous wife, even if he has to kidnap her...

She has a spirit that can't be tamed...

Brina Chattan has always defied convention. She sees no reason to be docile now that she's been captured by a powerful laird and taken to his storm-tossed castle in the Highlands, far from her home.

When a rival laird's interference nearly tears them apart, Connor discovers that a woman with a wild streak suits him much better than he'd ever imagined...

"Deeply romantic, scintillating, and absolutely delicious."—Sylvia Day, national bestselling author of *The Stranger I Married*

For more Mary Wine, visit:

www.sourcebooks.com

Highland Heat

by Mary Wine

--- ✎ ---

As brave as she is impulsive, Deirdre Chattan's tendency to follow her heart and not her head has finally tarnished her reputation beyond repair. But when powerful Highland Laird Quinton Cameron finds her, he doesn't care about her past—it's her future he's about to change...

From the moment Quinton sets eyes on Deirdre, rational thought vanishes. For in her eyes he sees a fiery spirit that matches his own, and he'll be damned if he'll let such a wild Scottish rose wither under the weight of a nun's habit...

With nothing to lose, Deirdre and Quinton band together to protect king and country. But what they can accomplish alone is nothing compared to what they can build with their passion for each other...

--- ✎ ---

"Dramatic and vivid...Scorching love scenes threaten to set the sheets aflame."—*Publishers Weekly* starred review

"A lively and exciting adventure."—*Booklist*

For more Mary Wine, visit:

www.sourcebooks.com

The Highlander's Prize

by Mary Wine

Clarrisa of York has never needed a miracle more. Sent to Scotland's king to be his mistress, her deliverance arrives in the form of being kidnapped by a brusque Highland laird who's a bit too rough to be considered divine intervention. Except his rugged handsomeness and undeniable magnetism surely are magnificent...

Laird Broen MacNichols has accepted the challenge of capturing Clarrisa to make sure the king doesn't get the heir he needs in order to hold on to the throne. Broen knows more about royalty than he ever cared to, but Clarrisa, beautiful and intelligent, turns out to be much more of a challenge than he bargained for...

With rival lairds determined to steal her from him and royal henchmen searching for Clarrisa all over the Highlands, Broen is going to have to prove to this independent-minded lady that a Highlander always claims his prize...

"[The characters] fight just as passionately as they love while intrigue abounds and readers turn the pages faster and faster!"—RT Book Reviews, 4 stars

For more Mary Wine, visit:

www.sourcebooks.com

Heart of the Highland Wolf

by Terry Spear

—⁓—

It's a matter of pride…
And a matter of pleasure…

Julia Wildthorn is sneaking into Argent Castle to steal an ancient relic, but reluctant laird Ian MacNeill may be the key to unlocking the one answer she really wants discovered…

From brilliant storyteller Terry Spear, modern day werewolves meet the rugged Highlands of Scotland, where instinct meets tradition and clan loyalties give a whole new meaning to danger…

—⁓—

Irish Lady

by Jeanette Baker

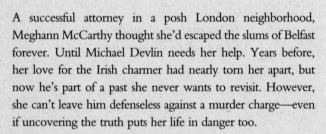

A successful attorney in a posh London neighborhood, Meghann McCarthy thought she'd escaped the slums of Belfast forever. Until Michael Devlin needs her help. Years before, her love for the Irish charmer had nearly torn her apart, but now he's part of a past she never wants to revisit. However, she can't leave him defenseless against a murder charge—even if uncovering the truth puts her life in danger too.

She'll risk everything to save Michael—and she's not the first of her family to put it all on the line for a man she loves. As Meghann delves further into Michael's case, further into the history that binds them so irrevocably, she slips into the unfolding drama of centuries before…of another woman's desperate fight to free her rebel husband from the clutches of Queen Elizabeth.

Stakes are high, but the reward is the love of a lifetime. And the Irish never give up.

"Wonderful…It grips from the first page to the last."
—Diana Gabaldon, author of the *Outlander* series

For more Jeanette Baker, visit:

www.sourcebooks.com

The Lure of Song and Magic

by Patricia Rice

~~~

Her voice was a curse...

When Dylan "Oz" Oswin's son is kidnapped, the high-powered producer will do anything to get him back. Desperately following an anonymous tip, he seeks help from a former child singing sensation called Syrene, only to find she's vowed never to sing again. Immune to her voice but not her charm, Oz is convinced she holds the key to his son's disappearance—and he'll stop at nothing to make her break her vow.

Only he can make her sing...

She knows the devastation her talent can bring. There's more than a child's life at stake, but Syrene cannot unleash her dangerous siren's voice upon the world, even for a man who is impossible to deny...

~~~

"So much attention to detail the characters truly seem
to come to life... [An] enchanting concoction of magic,
suspense, and an unlikely love."—*Booklist* starred review

For more Patricia Rice, visit:

www.sourcebooks.com

About the Authors

Connie Mason, who started her romance-writing career after she became a grandmother, once told *48 Hours* that she does her best work in bed—that work being writing, of course! For her newest releases, Connie has teamed up with Mia Marlowe, a rising star of steamy historical romance. Mia learned about storytelling while singing professional opera. A classically trained soprano, she knows what it's like to wear a corset and has had to sing high Cs in one, so she empathizes with the trials of her historical heroines.

Connie lives near Tampa, Florida, and Mia lives in Boston, Massachusetts. Credit for putting these two authors together goes to their editor, Leah Hultenschmidt, and their agent, Natasha Kern, who saw the creative potential in this pairing. Both Connie and Mia write sexy, adventurous stories with alpha heroes to love. They hope you'll enjoy the melding of their styles as much as they enjoyed collaborating to bring their new stories to life.

For more info, please visit www.conniemason.com and www.miamarlowe.com!